Sky Ambush

"My lord, ships on the scope, coming fast!"

Karne flashed a look through the flitter's canopy. One moment there were only tails of blowing snow, the next moment a heat-beam passed, betrayed by its purple tracer. The rear wing-edge of the nearest Halarek escort glowed red and sagged. The flitter nosedived and crashed in flames.

"Hold on, lord!"

Von Schuss banked the flitter sharply. He shot a glance at Karne. "There's a survival suit in the locker behind your seat. Get it on and grab a crash kit. We can't shake fighters; they're too fast for a flitter. There are some ruins"—von Schuss jerked the flitter violently over—"near here. You'll have a chance of safety there, milord."

Unarmed flitters, unmarked fighters, illegal siege. Rage burned away Karne's fear.

"Now lord!"

Karne jumped.

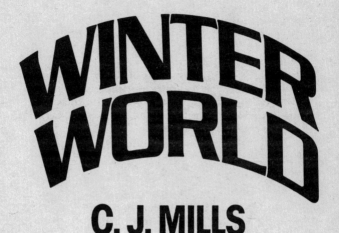

WINTER WORLD

C. J. MILLS

PAGEANT BOOKS

PAGEANT BOOKS
225 Park Avenue South
New York, New York 10003

Cover artwork by Hildebrandt

Printed in the U.S.A.

First Pageant Books printing: August, 1988

10 9 8 7 6 5 4 3 2 1

To Roberta,
who saved Karne Halarek's life

Prologue

The shuttle dropped away from the Gild merchantman *Aldefara* and fell toward Starker IV. Gild Captain Telek watched on the viewer as the shuttle disappeared into the storm clouds that completely hid the planet's surface. He ground his teeth in frustration. He was rid of the young Lharr, true enough, but too late.

"You bastard!" he snarled at the vanished Lharr. "You whining, insolent puppy! The Gharr kill each other in feuds all the time, yet *you* demand a Patrol investigation of what happened here!" Telek's nails were digging painfully into his palms. He forced himself to unclench his fists. He glared at the clouds below.

"If he had not demanded an investigation of the

1

'accidents,' I would already be on my way. If he had died in one of those accidents, I would be on my way. That other Gharr lord said Halarek would be an easy mark, that he had lived too many years on Balder to remember the ways of feud. A shooting on Balder's Orbital, bombs, poison, gas—the young lord survived them all!"

Telek shoved his bulk away from the viewer. His mouth drew tight. His thin mustache twitched. Three passengers had not survived the accidents, and the Gild did not look well on the loss of paying passengers. People were supposed to be safe on Gildships. Gildships were supposed to be completely neutral. Yet someone had brought Starker IV's feud aboard a Gildship. The Gild would lose vast sums of money because the *Aldefara* had to stay in orbit around this backwater world while the Patrol arrived, investigated, found the perpetrator, and tried him before a jury of his peers, assembled from wherever he was native. Telek's career in the Gild was over. He would be lucky to get command of any deep-space ship after this. If the Patrol missed his connection to this fiasco. If not...Telek shook his fist at the storm clouds below.

"I hope he gets you, young lord! I hope he gets you and does his worst!"

Telek stomped off the bridge, his robe swirling around his legs.

Chapter One

———◆———

THE GILDSHUTTLE SEEMED to drift through the thick, dark clouds for hours. The slender young man in the uniform of an Altarian Navy cadet stared out the shuttle's starboard window. For a time all he could see was the grayness. Then, off and on through breaks in the cloud cover, he could see the entrance shelters of Gildport huddled together in the twilight, whipped by blowing snow. The shuttle dropped lower. The narrow stone shelters reared stark and gray out of the whiteness. Gusts of snow hid them for a moment each time the shuttle passed over. Lower and lower the shuttle circled, waiting for the wind to die briefly. A clear stretch of landing pad, a lull in the wind, and the shuttle dropped with a bump to the ground. The pilot killed the engines. For a moment the only

3

sounds were the rattle of hard-driven snow against the shuttle's sides and the howling of the winds of Narn. Then the pilot lifted off her headset and turned toward her passenger.

"Sir, I've just been told you won't be permitted to leave this craft until you agree to submit to a complete med-psyche."

A flash of anger crossed the thin, tired face of the naval cadet. He stood and straightened to his full height. His golden eyes blazed in his brown face. "I am Karne Halarek, Lharr of House Halarek, head of one of the Nine Families! The Gild has no right to detain me!"

The pilot looked down at the headset and turned it over in her hands, then turned it back. She looked up at the young Lharr. "We must protect our neutrality, sir. The Gild recognizes no rank, class, or politics, and until now, that has been enough. All through the galaxy it has been enough. But someone brought your clan's feud, your world's politics, aboard a Gildship. We cannot risk the charge of helping to murder you; it would shake our reputation across all the known worlds."

"Gentlefem, a med-psyche takes a week, the Houses-in-Council holds its last meeting of the year in three days and the fate of my House hangs on that meeting. I must be there!"

"I'm sorry, sir, but the politics of Starker IV aren't the Gild's concern. Our continued neutrality is. The Gild cannot risk the possibility that you carry slow-acting poisons in your body."

The young Lharr spun and slammed his fist on the top edge of his seat. He looked down, took a deep, unsteady breath, and let it out very slowly.

"It seems I have no choice. Open the lock. I'll submit to your tests."

The lock slid open, Karne Halarek slid down the shuttle's ramp, and dashed across the pad to the customs house entrance shelter. The wind bit through his uniform, designed for the mild climate of Balder, and stung his nose and ears. Sharp, icy pellets slid under his collar and blew up his sleeves. The moment Karne ducked into the shelter a proxsensor opened the lift door for him and shut it once he was inside. Karne stamped the snow off his boots and scraped the ice out of his collar. He shivered in the unheated lift.

I've grown too used to fair-weather worlds, he told himself. If the Lifesguardsmen don't bring clothes more suited to Starker IV in the middle of Narn, I'm going to have a very cold flight home.

His mouth tightened, thinking of the warm clothes and other possessions that had been in his compartment aboard the *Aldefara* when the bomb exploded. *The clothes I can replace, but the painting Egil did for me—I could bring so little with me on such short notice and now I have nothing to remember Egil and his sire by.*

Karne turned away from the bitter thought. Egil Olafson had been closer to him than anyone but his brother Jerem, and Egil's sire, Odin Olafson, had treated Karne as if he were one of the Olafson boys and had shown him that powerful love can exist between a man and his sons without damaging their manhood. That's all in the past, like everyone and everything else on Balder, he reminded himself.

The lift had descended forty meters to customs

house check-in. It opened its door and the young Lharr stepped out into the warmth of Gildport and the slightly stale smell of constantly recirculated air. The First Merchant stood waiting, his red-and-gold uniform with the red rocket-and-gyro symbol identifying him beyond all doubt.

"Peace be on your House, Karne Halarek."

"And on yours grace, and peace, First Merchant," Karne responded.

"If you will come this way, sir, the Gildmeds are waiting."

The clinic was only a few strides from the lift. When Karne entered it, three physicians, dressed in white, bowed very slightly, the most recognition a Gildsman ever gave to rank. The oldest of the three, tall and gray-haired, smiled thinly.

"We'll begin by assuring you that no females will assist in any part of your exams, sir. We thought abiding by Gharr custom safest, even though you have lived long with other ways." He cleared his throat, as if aware he was treading on the edge of insult. "Also, the exam will be relatively quick, sir, much quicker than usual. The Medical Officer of the *Aldefara* sent down much of what we need. You were probably unaware of how thoroughly he examined you while you were unconscious after the accident with the gas."

Karne looked sharply at the physician. No, he decided, the man did not think the gas in the passenger compartment was an accident any more than Karne did. He was just protecting the Gild. The gray-haired man continued.

"The Medical Officer also sent a sworn statement that, since the poisoning, you neither ate nor drank anything he had not personally tasted first. You were very lucky he was aboard, sir. A lesser physician might not have been able to save you." The man motioned toward a small cubicle. "Most of the devices we'll use are in there. Please disrobe inside and sit on the table."

An incredible four hours later, the physicians dismissed Karne from ` the clinic. A Gildclerk guided Karne to the small park on the upper level of Gildport. The drooping features and short, silver-gray fur of the clerk did not startle Karne as they would have six years before. Six years before, the Gild had not posted XTs to Starker IV.

"The Gild invites you to wait here for your escort, sir." The clerk's voice was as furry as its body. "There is a storm and your escort has been delayed over Zinn. You know how Narn is, sir."

Karne sighed impatiently. "I know how Narn is. Arrange for me to talk to the manor house, please."

The clerk nodded and turned down one of the narrow streets around the edge of the tiny park. Karne watched the clerk pad out of sight, then turned to the small square of plants and grass, artfully landscaped to appear larger than it was. The park's bright greenness contrasted sharply with the graystone walls of the ceiling and buildings around it. A fountain splashed in its center against a backdrop of bluepines and tiny-leaved shrubs. The bluepines, which had been no taller than he when he left for the Academy almost six years before, now stretched toward the plant and day/night lights on the high, curved stone ceiling. Stepping-stones, with a fringe of delicate, green grass, led from each of the streets. Karne stared blindly at the water leaping up and splashing down.

Council called me home, saying only that my sire and brothers had been killed and that I was head-of-House, he thought. How did they die, my family? Who killed them? Only Asten Harlan would hire assassins so inept they failed four times to kill me. But Lharr Trev, my sire, was quick and clever and had outwitted Harlan for twenty years. Now all four are dead and I have not been trained to rule.

A hand touched his arm. He started and turned.

"Your pardon, sir," the clerk's furry voice said. "We've been unable to reach Halarek manor since the captain of your escort said they were leaving. Perhaps the storm is interfering with transmissions."

Karne felt a prickle of warning, an instinctive feeling even five years at the Academy could not dull. "Are you having trouble reaching other Houses?" he asked sharply.

"Not that I'm aware of, sir." The clerk turned to leave. "I will come for you when your escort arrives, sir."

"Thank you." Years of training in control kept Karne's face impassive, but could not stop cold sweat from trickling down his back. Something's wrong! And I've been away too long even to make a good guess what it is.

Karne looked again at the tiny park, trying to divert his mind from useless worrying. It would be better to think of neutral things until he had some data. House Halarek had no such gardens. When Ontar manor and city had been cut deep into the stone more than twenty generations past, no provision for gardens had been made. Surviving Starker IV's winter had been the colonists' sole concern. Ontar manor's only trees and flowers grew in tubs and window boxes. Karne walked to the edge of the fountain, stepping carefully on the stones of the path so his feet did not touch the fragile grass, and held one hand in the cool spray. The rhythmic splash of the water was soothing. Here, in the damp air, some of the green fragrance of the grass and trees lingered, in spite of the pull of the ventilating fans. For a moment Karne's mind flew to the misty greenness of Balder, its airy buildings with their glass walls and huge windows looking out on trees and hills and sky year-round, and he felt a sharp pang of longing.

"Your escort has arrived, sir."

The Gildclerk's voice broke into Karne's thoughts. Karne turned to find the XT standing at the edge of the park.

"If you would follow me, sir . . ."

Karne took one last look at the sparkling fountain, then followed the clerk through the maze of halls and passages, past warehouses, offices, and repair shops, to a lift. The doors slid shut and Karne stared at the red rocket-and-gyro embossed on them until they slid open again at the flitter pad. Above, snow piled against the curved sides of the pad canopy and gusted across the top of it in streams of white. Karne shivered and hugged himself to stay warmer. A cluster of black, two-man flitters crouched on the pad. Nine men, wearing the dark blue of House Halarek, came toward Karne. Their leader, his face seamed and scarred with years in the Lharr's service, sank to one knee before Karne and his men followed his lead.

"Peace be on you, lord."

"And on you, peace. Rise. We have much to do."

The leader stood, stepped one pace forward, and snapped a salute. "Captain Simms, at your service, Lord Karne."

How does he feel, serving the "woman" of my sire's sons? Karne wondered, feeling the old anger rise and shaking it off with difficulty. "Which ship is mine?"

Simms nodded toward the nearest flitter, then motioned forward one of the guardsmen, a dark, stocky young man with merry eyes and a crooked smile. The young guardsman saluted. "I'm your pilot, my lord."

Karne nodded acknowledgment and turned toward the flitter, already thinking about how to relearn the intricacies of Gharr politics very quickly.

"Milord?" Simms said sharply.

Karne stopped and turned back. He waited with barely hidden impatience for the officer to speak.

"Milord, House Harlan laid siege to the manor house only hours ago. We cannot take you home, lord."

Karne bent his head, appearing to study his boots, in order to hide the tension in his face. Harlan! Asten Harlan must be dead for his House to be this effective! When he looked up, he had his face under control. "Why didn't the Council summons that brought me back tell me a siege had been set? I was still on Balder when Harlan declared it."

"There was no forty-day notice, my lord."

"By my Sire's Blood!" Karne spun away and stared up at the gray light above the pad canopy. His thoughts whirled around the meaning of such an illegal siege. House Harlan must be out of that incompetent Asten's hands and into another's, Karne told himself. Richard's? The Four Guardians protect my House if Richard's older brother's dead!

Simms cleared his throat ostentatiously. "House Harlan has much support in Council now, my lord. As you know, your sire's Will made the Larga regent for the six months until your majority. Many on Council oppose a woman regent, even for so short a time. It is against all tradition, my lord. Beggin' your pardon, lord, but Harlan thinks to use that part of the Will to take Halarek Holding."

The unspoken conclusion to this summary was that Trev Halarek's frank contempt for his wiry, "weakling" son greatly strengthened Harlan's position. Karne's mouth tightened into a hard, bitter line. *We're not built like bulls, sire, my lady mother and Kathryn and I, but that doesn't mean we're weak! And I learned the basics of Gharr law in spite of you, at the Academy.* He knew what he had to do. He turned to his men. "Council must lift an illegal siege. We'll go directly to Council ground." The decision took some of his tension from him. Karne sprinted to his flitter, vaulted onto the wide wing, and slid into the passenger seat.

The pilot was only a moment behind him. He adjusted several knobs and switches, tossed a heavy coat and a stunner to Karne, and buckled himself into his safety webbing. Then he turned and extended his hand, Family fashion. "I'm Nik, milord. Nicholas von Schuss."

Karne clasped the offered hand and looked at the young man keenly. "Does the Baron know you're with me? Even acting as a pilot for my House can give your House the seeming of an alliance."

Von Schuss smiled crookedly. "He knows, because we *are* allied, Lord Karne. *Someone* has to support House Halarek. If one House can threaten another as Harlan is doing, no House is safe. Are you ready to leave, milord?"

Karne nodded, slid the stunner under his belt, finished pressing closed the coat, and fastened his webbing. Anger was bitter in his mouth. Even the essential knowledge of who Halarek's allies were had been kept from him. The flitter and its four escorts lifted off before the pad canopy had fully opened, slipping through the widening slit into the night and swirling snow. The moon, Tarval, had risen, and its pale blue light made the landscape below look even colder than it was. Plumes of blowing snow skimmed over the rolling hills, twisting, thinning, fanning out in the wind.

Karne looked over at the pilot. "You weren't in the Blues when I lived here, yet you fly the Lharr himself, a senior officer's job."

Von Schuss laughed, a deep, infectious chuckle that reminded Karne of the Baron von Schuss. "I may be only months in House Halarek's service, Lord Karne, but I'm the best pilot this side of the equator, and *that* makes me the Lharr's pilot. The Larga assigns people by ability, not seniority." He did not sound like he was bragging and his position as pilot to the Lharr suggested what he said was true.

Karne shifted to a more comfortable position. "If

you're von Schuss, and you clearly are by your looks and your voice, why haven't we met before?" And with his question, Karne realized he could already be in a Harlan trap. He knew none of House Halarek's officers. He stiffened and his hand dropped to the bulge of the stunner under his coat.

Von Schuss's eyes caught the motion and one corner of his mouth twisted wryly. "If I were Harlan's man, you'd already be dead, my lord. And you'd never have gotten hold of a stunner," he added quietly. "My mother married into House Kingsland and we've lived south of the equator the past fifteen years. Uncle Emil called me back two years ago when—but you don't know, do you? Karl's dead."

"Karl dead? How?"

"By Garren Odonnel, in a duel á outrance."

Karne suddenly felt very old. Karl von Schuss had been Jerem's closest friend. Now he, too, was dead, in a duel to the death. Jerem and Kerel and Liam and Karl and—he shook his head. Now was not the time for grieving, but for planning.

"My lord, ships on the scope, coming fast!"

Karne flashed a look through the flitter's canopy. One moment there was only the wrinkled blue face of the moon and tails of blowing snow, the next moment a heat-beam passed, betrayed by its purple tracer. The rear wing-edge of the nearest Halarek escort glowed red and sagged. The flitter nose-dived and crashed in flames.

"Hold on, lord!"

Von Schuss banked the flitter sharply away from the downed craft. He shot a glance at Karne. "There's a survival suit in the locker behind your seat. Get it on and grab a crash kit. We can't shake fighters; they're too fast for a flitter." Another tracer flashed past. "If we'd known Harlan was going to set siege, you can bet we wouldn't be out in these! I'm going to drop this thing twice. There are some ruins"—von Schuss jerked the flitter violently over—"near here. You'll have a chance of safety there, milord."

Karne sprang up, grabbed the back of his seat as the flitter banked, snatched a survival suit from the locker, and whipped the suit on over everything with greater speed than he remembered ever managing for crash drills.

"Out the cargo hatch on the next dip, lord."

Karne ignored the outraged voice of his sire's ghost, shouting in his head that he was letting a subordinate tell him what to do, and crouched beside the cargo hatch, gripping the crash kit between his chest and right arm. A small silver fighter with no identifying marks swept past overhead, banked, and started back. Karne watched the tracer leave the fighter and speed toward him. Von Schuss let the flitter drop quickly, then jerked it sharply upward.

"Open the door now. The ruins are to the left. Hold on!"

Karne clung to the loading arm with his free hand. The pilot banked sharply and then dropped the flitter. Through the canopy Karne saw a purple streak pass where they had been seconds before. Below, the snow, interrupted occasionally by jumbled rocks and mounds of rubble, streamed past at sinister speed.

"Now, lord!"

Karne swung over the hole and compelled his

straining fingers to let go. He hit the ground hard and rolled, coming up against the foot of a broken wall. He lay quietly in its shelter, shaken and afraid. He watched silver fighters dive after the flitter. The flitter wobbled, corrected course, swooped upward away from the fighters. A heat-beam touched its tail, Karne thought he saw a dark shape leave, then the flitter vanished in a flash of brilliant white light. Had von Schuss escaped? Through the swirling snow Karne could not be sure. The flitter crashed, burning, and two of the unmarked silver fighters followed it down. Blowing snow half hid them as they descended, then blotted them out completely.

Unarmed flitters, unmarked fighters, illegal siege. Rage burned away Karne's fear. They have orders to be sure there are no survivors! By the Four Guardians, I'd give half the Holding to know who's responsible and be able to tell the Council!

A break in the clouds let through a shaft of moonlight, light enough to hunt by. Karne scuttled along the ruined wall, looking for a door, a gate, or even a deep hole, any place where he could hide from the searchers. A dark patch on the wall ahead turned out to be the head of a stairwell. Karne looked over his shoulder. Gusts of wind were already filling his trail with snow and closing the gap in the clouds overhead. Darkness and blowing snow would make searching much harder. Karne said the soldier's prayer for those departed in battle in von Schuss's name and turned to the stairs. They were very dark, but the atomtorch from the kit would mark him like a beacon. He gripped the crash kit more tightly against his chest and started down the stairs with one hand on the wall, feeling the step ahead with his foot, cautiously putting his weight on it, hoping the Old Ones had put none of their traps so close to the surface.

His descent was agonizingly slow. The treads were cracked, broken, littered with rubble from the building above, and slick with dry, korn snow. The searchers had lights and numbers on their side. Karne licked dry lips. Any moment a light might shoot down the stairwell, outlining him against the blackness below. The tread under Karne's foot teetered. He windmilled for balance. The tread tipped and Karne fell. He grabbed at the darkness, desperate to catch a tread edge, a protruding stone, a chunk of rubble—anything to stop the terrible descent, but the stones he clutched tore loose and fell with him, showering him with dust and bits of masonry and a cloud of snow. He tumbled and slid helplessly into the darkness below.

Chapter Two

———◆———

A MAN-HIGH MOUND of rubble stopped Karne's fall with a crash. He lay very still, stunned with amazement that he was still alive. The fall had only knocked the wind out of him and bruised his knees, elbows, and cheek. He lay quiet, listening. His descent must have made a clatter, though he had been too busy trying to save himself to notice.

He heard nothing moving above. Perhaps the falling snow had muffled the noise. He reminded himself grimly that the snow could also muffle the sounds of pursuit until the pursuers were in the stairwell itself. Karne moved cautiously, first to see if his resting place was stable, then to see if cuts, scrapes, and bruises were his only damage.

He got to his knees, found the crash kit by touch, and felt his way cautiously around the mound of rubble. Below it, at least two treads were entirely missing. Was this the edge of one of the Old Ones' pits? Karne glanced over his shoulder. He saw no lights above in the storm. Carefully, shielding the light from searchers above, Karne swept the beam of the kit's torch across the stair. Below the two missing treads, the ruins above began to shelter the stairs and there they were in fair condition. A corridor crossed the foot of the stairs and vanished into the shadows beyond the reach of the light. Karne turned off the torch and descended with care to the corridor below.

He followed a wall by trailing his fingertips across it. Twenty-five paces beyond the stair, his fingers slid into emptiness. A corner, or a trap? Karne knelt and felt the floor ahead of him and to the side. It seemed solid. A corner. He crawled around it, feeling ahead of him, and, when he felt he was safely out of sight of someone at the foot of the stair, he sat on the floor and leaned against the stone wall. He listened. Still no one followed. He touched the face of the chrono to read the time, then let his head fall back against the wall.

Harlan must believe my House very weak, he thought bitterly, to lay an illegal siege and attempt gang assassination against all laws of feud. Is Council now so much in House Harlan's power the Harlans can act as they choose? Does Asten believe he can erase my Family before Council finds out? No, the plan is too good to be Asten Harlan's alone; he's never been a thinker. I *must* get to Council with this news, but if I elude the assassins now, how will I get there? The meeting is only three days away and I have no transport except my feet.

Karne reached for the kit. A light swept the foot of the stairwell, its gleam reflecting from the walls of the corridor. Karne froze, hand still extended, afraid of the sound resuming his position would make.

"Down here, my lord?" The voice was guttural, with a serf's accent and a definite tone of incredulity.

"I'm sure I saw him jump near here, Krand," came the reply.

Karne recognized the smooth, mellow voice, and broke into a cold sweat. Richard Harlan. He must be the Heir now, to come personally to see the Heir of House Halarek killed. Karne stood very, very slowly, silencing the metal objects on his belt with his hands. His mind raced. If the men came down the corridor, he would run. He was a dead man whether he ran or not, but it was better to chance the pits and mantraps of the Old Ones than the sure, ungentle mercies of Richard Harlan.

"I'm sure he jumped over there, lord," the serf continued. "Do you want me to go down here and look anyway?"

"What do you think, fool?"

The serf may have been stupid enough to question his master, but he was not stupid enough to argue. "I—I'm—the Old Ones—"

"Are you refusing an order, Krand?" Richard Harlan's voice was silky and all the more dangerous for it.

"You—you gave no order, lord. I—I—I just thought that if Halarek had come this way there'd be some sign."

"Go down and look, Krand."

The light bounced up and down as the Harlan soldier descended. Karne heard the man yelp, then heard the crashing and crumbling noises that indicated a fall. There was a long moment of silence, then Karne heard the man pick himself up and continue down the stair. Karne flattened himself against the wall and held his breath. Had snow falling from his boots left a trail? The serf's footsteps echoed from the stone walls.

"I'm not goin' into any of the Old Ones' Helholes," the serf muttered, not loud enough for Harlan to hear, but loud enough to echo to Karne. "Passages that go down and around so sneaky ya never know where ya are, and pits, and deadfalls and—"

"What do you see down there?" Harlan's voice was impatient.

The serf swung his light back and forth along the passages. "Nobody's been here, my lord."

"You'd better be right. Your life depends on it."

"I—I understand, milord."

Karne prayed the serf's fear of the Old Ones' treacherous and booby-trapped passages would outweigh his fear of execution. The man came a few steps down the corridor, dimming his light as

if he had gone farther. Moments later Karne heard
the soldier clumping and slipping on the stairs. He
heard Harlan's voice, but the men were apparently
already moving and the wind blew the words
away. Karne waited a long time before he sank to a
sitting position and let his head drop on arms
crossed over his knees. *Richard himself comes to
find me!*

Despair overcame the iron control he had kept
on his grief ever since he received the Council's
message and Karne wept, there in the dark and the
cold, for his brothers, Jerem and Kerel and Liam,
and for himself, the despised and untrained third-
born son, who now must deal with the consequences of the feud his great-grandsire had
started. Much later, cold penetrated even the survival suit, rousing Karne from his despair. His
joints ached with the cold, his fingers and toes
burned. Cursing himself for precious time wasted,
Karne reached for the crash kit. Clumsily, he
opened it with fingers that hurt at every movement. He set the thermo on its stand and huddled
close to its warmth until the pain in his hands and
feet eased. Then he unrolled the two-man shelter,
released a compressed-air capsule that inflated its
support tubes, and crawled into it with the thermo
and the rest of the kit. He connected the thermo to
the shelter's vent and pulled packages of klag and
dehydrated stew from the kit. He stared at them.
Standard crash-kit rations. Both required water.

Karne closed his eyes. Harlan and his searchers
were probably gone, looking elsewhere. Did he
want to risk a trip to the surface? The idea of
climbing the treacherous stairs and possibly ex-

posing himself to Richard Harlan frightened him
to his core. He had been too long away from
Starker IV. His instinctive feel for danger, his ability to instantly make the right reaction for his survival—these skills had been years unused. He
wondered bitterly if he still had them. And what of
von Schuss? If he had escaped the crash, he was
still out in the storm. As his commanding officer,
as a fellow human being, Karne felt a responsibility to help von Schuss if he could. And knew that
feeling was inappropriate on this world. He
opened his eyes and looked blindly at the white
shelter wall. He could wait for food, but he could
not wait to look for von Schuss. He had to go back
out to the surface.

Karne twisted the top off the one can of energy
rations and gulped the contents. He felt the
warmth of its alcohol content first, then the slow
surge of strength as the nutrients took hold. Karne
picked up his torch and the kit's collapsible
bucket, peeled open the doorseal, and crawled
slowly out of the shelter. He crouched in the darkness and listened. There was only the silence of the
dead stone building and the faint howl of the wind
above. He rose and walked carefully toward the
stairs, feeling his way with feet and fingertips. At
the foot of the stairs he stopped again and listened
for a long time. Unmuted by stone, the wind was
shrieking. He remembered how Starker IV's winds
could be in Narn, tearing at snowdrifts, ripping
branches from trees, freezing any warm-blooded
creature unfortunate enough to be caught out.

He crawled up the stairs on all fours, unwilling
to expose himself by using the light. When his

hands reached the top, he lay down, listening. He heard only the wind. He cautiously brought his head to the surface and looked. There were no lights. He crawled over the top and crouched there, listening still more, then crept silently along the base of the wall, keeping one hand on it at all times. Metal clinked against stone. Karne stopped in mid-motion. He heard another clink, just beyond a tall snowdrift. He set the bucket down carefully and drew the stunner from his belt. Then he flicked on the torch and pointed the light in the direction of the sound. The response was a rustling, sliding noise on the other side of the drift and a faint voice. "Lord Karne? I—" It was von Schuss's voice. A snow-covered lump at the edge of the light rose a little from the ground, then collapsed heavily.

Karne started toward the man, then remembered lessons in suspicion he had not needed for almost six years. He paused. Nothing else moved in the wind-whipped night. If he could see no one, no one could see him to kill him. Except von Schuss. Karne shook himself. That was not possible. The von Schusses had always been friends of Halarek. Karne returned the stunner to its case and quickly pushed through the snow to von Schuss's side.

"Von Schuss. Von Schuss!" He shook the man, but got no response. He turned the light on him. Von Schuss was unconscious, but clinging to the strap of his crash kit. The kit's fabric was wet and badly frayed.

"He's been dragging it!" Karne gripped the torch in his teeth with some difficulty and ran his hands

swiftly over von Schuss. A jagged point of bone
jutted through the right sleeve of von Schuss's uniform.

"Guardians!" Karne whispered, remembering
the agony of bone-end grating against bone-end,
and he rubbed the slight lump in his lower arm
where a similar break had been. He also remembered his sire's scorn because he had fainted when
the bone was set. He had been seven winters old.
Karne shook off the memory, dragged the injured
man as carefully as possible to the top of the stairs,
sat down with von Schuss's back against his chest,
and slid on his rear to the corridor below. At no
time did von Schuss release his grip on the crash
kit.

Much later, Karne sank back on his haunches
and looked at his work. He had sealed the two
crash shelters together because a two-man really
had no room for cooking if it had two men in it,
had splinted von Schuss's arm with a splint made
from the stand of the second thermo, dialed the
thermo up a decade to warm the half-frozen pilot,
then rolled von Schuss in his nightbag. He had
made a second trip to the surface for the bucket
and snow to melt in it. On that trip he thought he
heard fliers, but he had seen no lights. Now a two-
pot of stew and klag filled the shelter with warm,
fragrant steam. Karne set the pot off the thermo
and poured a mug of klag for himself from the
upper pot. He sipped cautiously, but the hot liquid
singed his tongue anyway.

Three days, Karne mused. Only three days between now and Council, and I'm three days' walk,
for an uninjured man, in tolerable weather, from

Halarek Holding. Karne looked at von Schuss. *I could leave him to survive if he can until I send someone for him from Council. It's what my sire would've done. But if the storms get worse or if Council denies my lady mother the regency . . .* Karne sipped the hot klag and stared at the steam still rising from the two-pot. Von Schuss's eyelids trembled. Karne's hands tightened around the mug. *He saved my life,* he told himself fiercely. *We go together, somehow.*

Von Schuss opened his eyes. "I didn't dream you found me." His voice was ragged and disbelieving.

Karne gave a short laugh. "Don't give me credit. I just snuck above ground for some snow and heard you by pure chance. I was afraid Harlan's men were still up there. Me, Trev Halarek's son, hiding in the dark of an Old Ones' place because I was afraid!"

There was a long silence. Then von Schuss stirred in the nightbag and pushed himself to a sitting position. He fixed Karne with his dark, serious eyes. "There's no crime in fear, lord, only in acting a coward because of it, or in showing it to your men. A commander's fear, and the care it calls forth, have won many a battle for the one afraid."

Von Schuss shifted position to ease his broken arm, winced at the movement, and cursed softly. "Harlan! Asten is failing and Richard takes the reins before his time. May his sire learn of it!" He looked down at the thin, smooth fabric floor of the shelter, then up at the shelter roof just centimeters above his head. "I tangled with two of Harlan's soldiers on my way here. They'd followed the flitter down. I killed them, too, but one of them kicked my broken arm as he went down, and I blacked out. I don't know how long I was out, but I was hellish cold when I woke up and heard you." Von Schuss shivered, remembering. "Do I smell klag?"

Karne nodded and poured a mug for him. While the pilot drank, Karne ladled out the stew, then sat watching the heat eddies bend and flow across the surface of his klag and wishing he were back on sunny, peaceful Balder. He'd had to come home. Much as he hated Starker IV's clan feuds and intrigues, he'd had to come home. His entire House and Holding would have been destroyed otherwise.

Third son and fourth to inherit, he thought bitterly. If women could inherit, I think my sire would've put Kit ahead of me. For her to have our lady mother's build and temperament was all right. The pain of that knowledge was as sharp as it had ever been. In the five years at the Academy, where he had been judged on his own personality and accomplishments, memory of Trev Halarek's contempt had been pushed to the back of Karne's mind. Now it was brutally vivid again. His mouth firmed to a thin, hard line. Well, he promised himself, my sire's despised third son will save something from Harlan hands, if saving is possible.

"My lord?"

Karne looked up. The pilot was studying him gravely. Karne hid his feelings behind a smile, which came out more of a wry grimace. "Doesn't it seem rather silly to you, one Heir calling another 'my lord'?" Karne asked.

Von Schuss lifted one eyebrow. "I'm a junior officer in your service, Karne Halarek."

Karne's hands tightened around his mug and he looked again at the minute ripple of heat flowing across the klag. "Right now I need a friend far more than another junior officer," he murmured. He could not make himself look up to see the pilot's reaction to this second breach of Gharr etiquette, so close on the heels of the first. This is the Altarian Academy's top cadet negotiator? he asked himself derisively. The cadet who never let his feelings show or influence him when dealing with an issue?

Von Schuss cleared his throat, hesitantly. "If that's the way you want it..." His voice was husky.

Karne looked at him then and von Schuss's eyes did not slide away from his in embarrassment as Karne had expected. In fact, the eyes brightened and the corners crinkled with good humor.

"Friends it is, then, 'my lord.' In private. What are you going to do now?"

"Get to Council ground somehow. Halarek Holding's the closest to us; maybe we can sneak in and steal one of Harlan's fliers for the trip."

Von Schuss chuckled. "Pull the Zinn bear's tail, huh? Wouldn't that be fun! We certainly can't get to the manor's fliers." He sobered. "I appreciate the 'we.' Your sire would've left me or killed me to keep me from slowing him down. I won't slow you down, Karne. There are painkillers in the kit. I'll keep up."

And he did. The storm had stopped by the time they climbed out of the Old Ones' ruins and started toward Halarek Holding, but gray clouds covered the sky, keeping the air cold. The sun was only a pale, green-white disk above them. The hard, wind-packed snow surface was a blessing, for they could walk much faster over the snow than through it, and a brisk pace helped fight the stinging cold. They talked little so they could hear approaching fliers, and there were several—small, fast, silver, and unmarked—scanning the rim of the Desert for survivors. Each time the young men heard one, they dropped to the snow, the white snow-textured back of the survival suits facing the approaching sound. Each time a flier passed over, Karne expected a sudden, deadly heat-beam. At no time did von Schuss mention his pain or ask for an easier pace. They traveled three days through open country, skirting the Desert, stopping only as necessary for rest, warmth, food, or sleep, driven by the need to get to Council in time.

On the morning of the fourth day, the day of the opening of Council, Karne and von Schuss climbed the low mountain pass that divided Halarek Holding from the Desert of Zinn and moved down the Holding side.

"Flier!" von Schuss cried sharply.

The men dropped flat and the flier passed over.

"Harlan green," von Schuss observed. "*Here*, at least, the fighters wear his colors. We must be near Harlan's outposts."

The two moved quickly through the foothills between the pass and the plain, using sheltered riverbeds where the snow was not deep and drifts were few. Fliers frequently passed over and the young men had to scuttle under the edge of a riverbank or drop facedown on the snow. Finally, from a ridge in the lower hills, they saw the entrance shelters of Ontar manor and city, all of them ringed by Harlan army units. Ontar was the center of the Holding, its heart. The sun broke through a gap in the clouds, throwing a painful glare from the snow. Karne squinted upward.

"It's almost midday. Council will be opening. We have to find a flier very soon."

They slid down the westward side of the ridge and slipped through the bluepines toward what had, from higher in the hills, looked like the outer ring of Harlan positions. Karne relied on von Schuss for educated guesses about likely spots for Harlan fliers to set down. Karne had had little military experience beyond armory practices, war games on Balder's open countryside, and the theories in books. The two young men moved almost silently through the snow, listening for men talking or the sound of a flier's engines. Karne felt time closing in on him. The regency of House Halarek had to be one of the first items on the World Council's agenda.

"Hsst!"

Karne froze at von Schuss's warning. In a hollow below them, two men in Harlan green leaned against an unmarked silver fighter. "Silver!" Karne whispered. "Proof!" He motioned von Schuss to stay put, then crept to the edge of the hollow and looked down on the Harlan soldiers. They wore beamers, but in belt-cases with snapped covers. While Karne watched, one of the men below pulled a flask out of his survival suit and motioned his companion to the low, inviting edge of one of the fighter's wings. Karne returned to von Schuss, who had taken advantage of the pause to wrap an arm around the flaky red trunk of a bluepine and rest his head and shoulder against the bark.

"You look done in, Nik."

A wan smile tipped the corner of the pilot's mouth. "Nearly. The kits have stim-tabs. Keep me going a little longer."

"The 'guards' aren't worried about being disturbed. Their beamers are locked up and they've just sat down for a little nip of something."

Von Schuss gulped a small white tablet and pushed himself away from the tree. He stumbled and caught at the tree to steady himself. "The stim-tab takes a few minutes to work, lord."

"I don't have a few minutes, Nik. Wait here a little while, then follow me."

"There are two of them."

"There are. But you aren't in any condition to help me. You can barely put one foot ahead of the other. Every moment here lessens my chances of reaching Council before it makes a decision. Imagine what tales the Harlans are telling, Nik! Or maybe they're consoling my lady mother for the loss of the Heir in the storm. I'll take those guards down, Nik. I have to."

Karne slipped away through the trees. He wished he were really as confident as he had led von Schuss to believe. He crouched at the edge of the hollow and examined the terrain. On his left, thick, low trees almost reached the side of the fighter. Bad strategy, he told the Harlan men silently. No good soldier plants himself so close to cover for the enemy. Karne circled toward the trees. The snow was dry; when disturbed, it would not send small betraying balls down the slope. Then he was among the trees, sliding toward the fighter. For several minutes, he could see the flier through the branches, but not the guards. He worried. Then he reached the edge of the trees. The guards had finished their drink and now stood by the craft's nose, looking up toward where he had been. Had they heard something? Had they seen Nik? Karne sat down and leaned against a tree trunk to steady his arm, then tuned his stunner to "long range" and swept its beam across the men. They folded up gracefully. Karne sprinted to them, felt each's jugular. The blood beat slowly, but regularly.

Soft! Too soft to kill them! Trev Halarek's ghost whispered. *Such softness will get you dead!* Karne shook off the warning and bent to strip the men of their uniforms.

Von Schuss skidded down the slope and grabbed the edge of one wing to keep himself from falling. "Dead?" He nodded at the two still forms.

"No. Someone will probably find them before they freeze."

Karne helped von Schuss into the fighter. In its shelter, they changed into the Harlan uniforms. Karne draped a uniform jacket over von Schuss's shoulders, arranging it so the crude splint was easily seen. He leaned back and studied the effect.

"You'll do. Invent some story about being injured in the siege or whatever. We are carrying important news for Lord Asten. Even if he has men looking for us at Council, and I doubt he does, he won't expect us in *his* uniforms."

Von Schuss pulled back in his seat, incredulous. "You're going to Asten Harlan?"

"*You* are. I'd give a lot to tell Richard to his face that he's failed to kill me, but, even in the Council chamber, I don't think I'd live more than a few seconds after he recognized me. It would be a stupid risk. *I* have a message for House von Schuss about its missing Heir."

Von Schuss grinned at some thought of his own. Karne belted both of them in, then lifted the fighter abruptly out of the hollow and turned it toward Council ground.

"That takeoff lacked a certain finesse..."

Karne did not respond to the humor in the pilot's voice. "Haven't flown since I left here. No need." He set the auto-pilot and was reaching for the dial to turn control over to it when the com crackled to life.

"Ship 30. Ship 30. Where do you think you're going!"

Karne flashed a look at von Schuss, who shrugged. Karne caught his lip between his teeth for a moment, then leaned forward and spoke. "We're heading for Council ground. We've just caught a skip-cast from that special patrol over Zinn. You know Lord Richard wants its report as soon as possible. Discreetly, not on the public channels."

"Those *are* the orders. Don't dawdle coming back. If Halarek finds that gap—"

"Yessir! We'll go silent." Karne snapped the set off.

"A string of lucky guesses, milord, all verified."

Von Schuss chuckled and settled himself more comfortably in his seat.

Karne sighed. "Lucky is right. I should just have mentioned Richard. That would've been enough. I took too much risk. I should've known better. If those hadn't been Richard's orders, we'd have had fliers all over us." He turned control over to the auto-pilot and let his head fall back against the seat's headrest. For a few minutes he enjoyed the feel of sitting down, then turned to von Schuss. "Let's talk about timing. I've never been to a session of Council and we're going to have to stop the meeting dead."

"*Never* been to Council?"

"My sire was sure I'd never rule, so he saw no need to take me. I had three brothers, after all."

"But you weren't the youngest."

"No," said Karne, in such a final way that von Schuss said nothing more on the subject.

A decade of Odonnel soldiers lounged outside the Council lift-shelters, eyeing stragglers going down to the Council chamber and stopping several, either to ask something or, once, to make a quick body search. Karne and Nik von Schuss watched the indignant search victim step into the lift and disappear downward. Karne saw in von Schuss's grim face and stiffened posture the pilot's outrage at this blatant disregard of the neutrality of Council ground. Karne was sure his own anger was not visible. The Academy had trained him well.

"You still want to try it, Karne?"

"Don't use my name!" Karne warned in a low voice. "I have no choice but to go in." He loosened his stunner in its sheath and walked briskly toward the lift. "Look important and rushed," he whispered. "We have a vital message for Lord Asten."

The Odonnel men moved to block them. The prefet in charge blocked the center of the lift opening, crossed his arms over his chest, and looked insolently down into Karne's eyes. The faintest ghost of taunting laughter drifted through the Odonnel men. Karne wrapped himself in an aura of authority and power. The illusion was effective —Karne had used it successfully two or three times when negotiations stalled—but it *was* an illusion. Inside Karne apprehension and fear churned his stomach and made his heart beat faster. He stalked up to the prefet. "Stand aside!" he ordered sharply. "We bear important messages to Lord Asten by Lord Richard's command!"

The prefet looked less sure of himself.

"Stand aside!"

The prefet moved out of the way. Karne brushed past him into the waiting lift and touched the control for "chamber level." The illusion of authority vanished the moment the door closed; Karne sagged against the lift wall.

"By the Guardians, you certainly set that prefet back on his heels, Karne!"

"A thespian's trick," Karne replied absently. The lift began descending. Karne gritted his teeth. "Searches! By a private army on Council ground! What's happened to the law?"

"It does look bad." Von Schuss's face was grave.

The lift's descent slowed. They had almost reached the Council-chamber level. Summoning again the control the Academy had taught him, Karne took deep, slow breaths to control his fury. *The successful pacification officer does not exhibit his feelings about an issue. On most worlds, such exhibitions influence one side or the other to feel an advantage.* The deep, slow breathing began to work. *The Navy pacification officer does not exhibit his feelings about an issue: he uses them, under appropriate intellectual control, to fuel effective action.* The lift doors opened onto the brilliant blue-green mosaics of the hall that encircled the Council chamber. Karne paused in the opening for a moment. *Effective action,* he repeated to himself. Guardians! My Academy training is all I have. Let it be of use to my House.

Von Schuss fumbled with his good hand in his breast pocket, pulled out another stim-tab, and swallowed it. "Last one."

"We'll be done, one way or another, before that one wears off, Nik."

The two strode toward the big double doors, looking to neither side. They entered the circular Council chamber and stopped just inside the doors to assess the situation. Bright overhead lights picked out details in harsh contrasts. Below the tri-d screen on the curved back wall, this term's chairman, the Duke deVree, leaned forward over his desk's glistening surface, his eyes intent on Lharr Timkin Odonnel, who was speaking. The Freemen's section, to the chairman's left, was half-empty. The benches of the minor Houses, to the chairman's right, were nearly full, and the lord of

one of these Houses was standing, waiting for his
turn to speak. Across the aisles separating the
semicircle of the Nine Families from the rest of
Council, House Halarek's segment was glaringly
empty. Only a few cousins from distant small-holdings sat on the benches, and no one sat in the front
row at the prep table reserved for the head-of-
House and his staff. Von Schuss rested his good
hand on Karne's shoulder encouragingly, then
walked down the circular aisle toward the benches
of House Harlan. Karne strode purposefully
toward the von Schuss prep table, hearing the disapproving buzz on his left made by the von Schuss
Family at the sight of the green Harlan uniform in
their area.

The Lharr Odonnel was saying, "House Odonnel
regrets, as do the rest of the Nine Families, the
death in the storm of Karne Halarek, the young
Lharr designate. However, it's imperative that the
House now left leaderless receive a new lord. The
only surviving males of that line are infants, sons
of Kerel Halarek, clearly impossible Heirs at this
difficult time, yet the Family Halarek has not chosen to take part in this debate." Odonnel waved
disdainfully at the almost-empty Halarek benches.

Karne stiffened, but he refrained from looking at
the speaker. The Lharr Odonnel had to know about
the siege, the reason Halarek was not represented.
Even Karne knew that Odonnel and Harlan had
been close allies for ten generations. Karne
stopped behind the first row of von Schuss
benches, keeping his eyes on the back of Baron von
Schuss's balding head.

Odonnel's righteous voice went on. "In spite of

her grief at the loss of her husband and sons, the Larga, at least, should be here with some male relative to speak for her and her House. Does she think we will actually appoint *her* head-of-House, whatever the late Lharr's Will said?"

An angry murmur swept the chamber. "No female regent!" someone on the deVree back benches shouted. Baron von Schuss shook his head despairingly. At that moment Karne gripped the baron's shoulder. The baron whipped around. His eyes met the green uniform and his face flushed deep red. "Your master's already—"

"Emil." Karne tipped back his helmet so the baron could see his face and telltale golden eyes.

The baron's anger faded and he started to rise. Karne put a finger to his lips and shook his head. The baron sank down onto the bench again and moved to make room for Karne beside him. A wondering murmur whispered through the von Schuss benches. Across the chamber, Nik had just passed the Justin benches and stood at the rear of the House Harlan's section. Karne touched the baron's arm and nodded slightly in Nik's direction. The baron sucked his breath in sharply.

"He didn't die in Zinn," he murmured after a moment. "We heard a 'cast from Gildport about an attack over Zinn and I knew Nik had been named the Lharr's pilot..." The baron's voice trailed away.

"My House is under siege. That's why you heard nothing from Halarek."

The two men returned their attention to the Harlan benches. Nik was brushing aside the hands of Harlan soldiers offering help to an injured comrade. He walked slowly down the aisle leading to Harlan's prep table, every movement that of a wounded and weary man. He bent and whispered something in Lord Asten's ear, straightened, and retreated to a cluster of young men on the Justin back benches. He removed his green helmet and kept his face turned from the Harlan table.

Even from across the room, Karne could see the blaze of triumph on Asten Harlan's face, and the suspicion on his son's. The duke turned quickly to Richard and began talking urgently. More and more eyes turned from the speaker to the duke or the mysterious murmurings on the Justin back bench. Nik and Karne exchanged small nods, then Nik slid off the Harlan jacket. Surprise rippled along the Justin bench, followed by a sudden rush of Justin and von Schuss men to Nik's side.

The chairman pounded his gavel on the polished desk top. "Quiet back there! We have a speaker on the floor. What's the meaning of this interruption?"

Nik stood. "Nicholas von Schuss, House von Schuss, here, my lord. I've just brought Lord Asten news that the assassins successfully brought down over Zinn all the Halarek flitters they had been sent to attack."

The chamber echoed with the shocked gasps of Council. Von Schuss waited for the sound to fade.

"I did not tell him there were two survivors, my lords. Two out of nine. I, Heir to House von Schuss, am one and Karne Halarek is the other."

All over the chamber, men turned to one another, repeating what von Schuss had said, commenting on it, some shouting at others, some standing and shaking clenched fists at House Harlan.

"Halarek's already dead!" someone shouted.

Nik motioned and his Justin friends closed protectively around him. He raised his head proudly and pointed to House von Schuss's front bench. "There! Halarek lives!"

Chapter Three

———◆———

KARNE SPRANG TO his feet and threw off the helmet and uniform jacket. The helmet spun across the polished floor toward the chairman's table—*whick, whick, whick.* The noise seemed loud in the suddenly silent chamber. Karne stood straight and proud. He turned slowly so everyone could see the golden eyes unique to the Larga's people. The chamber exploded into sound and motion. Halarek Family men leaped up and down shouting, "Halarek lives! Halarek lives!" Men poured into the aisles, yelling; pumping hands, brandishing fists, arguing. Friends of House Halarek swarmed toward Karne.

"Order! Order!" Chairman deVree cried, and his gavel made sharp cracking noises against his desk.

But the noise only grew louder. Nik von Schuss worked his way to the von Schuss benches, helped by a flying wedge of Justin friends. He gave Karne a triumphant grin and sank into the place Karne had just vacated. Justin men closed around Karne on three sides.

"We want you to live to tell your story, lord," one of the men behind Karne murmured.

Karne did not turn from the scene in the center of the chamber, but his "Thanks," was heartfelt.

He caught only a glimpse of Richard Harlan before the crush of Family men concealed the Harlan bench from his sight. The Heir of Harlan had been livid. Karne lost track of how long the shouting and shoulder-pounding went on. His head began to spin with weariness and the noise, motion, smells, and bright lights in the chamber. Suddenly the lights went out. There was a brief, surprised surge of noise, then silence. Karne heard the breathing of his neighbors and the sighing of the ventilator fans. His guard of Justin men pressed closer and several of them stepped in front of him.

"When you're quiet again, lords and Freemen, the lights will come on and we'll resume the meeting." The chairman's voice was hard.

No one moved or spoke. The chairman banged his gavel twice and the lights came on again. Lord Asten stood. His son appeared to be pulling down on his arm, to little effect.

The duke bowed to the chairman. His face was flushed and shiny with sweat and he was breathing rapidly. "It's a trick! Karne Halarek died aboard the *Aldefara*. Her captain will swear it. This boy's an impostor!" The sound system brought the harsh rasp of his breathing to everyone. "You know the Halareks. Do they breed slender, fine-boned sons?"

"No!" roared the benches of Harlan and Odonnel.

"Trev Halarek never brought his third son to Council. In fact, he exiled him to the Altair system as soon as the child was old enough to travel there alone. How many here know what that third son looks like?"

There were very few, and their memories of Karne Halarek were of a small child.

Our House now pays for your conceits, sire, Karne thought bitterly. I can't be personally identified even by my own vassals!

"He died in space, lords and Freemen, just as I reported." The duke struggled a moment for air. "Captain Telek of the *Aldefara* will verify what I say."

Karne waited for the roar that followed to die down, then walked into the open area between the chairman's desk and the prep tables of the Families. He faced the chairman, touched head and heart in respect as was the custom among the worlds of the Federation, and turned to the benches of the Nine Families. Even as he opened his mouth to speak, he heard voices from Harlan and Odonnel pointing out the alienness of that salute. He straightened and lifted his head with the pride expected of a Lharr. "The Gild itself will give the lie to the Duke of Harlan. Ask the First Merchant. I was *supposed* to die in space, lords and Freemen. The *Aldefara* is now confined to an orbit above us, waiting for Patrol investigators. There were assassins aboard that ship, gentlemen, and you all know how the Gild feels about it." He walked slowly around the circular space, looking across the ranks of Freemen and minor Houses as well as the benches of the Nine. "Look at my eyes, lords and Freemen. They are the eyes of my lady mother's people. Of all the Gharr, only my lady mother, my sister, and I have them. This is well known."

A low mutter of agreement swept the chamber. The sound affected Karne like a stimulant. I have more support here than just House von Schuss! For a few minutes he felt refreshed and wide awake.

Richard Harlan bent his smooth, dark head to his sire's and whispered something. The duke shook his head, pushed himself unsteadily to his feet, and pointed a shaking finger at Karne. "He's wearing special lenses that change the true color of his eyes. They're easy to find off-world."

Richard Harlan's mouth pursed in disgust. He turned away from his sire and crossed his arms over his chest. The Marquis of Gormsby rose and stalked around in front of his table. He pointed a quivering finger at Lord Asten.

"I'm no friend to Halarek, as you well know, Asten Harlan, but I'm not a fool! We're *Family* here, not serfs, and won't be put off with stupidities! Your House has already engaged in enough stupidities the last few days to last it a generation!" The Marquis pointedly turned his back to Harlan and sat down again.

"My lord deVree," said Karne, "may I still speak?"

The chairman nodded. Karne turned toward Harlan.

"Milord, we both know that who I am is not the issue. The issues are assassination and siege."

There was a sudden intake of breath in the chamber and then a wave of whispering in which "siege" was the most audible word. Karne waited for the whispering to fade, then spoke quietly, forcing his listeners to pay close attention. "The Harlans try to divert your attention to protect themselves, lords and Freemen. Unmarked fighters, directed by Richard Harlan, whose voice I myself heard, attacked my flight over Zinn and shot down my flitter and all of my escorts. With Harlan troops holding Ontar manor and city under siege, Halarek could tell no one what was—"

"Point of order," Richard Harlan cut in.

"What is your point, milord?"

"Lord Chairman, Karne Halarek isn't a member of Council and therefore has no right to speak."

A young man of House Justin stood. "Cinkaid of Justin, my lord Chairman. A man has his title and position on Council by blood right and not by Council permission."

"He's still a minor," Richard corrected smoothly.

"He's a legal representative of his House," Cinkaid retorted.

"Minors have no voice in Council."

Chairman deVree rapped sharply on his desk. "My lords! You have neither one been recognized except to state the point of order, and Frem Davin Reed has risen."

"A Freeman!"

"This is a question for the Families—"

"What business do Freemen have—"

"Let him speak!" deVree roared.

"Thank you, my lord." Davin Reed stepped down from his seat in the tiers of Freemen and walked to the speaker's post in the aisle. He wore the traditional tights and short-sleeved sark of Freemen. The badge on his chest said he was an alderman for the freecity of Loch. "Freemen, lords, and minor

Houses, Karne Halarek's right to the title and to a position in Council *are* the business of the Houses alone, but he said 'siege,' and that is *our* business."

Richard Harlan stood again and bowed gracefully to the chair and to Reed. "Frem Reed, we of the Nine appreciate the Freemen's willingness to guard the laws of feud, but this a minor matter, easily settled by discussion and negotiation."

Richard's polished manner and courteous speech impressed the older members of several of the Nine, who smiled and nodded agreement. Karne watched them and hoped savagely that some of them were smiling at Richard's inadvertent pun on his age.

"Out of order," Baron von Schuss muttered under his breath.

Reed leaned toward the pick-up so his voice came into the room louder than it had. "I did not yield the floor, milord Richard."

Reed stared at the Harlan heir coolly. Richard's eyes narrowed and his mouth tightened. He returned the stare, then shrugged and sat again in his place.

"Thank you," Reed said dryly. He turned slightly sideways so he could look across the tiers of Freemen as he spoke. "We have laws that govern feuds for the protection of the rest of the planet. We maintain our Freemen's neutrality only by insisting that these laws be obeyed. There has been no tri-d notice of siege, no forty-day truce for noncombatants to leave, no call for mediation. *There must be no secret sieges!*" He turned to look fully at Chairman deVree. "The Freemen insist the young Lharr speak."

DeVree spun his chair to face House Harlan. "Your

point of order is overruled. Halarek's position is not the question at this time. He claims to have witnessed an illegal siege and to have survived an illegal attempt at gang assassination. He may speak as a witness no matter his age. Lord Karne."

Karne swallowed the lump in his throat and spoke directly to Chairman deVree. "When my flight was shot down over Zinn, only Pilot von Schuss and I survived. We walked, lords and Freemen, for three days to reach my Holding, only to find Ontar manor surrounded by Harlan's armies."

"Liar!" Asten Harlan shouted.

Karne looked over the Houses in the semicircle of the Nine, from Kingsland to Harlan. "We stole a fighter, von Schuss and I, in order to get to Council. The fighter was silver, unmarked by the colors of any House, just like the ones that attacked us in Zinn, but this one was guarded by men in these uniforms." He kicked the green uniform jacket out to join the helmet in the center of the floor. "You all saw House Harlan acknowledge us when we came in. What other evidence of responsibility is needed?"

He waited for the outraged clamor that followed his question to die down. He stood a little straighter and looked around the chamber to gauge the reactions of the members of Council. The leaders of the Nine each conferred with members of their Family. Among the Freemen and minor Houses, men moved restlessly. Some had twisted in their seats and were whispering urgently to their neighbors. Many were staring in unconcealed anger at Asten Harlan. Karne spoke to the Freemen. "All of you know of the long feud between Harlan and Halarek. It has always been fought within the laws, until now. But Asten Harlan hates my House so much he has besieged us without notice. He even arranged assassination attempts while I was under Gild neutrality. *To kill me he risked Gild embargo for our entire world!* It is vital to our world that House Harlan be punished for breaking our laws!"

"Lies! Lies! I know nothi—" Asten Harlan gasped, then bent over his prep table, clutching its edge.

Harlan men rushed to his side. The few men on the Halarek benches roared their anger. Men of four minor Houses sprang up, demanding to speak.

"Lords and Freemen," Karne shouted above the uproar, "I haven't finished." Out of the corner of his eye he saw Richard Harlan's mouth form the words "You are finished," and knew his meaning. *There* is the danger in that House, he told himself. He looked away from the Harlan benches to the chairman. "My lord?"

Chairman deVree nodded and began pounding for order. When the noise had died down a little, Karne spoke. "I say again, House Harlan has broken the basic laws of clan feud. I demand the full punishment under the law—life in prison for the instigator and Council trusteeship for the House."

The room fell into utter silence. Asten Harlan lay on the front bench of his House, a black-robed physician at his side. Richard Harlan stood beside the prep table, rolling a stylus across the table and back, his eyes narrowed and fixed on Karne, his handsome face grim.

"You may go to the clinic for proper medical attention, milord," the chairman said. "An accused House may not vote on the accusation anyway."

"No." Asten's voice was thick and his breathing labored. "I'll stay and hear the vote out."

The physician whispered something to him, but Harlan just shook his head irritably. Richard moved to his sire's side. Davin Reed, who had been talking to a soldier in Council red, straightened and walked down the Freemen's aisle to the chairman's table. He spoke quietly to deVree, then returned to his seat.

Richard Harlan laid his hand on his sire's shoulder. "I'll speak for my House until my sire recovers his strength."

Asten shook his head weakly and made several small, floppy motions, as if he were trying to get up and his body would not obey him. Richard did not even look down.

DeVree motioned to a Council soldier stationed near his table. "Get the bailiffs, and see they prepare the ballots immediately." DeVree stood, so all members of Council could see him well. "Davin Reed, freecity of Loch, informs me that the Gild confirms by satellite pix that Harlan troops do, in fact, surround Ontar and Ontar manor. This siege violates our most basic laws, and action must be taken on this issue before any other. Have you other evidence for your charges, Lord Karne?"

"Only the word of the other witness, my lord." Karne's mouth felt dry, his hands were sweating, his knees felt weak. *My long walk and short nights, the tension—Guardians! Help me. I have to hold up a little longer. The debate must continue and I must appear strong and unafraid. Otherwise, the Families*

will fall upon my House like a Dur cat on a wom doe.
He looked over at the von Schuss table and wished
he could sit there again, with friends, but it was
important now to take physical possession of his
Family's place. He walked to the Halarek prep table
and sat down, alone, at the head of the nearly empty
benches.

The chairman gave him a small nod of approval,
for which Karne felt grateful. "Are there other witnesses, besides young von Schuss, willing to take
oath and testify on this matter?" the chairman
asked.

"Halarek was not sworn."

The chairman frowned. "I trust House Druma
recalls that minors need not be sworn."

"Heads-of-House always are."

"He is not head-of-House yet, Timkin Odonnel,
as you yourself pointed out not long ago. He may
not vote.

"Nicholas von Schuss, have you anything to add
to Halarek's testimony?"

"No, milord. It happened as he said."

The bailiffs arrived and scurried along the aisles,
passing blue ballot paper to everyone present except Karne and the men of House Harlan. DeVree
explained the vote.

"The law requires Council sentence. You, lords
and Freemen, must decide if Asten Harlan is guilty
of siege outside the law. If he is, and we now have
the Gild pix if you questioned Halarek's word, the
sentence is imprisonment until his death, plus a
Council trusteeship for House Harlan for as long as
Council deems necessary. Cast your ballots now."

The Council chamber became very quiet. Karne

watched members of Families cluster, quietly discussing their vote, and assumed such must be the custom. His hands, concealed under the table, clenched and unclenched. Do the members of Council hate my sire's roughshod tactics enough to doom his House? Karne wondered grimly. If the Harlans leave this room without penalty, Starker IV will have a war and House Halarek will be its first casualty. His eyes swept around the chamber. Rows on rows of men of the minor Houses and of the Freemen bent over their writing boards or sat motionless in thought. Those men are my hope, he reminded himself. They are two-thirds of Council, and if they vote against Harlan I have a chance to save my House.

"Voting time is ended," deVree announced. "The bailiffs will collect and count all ballots."

The red-coated bailiffs rapidly picked up the ballots and disappeared to count them. Karne spread his hands on the tabletop and stared at the long brown fingers. Baron von Schuss stood to be recognized.

"Emil von Schuss, House von Schuss. Will the Council discuss the assassins in Zinn while the vote is tallied?"

"We still have that issue on the floor, Baron."

Stubbornly Karne resisted the urge to clench his hands into fists, watching the muscles tighten and the knuckles turn white with the pressure he exerted against the table to keep his fingers still. To the left of the von Schuss benches someone stood for recognition, but Karne did not look up to see who it was. He concentrated on his hands and the table surface that lay beneath them. It was black with centuries of use and abuse, scarred, dented, and stained. Beside his right thumb someone had jabbed a hunting knife point again and again into the surface, exposing the bright red-brown wood beneath the polished surface. The mark had to be very old; weapons of any sort had been banned from the Council chamber for generations. Beside his right hand was a round dent, just the right size for a powerful man's fist, pounded hard in some ancient debate.

The cold, thin voice of the speaker just recognized broke Karne's absorption. "Brand Kingsland, House Kingsland. Hard evidence of an attack by assassins does not exist." Kingsland sat again.

Karne turned toward Kingsland. He studied the man's severe, patrician profile and wished he knew House Kingsland's alliances. *Is Brand the Earl? Surely, in his middle fifties, the man is too old. Although if Kingsland has no powerful clan enemies he might—*

Karne silently cursed Trev Halarek's arrogant refusal to give his third son a political education. All Karne knew about Kingsland was that it was related to House von Schuss by marriage, and he had not learned that from Trev Halarek. *You had four sons, sire,* Karne thought bitterly, *and I'm the one left to save our House.*

"Yan Willem, House Justin, lord Chairman." The man was only a little older than Karne, stocky, and short. "The evidence of the Gild hasn't been fully investigated, but the uniforms and the silver fighter give backing to Lord Karne's accusation. Personal armies or their members may not participate in assassinations, milord. It's the law. We all know it. Therefore, the attack in Zinn violates the

law, and a guilty verdict on this must influence the
length of Council trusteeship."

"Who says there'll be a trusteeship?" Garren
Odonnel sneered.

"We do, lords of Families!" said a harsh, angry
voice from the benches of the Freemen. "Hareem
Gashen, freecity of Neeran, lord Chairman. The
Gild satellite took pix of the illegal siege. Whether
or not there are pix of fliers over Zinn, the law has
set the sentence for illegal siege and the law must
be obeyed."

"The Freemen have never interfered b—"

"We don't 'interfere' now, Lord Timkin. Alderman Tashak, freecity of York. The law the Families
made will be obeyed. We, the free people of Starker
IV, will see that it is."

"Reed, freecity of Loch. 'Noble' Nine, your serfs
are rebelling, your duels and feuds are escalating.
We won't permit your lawlessness to draw Freemen into war, nor will we permit you to alienate
the Gild. We'll enforce the laws of feud, my fine
lords, to protect *our* families and cities."

A bailiff hurried down the aisle between the
Freemen and the minor Houses. DeVree held up
his hand. "Lords and Freemen, the verdict."

The angry Freemen sat reluctantly, glaring at
their opponents among the Families. DeVree read
the tally sheet to himself quickly, then held it high
for all to see. "Asten Harlan has been found guilty
of illegal siege and is therefore sentenced to spend
the rest of his life at Breven, the Retreat House
nearest his Holding. The floor is now open to discuss the name of the trustee and the length of the

trusteeship for House Harlan. Earl Nellis Kingsland may speak first."

Karne felt relief at the sentence, which promised breathing time, but the wave of relief broke the iron control he had kept on his exhausted, over-tense body. He had to leave before he shamed his House. He left the chamber as quickly as propriety allowed and, once alone in the hall, ran to the nearest sanitary, where he was miserably sick. He retched past emptiness, then sat on the cold tile floor with his drumming head between his hands. When he felt a little better, he leaned back against the wall and focused on the gypsy-flower on a tile across the room. He set himself into the pattern-for-stress that every Altarian cadet learned his first year, centering his attention on the flower, and let the tension slowly drain away. When his head stopped hurting and his shoulder blades no longer felt pinched together, he got slowly to his feet and went out into the hall.

The Council had adjourned, for the hall flowed with lords and Freemen. Karne forced away both hope and despair and looked around for someone he knew. Watching the brightly dressed Council members was a little like looking through a kaleidoscope, and he did not want to test his stomach against the swirling, shifting colors for very long. Several paces down the hall, a brown-sleeved arm waved to him over two heavily feathered blue hats. The hats swayed apart and Karne saw the baron, who beckoned him to join a small group of men clustered along the glazed wall near the central doors to the Council chamber.

The baron drew Karne into the group. "You already know Allet, Earl of Justin, don't you, Karne?"

Karne nodded. Allet Justin had been one of Trev Halarek's favorite hunting companions.

The baron turned to the other men in the group. "Wilden Freeson, Childreth Konnor, and Van McNeece."

Karne nodded acknowledgment.

Von Schuss continued in his brisk way. "Council demanded Harlan lift the siege at once, of course. Blanket embargo against his House if he doesn't, you know. Trusteeship only lasts until the Gild reports its findings about the *Aldefara* incidents or until the Thawtime Council, unfortunately."

"By the Four Guardians!" Karne exploded.

"A light sentence, true. Harlan has powerful allies and the Freemen wouldn't take sides in 'Family' business, you know. But you gained yourself time. And Asten's paralyzed. Won't live out the trusteeship, physicians say, and Richard can't rule, officially, till Asten's gone, you know."

"Not 'officially,' but he will rule. Richard I remember." Karne's voice was bitter.

"Kingsland is trustee, not the worst choice for you," Konnor offered.

"Council also accepted Trev's Will," McNeece added. "The Larga is regent until you come of age. But Council will give your House no protection." McNeece's voice shook with anger.

Karne felt the blood leave his head. Baron von Schuss shot out a steadying hand. "That's why we're here, you know." He shook Karne gently. "My House will send a Century right away."

"I'll send anyone who volunteers," Justin said.

"The rascals on my back benches, most likely. I couldn't stop them if I wanted to, short of disinheritance."

"We'll send what we can until you can hold your oath-feast," Freeson said, and McNeece and Konnor nodded agreement.

Karne drew a deep, shuddering breath of relief. He was no longer alone in his fight to survive. "Thank you," he said, but his voice shook. *You're showing weakness*, the harsh voice of Trev Halarek's ghost snarled. Karne straightened by force of will, his knees shaky and unwilling, and looked at the men around him. He summoned a smile. "Believe me, I haven't the words to thank you enough. My House is at your command if ever you have need of one of the Nine." As he spoke, Karne backed, ever so casually, against the wall just centimeters behind him. The smooth, firm tile felt good to his tired back and relief-weak knees, but he knew he could not hold together much longer. He ran a hand through his already rumpled hair. "Your men will receive all the hospitality my House can afford them." The hall began to spin slightly, in spite of the wall's support. "I must excuse myself, friends. My personal family is waiting for me at home." Karne let the warmth he felt for these new allies flow into his words. Then he bowed formally to the men and turned carefully toward the exit and the flitter pad.

Baron von Schuss accompanied him, walking close but not shaming him with actual help, reeling out bits of Family gossip and political tidbits in a deliberately monotonous fashion quite unlike his usual manner, but which Karne found strangely calming. Halfway to the lift, Nik joined them on Karne's other side, his head down, his mouth twisted in thought. The baron kept up his monologue all the way to the pad and a brown-and-gold von Schuss flitter.

The baron stood at the flitter's wing, available, if necessary, to help his nephew or Karne up. The inane string of stories flowed on, but the baron's eyes were sharp, his posture alert, as he watched the two young men. Karne hauled himself onto the wing, then extended a hand to Nik. The pilot hesitated, but allowed sense to win out and accepted the assistance. The baron's face turned grim.

"I wish you'd let a Council physician set that arm properly, Nik."

Nik's mouth twisted into a wry grimace. "It's not so bad. Dr. Othneil can take care of it when I get to Ontar; a pilot's place is with his lord, Uncle Emil."

"But you can't fly him home."

"Nonetheless, Uncle."

Unstated but understood by all three was the likelihood that if Nik stayed behind, he might not be able to get into Ontar manor at all. Richard Harlan might not obey Council orders unless militarily forced. The tightness in the baron's features lasted a moment longer, then his monologue continued. Karne looked down at him, caught his eye, and winked. The baron's bland social expression dissolved into laughter.

"You're sharp, Karne Halarek. Thought you needed a cover for your condition. You stood up amazingly. Don't know anyone else who could have done as well. Set the auto-pilot and sleep, Son. You'll be safe till you get home, you know, and likely be safe there for awhile, too. Even Richard Harlan needs time to think about the new conditions in his House. The Lord be with you."

Karne smiled and lifted a hand in respectful salute. "And with your spirit." He ducked into the flitter.

Nik had already reclined in the passenger seat, arranged his splinted arm as comfortably as possible, and closed his eyes. "If he'd known we were coming," he said drowsily, "he'd have brought a transport, but since he didn't the Justins have promised to fly escort. Yan and Dennen Willem plan to stay." Nik settled deeper into the seat. "As Uncle Emil said, not even Richard would attack you again so soon after Council sentence."

Moments later, von Schuss was asleep. Karne brought the flitter up off the pad and set the autopilot's course for Ontar. He took one last look at the sparkling white landscape below, then he, too, closed his eyes.

Chapter Four

———◆———

HOURS LATER THE destination alarm rattled Karne awake. He sat up groggily and looked outside. Below, the land glittered in the frigid, blue moonlight. Smoky plumes of blown snow floated like pennants from the mountain peaks. Karne could see the rough, black texture the mountain pines gave the foothills. Then, on the plain below, a U-shaped ridge of trees appeared, marking the boundary of the manor's surface garden.

"Set the blue guidance controls," von Schuss reminded him sleepily, then settled again in the seat with his good arm flung up over his eyes.

Karne leaned close to the wide window, waiting to see the gates over the flitter pad slide open. Home. After six years.

Slowly the gates slid aside and Karne's craft dropped through them, safe on guidance control from the manor below. As soon as the gates closed, Karne turned on the flitter's exterior beacons and watched the rough-hewn walls slide past, remembering imagining as a child that he could see the stonecarvers' chisel marks. The shaft was thirty meters deep, and the first Halarek had been too proud of the achievement to allow the stone to be smoothed and painted as it had been in other manor houses.

The flitter bumped lightly against the pad surface and, after a few minutes' wait, Family, retainers, and a contingent of Lifesguardsmen filed out from behind the blast shields. They formed a corridor through which the Larga Alysha Halarek passed. In honor of the occasion, she wore a gown of the rich, dark blue that was the Halarek color. Beside her, dancing with impatience, was Kathryn.

Karne stepped out onto the flitter's wing and stood a moment, swaying slightly. His nap had lessened his weariness only a little and had left him groggy and unsteady. Von Schuss slid out onto the wing beside him. Karne grinned at him. "I'll be talking to you later, Nik. Get that arm looked at."

Karne jumped carefully down, keeping one hand on the wing-edge for balance, then stood still a moment, waiting for the shameful weakness in his knees to go away. He met his mother's eyes. She smiled gently and held out her right hand to him. He went to her, dropped on one knee before her, and lifted her hand to his forehead. "Lady Mother."

The Larga looked down at his bent head and the strained lines in her face softened. She put out a hand as if to touch his hair, then quickly changed the gesture into a motion to one of the Lifesguardsmen to help von Schuss off the wing.

"Rise, my son. Welcome home."

Karne stood and looked down at her. "As stylish as ever, Lady Mother." He felt a twinge of amusement at his mother's vanity. It had been said of Trev Halarek that he did not care much for women, but would have married a wom doe if necessary to get an heir. Trev had surprised everyone when his Black Ship brought back from a neighboring star system this tiny woman with her warm golden skin, honey-gold hair, and dark gold eyes. She was so different from the brown-haired Gharr that Trev Halarek was clearly flaunting not only his wealth and power—any noble who lifted off in a Black Ship to steal a bride from another world had to have great wealth and power in order to finance the trip—but his contempt for Black Ship traditions. After the Sickness wiped out most of the women of the Families and left a taint in the seed that killed one-third of Family females in infancy, the Black Ship flights had begun. They had taken only women who blended with the Gharr in appearance and culture. There were worlds enough for that. Alysha Halarek's golden beauty, and the knowledge citizens of her world considered the Starker system barbaric, was like a constant insult to the men who had kept tradition. It accused them, without words, of timidity and cowardice.

The Larga took Karne's hands. "Come. The staff waits for you in the Great Hall. There were so many rumors of your death, and serfs are so gullible. They need reassurance that you're truly alive. You can see the rest of the Family later."

Karne nodded numbly, made a polite bow to the cousins standing behind the Larga, gave Kathryn's cheek a quick, affectionate stroke, and turned toward the door to the manor proper. Lifesguardsmen moved to guard him on both sides and behind. He was too tired to object.

The lift to the upper levels was only a short distance from the pad entrance, yet Karne began feeling trapped from the moment he entered the corridor, and the feeling intensified with each step he took. Tons of stone floors and ceilings above him; cold, gray stone walls around him, smoothed gray stone underfoot; no windows, no sunlight, no fresh outside air. He heard acutely the constant, soft whirring of ventilator fans, pushing air from outside through the manor and town, recirculating and recirculating it over the charcoal grids. It had no smell, no feel, no life. Karne shook his head, as if that would clear it of the grayness, the pressing stone, the lifeless air, the strangling fear. Duty had brought him back to duties he knew nothing about. And to death.

Duty and death, Karne thought. Death is the fate of the heads of this House.

"Karne!"

Karne looked up. The Larga stood waiting for him in front of the open lift. When had she passed him? She came back, put one slender hand lightly on his arm, and looked up at him. "I'm sure it was very hard for you to come back, Son," she said, so softly only he could hear. "Trev gave you very little reason to feel loyalty to this House or this Family. He *certainly* didn't mean for you to lead us. I'm glad you came back to try."

Karne knew from her face that if they had been in private, she would have put her arms around him.

"It's taken great courage, Son. I'm proud of you." Alysha Halarek brightened with a visible effort. "The lift's waiting, Karne. It's time to show our people their new lord." She twined her arm around and over his in the formal lord-and-lady manner and squeezed his arm against her side. "I'm so glad to see you," she said very quietly. "I've really missed you."

They entered the lift with four Lifesguardsmen. Kathryn threw her arms around Karne's waist the moment the gate closed. She hugged him ferociously. "Karne! Karne! I'm so glad you're home."

"Ah, kitten, that hug feels so good!" Karne hugged her until she squawked, then put hands to her waist and set her a little away from him. They shared the brown skin and dark brown hair of their sire's people, but they had their mother's wiry build and brown-flecked golden eyes. "You're not a little girl anymore, are you, Kit?"

The girl stood as tall as she could. "I'm fourteen winters old!"

"That's not what I meant," Karne teased. "You were flat when I left."

Kit smoothed her kirtle over her slender hips and flushed. "I was only nine! I'll be fifteen this Kerensten. Marrying age, Karne."

Karne slid an arm around Kit's newly acquired waist. "Anyone in mind?"

Kit shook her head.

"I'll have to do something about that when the world stops falling in around my ears."

"Karne!" Kit said, laughing and blushing.

But the world has not stopped falling in, Karne reminded himself. I have a breathing space before Richard comes up with something, but he will come up with something, before I have time to learn my way through the political morass here. Everyone knows my sire did not prepare me at all for ruling. Richard will take quick advantage of that.

Another quick squeeze from Kit brought Karne's attention back to her.

"You'll have to make a speech to them, Karne, you know. How's my shy big brother going to do that?"

The Larga looked severely at her daughter. "Don't tease him now, Kathryn. And don't go hugging him like that in public either."

"This isn't public. It's just us and the guards, personal family, Lady Mother. Besides, I love him and I've missed him terribly."

The lift stopped. Karne lifted Kit's arms away just as the door opened. "You know she's right, Kit." Then he bent and whispered in her ear, "I've missed you terribly, too."

The guards stepped out, the Larga followed and walked briskly down the corridor toward the Great Hall. Brother and sister hung a few steps behind her. Karne leaned close to Kit. "I talk to groups all the time, Kit. I was going to be a Navy pacification officer, remember?" The irony of that struck him, and Karne's face hardened for a moment.

They turned the corner by the courtyard, now darkened because it was "night" in the manor as well as on the surface, and stopped in the main entrance to the Great Hall. It was packed with everyone from the library staff to the stable helpers of level one. Karne even saw the gardener, who had a legendary reputation for never leaving the conservatory area on level six. Cousins of various degrees filled the galleries down both sides of the Hall. Along the rows of columns that supported the galleries, soldiers of the household Blues were setting flaming torches in ancient wall brackets. Torches of fire, ritual accompaniment to House Halarek celebrations for at least twelve generations. Karne reached out and brushed his fingers across the faded paint on one of the columns. Were there as many people in the gallery above the door as in the others? He looked at the murmuring crowd, surging and swaying in the smoky light, and felt a flutter of fear. These were not strangers whom he would leave behind when negotiations were over, whether he succeeded or failed in making peace; these were Family and staff and whether they lived or died depended on him. He beckoned to three Lifesguardsmen, tweaked Kit's nose, and pressed into the crowd.

"The Lharr. Make way for the Lharr," the Lifesguardsmen ordered, shoving a path through the excited throng.

Hands reached out to touch Karne. They patted, stroked, held on a moment. The guardsmen pushed bodies aside. Sometimes they even had to tap heads with their stunner butts before the obstruction would move.

"A Lharr again."

"Good health, my lord."

"Live long, lord!"

"Lord Karne! Lord Karne!"

Karne felt the excitement and the reverence of the serf-servants for their lord and resolved to be worthy of their belief in him. He reached the dais and climbed the three steps onto it.

"Halarek lives! Halarek lives!"

Karne looked out through the smoke at the shouting crowd. He looked up and across the Hall to the gallery above the main entrance. The Larga stood, small and golden, at center front. She smiled encouragement. These are *my* people, Karne told himself. I don't feel it yet, but they are mine and they depend on me. He cleared his throat. "The rumors of my death were ahead of time, as you see."

A relieved chuckle ran through the crowd.

"We're pressed hard, right now, but while I live, you're safe. I promise you that. House Harlan will take this Holding only when there is no Halarek Family left!"

The serfs shouted, and stamped, and cheered, and whirled caps or aprons in the air. Karne could have said no more had he wished to. He stepped down from the dais and said quietly to the guardsmen, "We're leaving. Now, by the nearest door."

Karne and the three guardsmen pushed under a side gallery and out the door there into a hall.

"I'm taking four hours' sleep," he told the guards. "You—"

"Treen, my lord."

"Treen, tell my generals to meet with me in the library in four and a half hours.

"You, with the nonregulation boots, go find the household officers and tell them to meet me in the library in five hours."

The two soldiers saluted briskly and left. Karne turned slowly to the lift and his room. He felt as if he were moving through deep drifts of snow that dragged at his feet, pushed at his legs, resisted his every move.

"My lord?"

Karne looked at the third soldier, walking beside him now.

"My lord, I'll go with you to your quarters."

Karne looked at the man through a fog of weariness. "My quarters?"

"You've been attacked four times already, lord. Don't you want a guard?"

Karne stopped and studied the man, suspicion stirring. "The Lharr Halarek has never had a guard. I'm not going to be the first."

"Yes sir!" The soldier flushed, snapped a salute, and left.

Karne watched him, groggy and confused. Had he been wrong to suspect a trap, if only the trap of public humiliation, the spreading of word that the Lharr-designate dared not move, even about his own manor, without guards? The soldier could not have been an assassin. An assassin would not offer boldly to come with him. Or would one? He had been long away from the savage game that was life on Starker IV. He did not remember all the rules anymore. Karne stumbled into the lift and leaned against the wall in the dim compartment until it stopped at level five. He walked slowly down the hall to the door of his room. It was the last of the line of doors into what had been first the nursery and then the children's rooms. Now, only two of the children still lived. He pushed open the door. The room was just as he remembered it—long and narrow and gray, with a narrow, hard bed, a single chair, a small table, and a shelf of worn and tattered books. The only bright colors in the room were in pictures of other worlds, some of them framed prints and paintings, some torn from books and school papers. Karne sank onto the edge of the bed and tugged off his boots, lay back, and closed his eyes.

A segment of the white, furry bed-throw moved under his arm. It squirmed and struggled, then began shrieking, "Uhl! Uhl! Uhl!" Karne leaped from the bed. Grogginess swept away by fear, his hand dropped briefly to his stunner. Then the hand fell away from the grip and he pounced on the

lump. He wrestled it out from under the edge of
the throw and held it up in the air near his face.

"Wiki! Is it really you, old fella?"

Six skinny arms/legs and a long, thin tail
emerged from the white ball of fluff, and two enormous gray eyes, ringed with sooty black, opened
and stared at him. The little animal struggled
from Karne's hands and wrapped all six limbs and
its tail around Karne's face and neck and began to
purr.

"Hey! I can't breathe!" Karne pried Wiki off and
spat out a mouthful of white fur. He lay down
again and tucked the little animal into the crook of
his arm. "Am I glad to see you," he whispered into
the area where he had always imagined the uhl-
uhl's ears to be. "I was sure an old beast like you
would already have joined his ancestors." The uhl-
uhl arranged itself comfortably, laid its tail along
Karne's arm up to his shoulder and, purring con-
tinuously, closed its eyes.

Much too soon, pounding on Karne's door awakened him. He lay, eyes open, several minutes before he remembered where he was and what he
was supposed to be doing. He got up sluggishly,
brushed at the wrinkles in his cadet uniform, ran a
hand perfunctorily through his hair, and went out.
The soldier Treen waited for him in the hall.

"The generals await you in the library, my lord."

"Thank you, Treen. Have someone bring me
breakfast."

Treen snapped a salute and hurried away. Karne
walked down the flight of stairs to the next level to

wake himself up. He paused in the privacy of the landing to stretch and to bend, bouncing, several times to feel the blood moving in his veins again. The fog in his brain thinned. He descended the rest of the way to level four and crossed the corridor there to the heavily carved door of the library, where he paused a moment to tug down his uniform tunic and run his hands quickly through his hair one more time. He closed his eyes and imagined himself filling with authority and strength. *A pacification officer must be authoritative, or create a convincing illusion of authority. Learn the techniques of illusion, play your part as convincingly as a good actor, and soon the illusion will become reality. You will* be *authoritative.* He needed the reality now, but illusion would have to do. Karne pushed open the door.

His eyes swept around the room—book-lined walls two levels tall, a door onto another corridor, the graceful, curved iron stair that rolled on a track around the room, the long table where Trev Halarek had done much of his work. The table's worn, polished surface was empty now. The iron stair waited outside a heavy door on the next level, the back entrance to the Lharr's official quarters. Karne turned away from that door; Trev Halarek was dead and Karne Halarek was not yet accepted in his place. The Larga Alysha sat in a winged chair beside the massive stone fireplace. Asroth Brinnd, Trev Halarek's trusted adviser for more than twenty years, was bending over her with a sheaf of papers. General Shen, who had grown up with Trev Halarek, and Brinnd were the two House officers Karne had been sure of recognizing.

The others—he would have to decide how to handle his ignorance of the others' names and faces as his need for one or another came up. Already Karne was feeling like a man on a high wire over a deep gorge. A wrong choice in any direction meant disaster.

"Excuse me, my lord," said a young voice behind Karne.

Karne stepped aside and a page of about seven years slipped through the door, carrying Karne's food on a tray. The boy set the tray on the long table, bowed smartly, and left by the other door. A short, plump officer in his fifties and a tall, square officer of about the same age came in immediately after the page left. The short officer was breathing hard.

"My lord, you awakened early. We came as soon as we could."

Karne decided to let the excuse pass. "Sit down, gentlemen. I assume you're General Zicker," he looked at the plump officer, "and you're General Shen," he added to the tall officer. "We have a lot to do in a short time. I know my sire trusted your judgment—" Then Karne remembered the Larga and Brinnd. He turned to them. "We'll be using the library for private conversation, Brinnd. Please leave us. We'll send word to you when we're finished. I'll need to talk to you later, as I hope Prefet Treen told you."

"Yes, the prefet told me." Brinnd bowed stiffly and left the room.

"Lady Mother." Karne smiled at her. "You are the regent. Would you sit there or here with us?"

"Must I stay, Karne? I know nothing of military matters."

"You are the regent. You must stay."

The Larga inclined her head in agreement and Karne turned again to the generals. They were watching him with boredom and a hint of contempt. Karne could imagine what Trev Halarek had said to them about him. "Gentlemen, my first question is, how did Harlan surprise you with a siege?"

General Shen's sleepy eyes widened. His glance sharpened. "It was the middle of Narn, lord. Sieging is a lengthy business. No one sets siege in the middle of Narn!"

"It was my imagination, then, that saw the manor ringed with Harlan tents and fliers?"

General Zicker flushed, stung by Karne's sarcasm. "No one has ever done it before, lord."

"With no head-of-House, the two of you were in charge of the defense of Halarek Holding. How long have you been in Halarek service, General Shen?"

"Twenty-seven years, lord."

"And you, General Zicker?"

"Close to forty, lord. I began under your grandsire."

"In all that time, neither of you has studied House Harlan? Our clan's most powerful enemy? When has House Harlan stuck to the 'rules' if it could gain advantage by cheating? Even I know *that* much. Were you unaware Richard Harlan has taken control of that House? I've been on Starker IV only five days and *I* know it!"

Karne watched their feelings play over their

faces with an eye trained to understand subtle changes of expression. What they wanted to say to him, they dared not. He was the Lharr, but they were furious to be sarcastically scolded by a boy not yet of age. Yet they knew that if he lived to his majority, he would be in a position to reward or punish greatly. Karne reached for the klag on the tray, forgotten in his anger at the generals' carelessness. He sipped absently at the tepid liquid, never taking his eyes from the two angry men. The generals would have to be replaced, as soon as possible. It was most unlikely they would attack him, but they might. At the least, they had shown a fatal lack of good judgment. Until he found qualified men, he would have to do the tactical planning himself, perhaps with Nik's help. Textbook planning. Karne grimaced. It was not a good solution, but it would be better than leaving the Holding's defense in the hands of these two. For the moment he would leave them their titles because they still had vast stores of useful knowledge he might be able to use. And he had no desire for an uprising by the generals' loyal aides and officers.

The generals' color returned to normal. Karne set down the mug. "Here's what I want you to do in the next four days: General Shen, check our stores, see what we need to add in order to withstand a long siege, and report to me; General Zicker, House Justin and House von Schuss are sending us reinforcements and I want you to find and prepare quarters for them. Houses Konnor, McNeece, and Freeson are sending aid until I can hold my oath-feast. Those men will need comfortable, but temporary, quarters. I haven't talked to

Brinnd about the feast yet, but I'm guessing he'll need at least a week to prepare it. That's ten days, leaving four days till the start of Uhl. I don't think even Richard will risk his troops in those storms." Karne looked up at the door to the Lharr's quarters and paused for a long moment. He looked again at the two generals. "I'm not going to wager my Family's survival on Richard's predictability, however. I shamed his Family before the entire Council. He won't wait till Thawtime to avenge that, trustee or no. Prepare us for a long siege, gentlemen. You're dismissed."

Karne walked to the end of the long table, pressed an opaque panel in its side, and walked back to sit down to his cold breakfast. He looked up at the motionless generals. "Get to work, gentlemen."

Both of them stiffened, but they obeyed. Karne picked at the dried bread and crumbling cheese. His nose wrinkled, but he was two-days hungry and in the end he ate the food, washing it down with tepid klag. He leaned back in the chair and closed his eyes. Shift to another level, he told himself, there'll be a new set of problems in a minute. He drifted to sleep, to be awakened almost immediately by the loud shutting of a door. Brinnd and three other men had entered.

The Larga rose and greeted them courteously. Karne caught her eye and smiled appreciation for the brief time she had given him in which to get a grip on his thoughts again. He inspected the new arrivals. Brinnd was tall for the Gharr, and lean, with an air of confidence and power. His companions included a short, sharp-featured man in his late thirties, a younger man perhaps ten years older than Karne who had the darker hair of north country people and a familiar face, and a boy, also from the north, who was so eager or nervous he was trembling. Brinnd ordered the men into positions in front of the work table. His tone, his directing motions, the very act of ordering the men into places, proclaimed his intention to take control of the meeting and keep it. Karne felt that control and resented it: He was ignorant now, but he would not stay that way and *he* was going to control his own House. He motioned the sharp-featured man to come forward and looked to Brinnd for an introduction. Brinnd looked distinctly surprised.

You listened to my sire too much, Karne told him silently, with a powerful feeling of satisfaction. You will not get the reins of this meeting back. Karne stared at Brinnd, pointedly, yet courteously.

"Frem Weisman manages the household staff and purchases supplies for the Holding," Brinnd finally said, reluctantly.

Weisman knelt. Karne acknowledged the gesture and said, as Weisman stood, "I remember you, Freeman. You used to wear the sark and badge of your freecity."

"I consider myself a member of this House now, lord. I've worked for Halarek twelve years this coming 9 Aza." Weisman stepped back to the exact spot Brinnd had originally shown him.

So, Karne thought, Brinnd has *you* thoroughly cowed.

"This is Tane Orkonan." Brinnd indicated the dark-haired man.

Karne came around the table, hand extended, and met the man halfway. "I don't need an introduction to Tane, Brinnd. He taught me Galac and Sternlangue."

Orkonan dusted his hands against the back of his tunic and made a small bow. He winked at Karne as he straightened and flicked his eyes in Brinnd's direction. "You're a welcome sight, my lord." He grinned. "That's going to take some getting used to, 'my lord.'"

A brilliant smile lit Karne's thin, serious face a moment and then was gone. Orkonan motioned the very young man forward, before Brinnd had a chance to. "Here, my lord, is my cousin Gareth. He's apprenticed to Frem Brinnd, started just last month."

Karne glanced at Brinnd. The man's whole face had stiffened, but he said nothing. His eyes glittered as they flicked back and forth between Tane and Karne. Gareth was sketching a bow. Looking at the young man carefully, Karne guessed Gareth was closer to Kit's age than to Orkonan's or his own, and that would be more usual. He was also likely a younger son of House Konnor, as Tane was, and required to earn his living with his mind or his hands.

"Is your personal family aware of the danger to you, Gareth, working for my House?"

The young man nodded. "You are our liege, Lord Karne."

I should have known that! Guardians, sire, how could you have been so sure one of the other three would survive! Karne forced down the rage inside and hoped his face had not betrayed his ignorance or his anger. "I'm glad you've come. We need every hand that's offered. Let's get to business." He walked around the table again and toyed with the edge of the breakfast tray for a moment. "As I remember, an oath-feast must be held before my vassals feel legally bound to the tie between us. Is my memory accurate, Brinnd?"

The tall man nodded slightly.

"Is—say—eleven days enough time to prepare such a feast, Brinnd? Maybe 36 Narn?"

"It can be managed."

"The cost of hosting the promised volunteers from von Schuss and Justin?"

"That involves a little guessing, but it can be done."

"I also need to know how much money is available to hire mercenaries, should that become necessary, and what kind of military effort against Harlan the House can afford."

"That can be done right now."

"Then set the men to it, Brinnd. I want to talk to you privately for a moment."

While the three younger men assembled the materials they would need, Karne took Brinnd to the side of the fireplace. "You don't address me by my title when you speak, Brinnd. I demand that sign of respect from all my officers."

Brinnd stiffened, seeming to grow taller and thinner. "I've been the administrator here longer than you've been alive, young man, and—"

"My title, Frem Brinnd." Karne put all the authority he had learned into his voice. "My officers

must show the respect due a Lharr if I'm to have
the respect of outsiders. Say it, Brinnd, or by the
Four Guardians, you'll be out of this House by
morning!"

An angry flush crept into Brinnd's hollow
cheeks. He swallowed. "You're not the Lharr until
the tenth day of Aden next," he spluttered.

"He *is* the Lharr, in all but age." The Larga rose
and came to stand beside Karne. "Our present political position is too precarious to risk even the
appearance of disrespect for Karne, especially
from the administrator of his House. You, of all
people, should know that."

Brinnd straightened the heavy bead necklace
that was his sign of office and ignored the Larga.
"You can't do anything now, young man. You come
to our world ignorant of our ways and of what is
needful to survive. I have the knowledge House
Halarek needs to live."

Karne stood very still, watching the older man.
Did Brinnd speak from arrogance or belief or for
betrayal? Karne and his administrator would be
together much in the coming days, most of the
time Karne did not spend with his army officers,
in fact, and the deliberate omission of Karne's
title, the faint but obvious contempt with which
Brinnd treated Karne—these together would do
small damage at first, but the effect would grow. If
House Halarek's chief executive officer were allowed to behave so, others soon would, too, and
the House would fall. Karne pondered the problem. He could imprison Brinnd until he yielded,
but that would also imprison his knowledge. Ignoring the omission would be disastrous. The only

way Karne could force Brinnd to obey would be
torture, and Brinnd would surely know Karne ordered torture for no one. Karne turned to the
Larga. "Is anyone else in the manor qualified to
take over as administrator, Lady Mother?"

The Larga's lips were drawn tight and she was
tapping one foot on the floor angrily. Her eyes
blazed. "Tane can. He's been Brinnd's right hand
for four years. He'll do the work well." She whirled
on Brinnd. "You, Freeman! You've behaved in an
impossible fashion! No one has dared to so ignore
me in all the years I've lived here. And I am now
regent! Nor has anyone, *ever*, spoken so to the
Lharr Halarek!"

Brinnd's lip curled. "He's not a Lharr. He never
will be. He's too soft and weak. The 'woman' of his
sons, Trev called him! Why, even Lady Kathryn
would be—"

"Enough!" Karne said, in a far more quiet voice
than his feelings clamored for him to use. "You,
Frem Brinnd, are out of a job and I want you out of
this House by dawn tomorrow. You will get the
pension you earned in my sire's service, but no bo-
nuses, nothing extra."

Brinnd shed his contempt like a cloak and
looked Karne in the eye. Karne stared back,
stunned at the change. Brinnd set a hand on
Karne's shoulder. "I have loved and served this
House a long time, my lord. Even my freecity no
longer means as much to me as House Halarek. I
did not want to see it lost by a weakling, so I decided to test you, in a safe place. If you had been
the 'woman' your sire thought you, I would have
stayed and attempted to correct that in you. But

I'm getting old. What I really wanted to do was take my pension and move to Neeran, where I can enjoy my grandchildren." Brinnd's stern face loosened a little, into what might have been a smile. "A man cannot control others if he cannot control himself, Lord Karne. You, in spite of provocation that would have set many a lord of the Gharr at my throat, controlled your pride and your anger. You surprised me, lord." He bowed respectfully. "Because of your sire's aberration regarding yourself, you have a lot to learn before the Thawtime Council, but you have begun. You will rule, Lord Karne, and rule well, if your enemies give you the time." He bowed and left the library.

Chapter Five

———◆———

BRINND LEFT THE library, dropping his necklace of office on a chair and gently closing the door behind himself as he went out. Karne watched in mute amazement. The old man had not meant his harsh words. Karne glanced at his mother. The Larga, too, seemed stunned. She spoke slowly.

"Karne, I've known him for what—thirty years? —and I've never known him to use his devious mind on a Family member before."

"He's an old fox," Karne said with grudging admiration. "The signs of a performance were all there, but he was so convincing I ignored them."

He laughed ruefully. "That ought to teach me not to be complacent. Well, let's get on with business, regent. Tane needs to be officially told he has new duties." Karne looked over at the men around the long table. Weisman and Gareth were rustling through papers busily, too busily, but Orkonan was frankly watching. How much had they heard? he wondered.

"Who asks Tane if he'll take on the administrator's job, you or I?" Karne spoke too quietly for the others to hear.

"Well, you are Lharr but you aren't of age yet. We're making a contract with Tane, so I suppose I'll have to make the legal agreement, but you rule here, so you ask him and you set the terms. I'm sure he'll accept. I'll sign whatever paper the two of you draw up."

Karne nodded and walked to the worktable. He touched Orkonan's shoulder and drew him a little away from the others. "Tane, the job of House administrator is yours if you want it. You know the duties and I'm willing to make a written contract with you. The Larga says you'll do the work well. Do you accept?"

"No!" Weisman burst out. He was quivering from nose to fingertips. "No! You can't give the job to him. I've worked for this Family twice as long as Orkonan has. You owe this job to me! To me! Not to this upstart son of a minor House!"

"Frem Weisman," the Larga began soothingly, "I can see you believe you have reason to be upset—"

"Reason! I've been done out of the job I've worked years for, and by a woman's whim!"

Alysha Halarek opened her mouth to reply, but

Karne made a sharp cutting motion with his hand to silence her. "You forget yourself, Frem Weisman," he said coldly. "Perhaps Freemen speak so of their Freemen superiors, but you will not talk of the Larga of House Halarek with such contempt. Is that clear?"

"Aye, my lord."

There was a subtle sneer in the reply, so subtle that Karne knew if he called attention to it, he would appear petty and ridiculous. He snapped his mouth closed on a biting reply. "Lady Mother, did Frem Weisman have grounds for thinking he would be given the job when Brinnd—retired?"

"Certainly not!" The Larga flashed a look at the offending secretary and then away. "The Freeman has no ear for languages and cannot handle complex accounts at all. He does his present job very well, but he hasn't the skills to move higher. Trev hired Tane to take over Brinnd's position. I'm sure he made Frem Weisman no promises at all."

And if he did, Weisman was a fool to believe in them, Karne added to himself.

"My lord." Weisman made a full bow and looked at Karne with pleading eyes. "I can learn Galac and a hired accountant could handle the figure work, freeing me to do other things. I know the business of this House, lord!"

"You haven't been able to learn Galac in twenty years. I can't believe you'll do better now." The Larga ran a paper from the table through her hands again and again. She kept her eyes on the moving paper when she spoke. "Our House survives on its exports, Freeman. We must have an administrator who speaks both Galac and Sternlangue well and who handles numbers easily. *You* would have to deal with most of the First Merchants stationed here through an interpreter and an accountant. That is inefficient and expensive, Freeman." She looked up and pinned Weisman with golden eyes gone hard and cold. "You do not qualify for the job. It's that simple. *You do not qualify.*" The Larga turned her back to him, picked up a stack of plasti trade sheets, and pretended to read them.

Weisman reddened and shot the Larga a venomous glance. "I'll never forget this. Never! I'll—"

"Weisman!" Karne broke in sharply, "say not one word more or you'll follow Brinnd out of this House's service. Go to your quarters and calm down. If you wish to resign, you may. However, you've done this House valuable service and I'd like to see that service continue."

Weisman stomped from the room. He'll bear watching for awhile, Karne told himself, and added Weisman's name to his mental list of people to check on in a few weeks' time. Karne hunched his shoulders, then pushed them back and heard the small cracking sounds as his back slightly rearranged itself. If I expelled everyone with a motive for treachery, he thought bitterly, there would be too few people left to keep the House and manor running. He suppressed a sigh, aware of the eyes of Orkonan and his cousin. "I'm going to my room for a time, Lady Mother. Have a page bring me midday there. Tane, I want to know the names of all my vassals, their financial standing, the financial standing of this House, the cost of restocking for siege—Generals Shen and Zicker are preparing a list for you—and the soonest my oath-feast can be held. Later you can start teaching me about imports and exports and wages and..." He smiled slightly. "But then, you know what I need to learn and how to teach me, don't you? One clue. The Academy trained me to learn very quickly by ear."

Karne ignored the strange look his mother gave him when he did not go to the curving iron stair to the Lharr's quarters but headed for the hall door. He mounted the stairs to his tiny room two at a time, locked its door, sent a message by com to the Family's clinic that he wanted to see Nik von Schuss in his fifth-level quarters in an hour, and lay down on the narrow bed. Wiki crawled out from under the bed, curled, purring, under Karne's chin, and they both went to sleep.

Karne woke with a start in a rush of fear. Something had touched his cheek. He rolled away from the touch, grabbing for the stunner that was not in his belt, and opened his eyes. Wiki was sitting on his pillow, reaching to pat him with the bare toes of one tiny paw. Just Wiki. Karne willed the tension out of himself. His survival instincts were coming back, but his reactions were slow and incomplete. He should have heard Wiki move, should have had a weapon at hand, should have been able to aim and fire that weapon in a fraction of a second. His life would depend on it. He glanced at his door. At least he had locked that. Wiki nudged Karne's hand demandingly. Karne rolled the uhl-uhl over onto its back—at least he presumed it was Wiki's back, it was hard to tell with an uhl-uhl—and tickled its belly. The uhl-uhl let two more legs sprawl out of its fur and purred loudly, briefly, then it rolled off the bed and over to the door. Its movements resembled those of a dust-ball in a light breeze. It sniffed at the crack under the door.

Karne smiled at the little creature. "Hungry? So'm I. Let's see what they sent."

A tray lay on the floor outside. A note on top said, "Pilot von Schuss will be unable to accommodate the Lharr because he has not yet awakened from the chemical sleep necessary for setting his arm. H. V. Othneil."

So, Karne thought, sighing, I can't get your advice for awhile, Nik. He carried the tray into his room, shut the door, then shared the food with Wiki. He sat long after he had finished, staring blindly at the wall in front of him, trying to make connections between what he had just learned and what he remembered, trying to make high-proba-bility estimates of what his enemy's next move against him would be, and when.

For the next five days, the conviction hung over Karne that Harlan would act against him at least once more before the storms of Uhl stopped all movement on the surface. During that tense time, the manor's military and household officers crammed Karne with vital details of political alli-ances; vassals' names and obligations; the laws of siege, duel, and assassination; and reviewed the history and tactics of the Halarek/Harlan feud, be-ginning with the theft by Karne's great-grandsire of Lord Richard's great-grandsire's Black Ship bride. In the evenings, he sat with Nik privately in the library and went over the day's information, summarizing, condensing, trying to remember everything vital to his House. He felt saturated with vital information. He also felt adrift, without the experience to judge which bits of information would be essential to the survival of his House. On the night of the fifth day, he came slowly into the library, closed the door, and leaned against it, head hanging, shoulders drooping. He rubbed his eyes wearily. The only other occupant of the room, Nik von Schuss, who was crouching by the fire, studying it, looked up in concern. "Karne?"

Karne slumped into the big leather chair by the fireplace and stared dejectedly at his feet. "I don't know enough, Nik. I can't learn fast enough. I'm going to make a wrong choice in a tight place and damage my House or even take it down. And the history of my House is one tight place after another." Karne let his head drop into his hands and was silent for a long time. When he looked up, his golden eyes were blazing. He pounded his fist on the arm of the chair. "How could my sire do this! Did he hold Asten Harlan in such contempt that he thought his sons were safe? That *he* was safe? House Harlan intends to take this Holding from us and I've been Academy-trained to keep peace!"

Von Schuss's usually merry face was serious. His dark eyes held Karne's. "From Asten, you *were* safe, considering his incredible ineptitude. Asten wasn't responsible for your sire's death. Hasn't your lady mother told you that? Richard killed them all with his own hand, first Trev and Jerem, right after Thawtime Council, then Kerel and Liam when they attempted to avenge those deaths. He killed Kerel and Liam and all their raiding party but two from ambush. He left two Blues alive to tell what he had done."

"Guardians!" Karne stared, unseeing, at the book-jammed shelves across the room. For a long time his mind was a dark emptiness, too stunned to think at all. When his mind did stir again to thought, it was to Jerem—his wit, his charm, the deep love he and Karne had felt for each other. Grief came then, sharper and darker than before, and then a savage anger. The Heir of Harlan had killed the Heirs of Halarek with his own hands!

Karne's muscles cried for swift, violent action. He had to *move* before his rage tore him apart and he could not move against Harlan. Not yet. His knowledge was too little. Karne sprang from the chair, sprinted to the nearest lift, and rode down to level two and the flitter pad. He heard Nik behind him only vaguely. The com-center officer's face dropped with surprise when he saw Karne running across the pad toward a flitter.

"My lord!" he called. "My lord, you can't take a flitter up! There's a storm'll blow you to Kingsland Holding!"

In that moment Nik caught up, wrapped his good arm around Karne, and whapped him on the side of his head with the cast. "Lord," he said urgently into Karne's ear, "stop! I can guess how you feel, but you can't behave this way in front of your staff. Karne, listen to me!"

Karne stopped struggling and a measure of sanity returned to him. Nik loosened his hold but did not let go.

"Milord," he said, louder and more formally, "come. You could use sword practice now."

Nik hustled Karne into a lift, down one level, and into the sand-surfaced arena. Karne followed him like a child. The sword dummy stood in a raked circle of sand, and beside it, on the low arena wall, lay two battered swords. A rok-hide tunnel lay over the dummy's power cord to protect it from accidental damage. Nik pressed one of the swords into the dummy's grip, the other into Karne's, turned the dial on the dummy's back to "8—expert," and stood Karne in front of it.

"Imagine that's Richard. It's at his skill level. Kill him, Karne!"

The dummy turned slightly, following Karne's heat, and slid forward. Karne parried the first blow, then lunged for the dummy's heart. The dummy brushed his sword aside easily. The dummy's setting was beyond Karne's usual level of skill, but Karne's rage gave him speed and daring. Nik backed against the low arena wall and watched Karne lunge, thrust, parry, twist, dodge, thrust, parry, turn, thrust. At last, when Karne was drenched with sweat and bleeding from many minor cuts, he scored a "mortal" blow and the dummy stopped moving. Karne came to lean against the wall next to Nik, panting and steaming sweat.

"Thanks—friend," he said, and sank to sit limply at the base of the wall.

"Didn't think you wanted the padded jacket tonight," Nik explained. "The dummy can't hurt you badly and a little pain could spur you on to get rid of that—that—"

"Yes," said Karne.

He rose slowly, pulled his wet tunic away from his skin, and headed for the sanitary. Shortly afterward, washed, and dressed in an exercise suit borrowed from the military storeroom beside the sanitary, Karne joined Nik in the hall outside the arena. Behind them was the armory, with its smells of sweat and weapons' oil. Karne tipped back his head and sniffed deeply the powerful smell of the "horses" stabled along the two halls on the other side of the arena. He stared at the arena's stone wall, stared at it hard, as if he could by will see through the manor's central core to the stall where Brenden stayed over winter. Brenden. Karne resolved to make time to come down and exercise Brenden.

His sight and mind returned to the stone wall in front of him, to the stone walls of the rooms behind him and above him. Above him. The kitchens in the core above the arena, the Great Hall above the kitchen, the library and Hall galleries above that, the Lharr and Larga's quarters above that, the conservatory above that—hundreds of meters of thick, gray stone. And the ventilator fans. And—

He made an impatient gesture. There was that to deal with, too, the weight and the grayness and the months of confinement. He strode down the hall, around the corridor past the quarters of the animal workers, and past the first two of a row of colored doors. He pushed open the third. Nik put a restraining hand on his arm.

"Karne, what are you doing?"

"I have to go outside."

"Outside? Outside! You're still out of your mind!"

"It's something I have to do. Now. But I'm no fool, Nik. I'm going out through one of the city's escape lifts, not through a manor lift where one of my disapproving cousins might see me. I won't go beyond the surface shelter, and I'm taking you with me, at least as far as the lift."

"There's a storm outside."

"There's a storm inside, too. Nik, I've been away from here too long. I've learned to need fresh air and wind and real sunlight and openness. Ontar no longer feels like home to me, it feels like a trap. Even if there were no Harlans, Ontar would feel like a trap to me. That's part of the rage, Nik. If I can get rid of that part, I can *use* my anger instead of letting it use me, like it just did." Karne gripped von Schuss's upper arms. "I can't afford to lose control of myself, Nik, not now. Not with Richard waiting to catch me in a serious mistake." Karne looked into his friend's doubtful eyes. "Trust me, Nik. I've learned a lot about myself in the last five years. You don't have to understand my need, just come with me. Please."

Nik looked very dubious, but he followed Karne through the door, down a flight of steps to the hovercar garage, and into a car. Karne spun the steering wheel and drove into Ontar.

The city slept in the blue glow of imitation moonlight. For the first time in his life, Karne felt

impatient with the pretense of surface light.
Ontar's buildings seemed more crowded together,
dirtier than he remembered them, the streets
seemed far narrower and rougher and more winding. The hovercar sometimes brushed against the
potted trees along the walkways. In some of the
narrower streets, pedestrians, had there been any
that late at night, would have had to take shelter
in doorways to avoid being run over. The air felt
thick. Karne had forgotten the smell of Ontar, the
sour, musty smell of too many people crowded into
tight quarters whose filters were seldom cleaned.
The buildings loomed over the car, dark, heavy,
suffocating. Karne felt confined, bound, at the
edge of panic. He flung the car down a painted yellow path that led to one of the city's emergency
exits, his hands shaking. The cobbled street turned
and twisted, narrowed, broadened again, and
ended in a stark, empty emergency plaza. Karne
sprang from his seat, wild with the need to get out,
and strode across the plaza to the long equipment
rack beside the lift, Nik close behind. Their boot-
steps bounced echoes from the smooth stone walls.

Karne grabbed a survival suit and a breathing
mask from the rack, then spun, breathless, tense.
"Guard the lift, Nik?"

Von Schuss nodded. Karne rode up to the surface, putting on the suit and mask as he went. He
knew what he must do and wondered if he had the
strength to do it. The lift stopped. Karne stared at
the heavy doors. Outside was all that Starker IV
was and Balder was not. Slowly, he stretched out
his hand and pressed the button that opened the
lift door. Wind and piercing cold swirled in. Karne

stepped out of the lift and walked to the edge of the
entrance shelter. This was Starker IV. A storm blotted out the sun, the sky, the landscape, everything
beyond the shelter entrance. Karne shoved his right
hand into the grip at the edge of the shelter. Beyond
was only a gray-whiteness striped with wind-driven
snow. The wind screamed across the plain, scouring
down to the frozen ground. It tugged at Karne, pulling him toward the mountains. He clamped his free
hand onto the grip on the opposite side of the shelter
and resisted the insistent tugging. Ice bits rattled
against his face. Frost covered the mask and crept
over the lower edges of the suit's goggles. Men had
died in that wind, the breath sucked out of them.
Karne listened to the wailing wind, the scraping
sound of ice pellets streaming past, the shush of snow
driven into and over the drift against the shelter's
side. He knew the next five months would be like
this—storms and cold and screaming wind. For
three of those months no one went onto the surface
for any reason.

Karne let himself think of the emerald green of
Balder—trees, grasses, hills, plains, bathed in sunshine or frequent gentle mist, rainstorms that did
not destroy, snowstorms that lasted only hours instead of days, winter sports impossible on Starker
IV. He saw the huge, gentle snowflakes of winter,
pale green springs that stretched into bright, mild
summers, and summers that slowly turned into
autumns blazing with colored leaves. He thought
of walking and playing with friends without fear of
assassins, of friendships with young women with-

out outraged cries for marriage or blood, of Egil most of all. Big, blond, powerful Egil, who had been closer to Karne than even Jerem. Jerem, who should have been Lharr.

Karne bit back a surge of grief and took advantage of a momentary lull to move deeper into the lift shelter, out of reach of the clutching wind. Between protecting walls, he removed the mask and breathed the sharp, cold air. It pinched his nose and made his lungs burn, but it was real, uncirculated. Until Kerensten, this harsh, killing wind would be all the unprocessed air there was. He replaced the mask and walked out again to the edge of the gray light and racing snow. He clung to both hand grips. It was Balder and my own freedom for the life of my House, he told himself. I've traded warmth and sunlight and joy and friendship for duty and Family and this unwelcoming world. I've made my choice. I must make that choice worth the price.

He lost track of how long he stared blindly into the fierce night. He was painfully aware how far he had to go to become an effective Lharr. He was also aware Asten Harlan's paralysis drastically shortened the time he had in which to learn. At last the cold penetrated even the survival suit, and Karne turned away from the storm and walked determinedly through the thin layer of snow inside the shelter to the lift.

Nik and Karne did not talk on the ride back to Ontar manor. Karne was preoccupied with his thoughts and Nik had the wisdom not to interrupt him. Karne hopped out in the manor house court-

yard and, rather curtly, asked Nik to garage the car
for him. He glanced up at the nursery windows,
their window boxes dim shadows in the "night" of
the courtyard, the gypsy-flowers and trailing ferns
in them mere lumps in the darkness. He paused in
the dim corridor outside the Great Hall to smell
and feel Ontar, then he charged up two flights of
stairs to his room and flung open the door. He
stood in the doorway and looked at the prints and
paintings of other worlds. They had been his
dream, his escape, for as long as he could remember. When he had failed to meet Trev Halarek's standards on the target range or in the
arena, he had spent the hours of punishment here,
visiting in mind the windy plains of Beta Sigma
III, the vast bazaar of Rigel IV, the Altarian Naval
Academy on Balder, and other places on other
worlds. Well, he had seen those windy plains from
orbit and had bought a rok-hide chest in the bazaar on Rigel IV.

He walked the few paces that separated him
from the large painting of Balder and its two tiny
moons. He reached out and brushed his fingers
lightly across the quiet, blue-green face of the
planet—calm, peaceful, the Quadrant headquarters for the Federation of the Inner Worlds.
His hand dropped to his side and he stepped back,
away from the painting. For several minutes he sa-
vored its colors and its memories, then he carefully took it and all the other pictures down,
stacked them neatly, and tied them into manage-
able bundles.

Chapter Six

———◆———

THE NEXT MORNING, Karne carried a few valued small possessions, and Wiki, to the Lharr's official quarters at the end of an adjoining hall. He paused in the hall door, looking into the sleeping room, which was almost as bare as the one he had just left. Straight ahead across the room was the door to the sitting room of the Larga's quarters, and on his left the door to the movable iron stair down to the library. The large wood bed, without carvings or decorations of any sort, was curtained in Halarek blue and green. The bed, a desk of severely plain design, and a night table were the room's only furnishings. No rugs, no tapestries, no paintings softened the hardness of the gray stone. Karne almost turned and went back to his boyhood room. Instead, he squared his shoulders, carried his load of possessions to the bed, and rang for one of the fifth level's servants. He ordered the Rigellian rokhide chest and the old leather chair brought from his old room to his new quarters. He called for fast-breaking and then for the tailor to measure him for a new wardrobe.

"I couldn't spend the rest of the winter in my cadet uniform and clothes from the armory," he told Nik later, wryly.

The first item on the morning's agenda was a meeting with Orkonan to go over procedures for the oath-feast, which was to be held on 36 Narn. While Karne practiced his speeches for the ceremony of fealty, he was also standing still, mostly, for the tailor, who was pinning and basting elaborate feast clothes. Kit and the Larga Alysha sat watching the proceedings with considerable amusement, to Karne's annoyance. He had just jerked, and cursed, because the tailor had stuck a pin into him for the twenty-third time, when someone knocked at the door. A prefet of Blues was inside almost before the Larga finished saying, "Come in."

The prefet saluted Karne, then the Larga. "Milord, milady, the com center has just received an emergency call from Farm 3. The agslaves have risen, killed all five manager-assistants, and captured the manager. The manager's wife made the call, says she and the children and the serfs are sealed into the manager's building. They can't be hurt there, but they're besieged and some of the slaves know how to turn off the power. General Zicker is on his way down to talk to you, Lord Karne."

"Good. Send for Pilot von Schuss and General Shen, prefet. Dismissed."

"Sir!" The prefet spun on his toe and left, passing General Zicker at the door.

The general saluted with a flourish. "Milady. Lord Karne."

Karne dismissed the tailor with an abrupt motion of his hand.

General Zicker settled his portly body slowly

into the nearest chair. "Gout's bad today," he said apologetically.

"General," Karne's voice was very quiet and rigidly controlled, "you will ask permission before you sit in my presence or the regent's. Now stand and do it properly!"

The general glanced at Karne with surprise, then his face flushed with resentment, but he stood as ordered, asked permission, and sat again.

A captain in the uniform of the Lifesguardsmen entered through the door the general had left open. "Milord, General Shen begs to be excused. He is abed with fever."

"Thank you, Captain." Karne watched him leave. He turned again to the general. "Sir, the prefet who brought the message said you already knew about the situation at Farm 3. What do you advise?"

General Zicker cleared his throat. "Milord, milady, something should be done at once. A quick attack—shut off all the entrances to the farm buildings and trap the slaves on the surface—is my best advice. Then kill all the ungrateful rabble. If we don't, other agslaves will try taking hostages, too."

Nik had slipped quietly into the room while the general talked. He tucked a note into Karne's hand as he passed. Now he leaned forward intently and asked, "Where are the slaves now, General?"

"Who are you to be asking me questions, Pilot?"

"He's my tactical adviser," Karne said in a warning voice. "He is also Heir in von Schuss and requires the respect due his blood rank, General, at least in such discussions as these. You do yourself no good by being—discourteous, General."

General Zicker's eyes narrowed and his lips thinned. He nodded agreement.

"Where are the slaves now, General?"

"That was not reported, Pilot."

"Would they still be on the surface this late in the year?"

"I doubt the herd animals are yet all fenced, milord. A great many slaves should be needed to finish that before the storms really hit. Of course," Zicker added as an afterthought, "if they've killed the managers, who's to tell them the animals need protection? Slaves don't know enough to wipe their own noses without orders."

"Have you put an appropriate number of men on alert, General?"

"Yes, milord. The transport stands ready to leave at your command."

"Load the men, General. I'll be there as soon as I put on some decent clothes."

"By my Sire's Blood, lord! You can't mean you plan to accompany the men! Not to put down slaves, milord. That is a task unworthy of one of the Nine. You'd never be able to hold up your head again if you lowered yourself to fight *slaves!*" The general's face purpled with distress.

Karne looked to Nik for confirmation or denial.

"He's right. A lord fights only men of his own class, short of an absolute disaster, like slaves attacking the manor house itself. You have enough problems without compounding them, Karne."

Karne sighed. He would get no battle experience

this time. "Get the men you need and settle this, General."

General Zicker nodded, levered himself out of the chair, and left.

Karne opened the note. "There's a visitor for you in your quarters." Karne looked questioningly at Nik, who just grinned, shrugged his shoulders, and turned away. "I don't know who your visitor is. Go up and find out."

Karne thought he heard laughter in Nik's voice, but he could not be sure. He looked at von Schuss's quivering back for a moment, then bounded up the iron stair, which rattled and clanged under his feet. He shoved open the ornate wood door at the top of the stair. There was no one there. He burst into the adjoining sitting room. A blond head and powerful neck showed above the worn leather of the old chair from his upstairs room. The moment the door banged against the wall, a blond giant sprang out of the chair and whirled to face the sound.

"Egil!"

The two embraced, laughing, pounding shoulders, talking at once. At last Egil set Karne a little away and looked down at him with dancing blue eyes. "I missed you and your 'Go away, I'm studying,' so I twisted my father's arm, explained that I hadn't heard from you, that you needed friends right now, and that I hadn't done that well on last term's exams."

"But your career!"

Egil shrugged. "I'm not cut out for a Navy man. Too many rules and orders."

Karne grinned, remembering some of the scrapes Egil had gotten them into.

"My father can find a place for me on one of his merchantmen when I get back," Egil added.

"When you get back," Karne echoed, instantly sober. "If you show yourself my friend, your life is in as much danger as mine. Stay out of this fight, Egil. The Guardians alone know how glad I am to see you, but I want to see you alive. Come back when the war's over."

Egil shook his head. "I remember what you said about not daring to trust anyone, about friends betraying friends for money or land. You need someone who'll stand by you no matter what."

"It's your *life* we're talking about, Egil!"

"It's your life, too." Egil grinned. "'No one knows their time of dying, so why cower in a safe place,' or so the ancient ones said. Death finds everyone sooner or later. How goes being Lharr?"

"Very bad. I'm not yet Lharr legally because I don't yet have eighteen winters and you know what my sire thought of me."

"Your sire was an ass! If that's your worst problem..."

"It's not. I'll tell you more later. I last felt pressed this hard when my Navy team faced the opponents in the Urtek-Cyrilla dispute and both sides wanted to kill us. Remember? There were a lot of nasty surprises in that situation, too, but there I was only a junior officer, for which I was very grateful. Here, I'm the officer in charge. And there's a slave revolt in progress."

Egil looked very thoughtful for a moment, then he brightened. "You managed then, you'll manage now." He slammed Karne between the shoulders, then caught him with a practiced hand as Karne staggered from the blow. "I'm here now, and there's never been anything the two of us couldn't handle. Right?"

Karne grinned and threw an arm around his friend's back. "Let's go downstairs. I'll introduce you to my lady mother and she'll introduce you to your quarters."

Karne thought the iron stair would come off the wall when Egil came down it, but it did not. The people in the library looked up at the clatter and Kit's mouth fell open. Karne laughed inside. *I've told her about Egil, but she didn't believe he could really be that big, or that fair.*

The Larga rose in a swirl of bright burgundy-colored skirts and held out her hands to Egil. "Welcome, Egil Olafson. I've heard so much about you."

Egil strode forward, went down on one knee, and lifted the Larga's hand to his forehead. He stood, then, and looked down appreciatively at her. Her head came just above his elbow. "Peace be on your House, Larga Alysha."

"And on yours grace, and peace, Egil." Alysha Halarek smiled and the dimple in her right cheek appeared. "You've been studying our customs. Here, let me introduce you."

Egil stopped her after only two or three sentences. "I'm sorry, Larga, I thought I'd be able to follow you, but I can't. I speak only a little Rom."

The Larga laughed. "You fooled me," she said in Galac. "You have a good accent." She looked across the room. "Tane, get translits for us, please."

Egil made a small bow. "Thank you. I won't need

one long. The fourth language always comes easier than the second, and I have teach-tapes with me."

The Larga nodded approval. "It sounds like you plan to stay a long time. I'm glad. Karne needs a friend who's not tied up in the political mess here." The Larga took a translit from the rack Orkonan held out to her and clipped the chain around her neck so the round talk-box lay against her throat. "Translits are awkward, but not nearly so awkward as not being able to understand. Here on Starker IV, few people know either trade language. You'd be in real trouble if you got stranded without at least a pair of them with you." She looked over her shoulder. "What did you set them for, Tane?"

"Rom/Sternlangue."

"Thank you. Now, Egil, if you'll follow me, I'll show you to guest quarters."

In the late afternoon the transport for Farm 3 lifted off with the best men of eight Centuries on her, but it was the next morning before General Zicker sent word he had arrived at the farm, was deploying his men, and expected to meet the enemy any time. Karne checked with him that afternoon and Zicker had not yet seen any slaves. The next day and the next the general still had not found the "enemy" and had made no attempt to descend to the farm buildings, had made nothing, as far as Karne could see, but excuses. That evening Karne read the comcopy of Zicker's last message of the day, swore savagely, tore the message into ragged pieces, and hurled them into the library fireplace. "He's refused to attempt to clear the farm entrances and send men down! He says the losses would be too great! By my Sire's Blood!"

Karne looked at Orkonan, Nik, Kit, Egil, and the Larga Alysha, all of them watching him in silence. "Zicker *can't* expect those slaves to come to him! They're already where they intend to stay. It's the end of Narn! Day after tomorrow's my oath-feast and my soldiers are sitting on the surface above Farm 3, in vicious weather, waiting for Zicker-only-knows what! The slaves are cozy and our only casualties are from frostbite!" Karne drew back to kick a log in the library fire farther toward the back, then remembered it was not the sort of fire he had enjoyed the last five years and put his foot back on the floor. This fire was only an imitation—realistic logs with realistic flames and a realistic smell—that would look and smell no different in fifty years. Karne's mouth tightened until his lips were only a thin line. He looked at the Larga and at von Schuss. "General Shen has pneumonia and Zicker won't move. Well, he has to move on orders given in person or be tried for mutiny. He's in mutiny now. I'm taking a Century of Blues to break open that farm however I have to. Tane, send for Troopleader Gregg. Tell him to pick the men. One hour before sunrise tomorrow, battle dress, on the flitter pad. Nik, I want you to fly the transport. If anyone can safely fly in Uhl, you can."

* * *

Troopleader Gregg saluted Karne outside the door of the flitter pad. "All you ordered are aboard the transport, lord."

"Good. Detail four men for fighter escort. I want Zicker and all his officers taken as quickly as possible. Be sure the men on the transport split up to take all the troop shelters. No one is to use com equipment until we land at Farm 3: there are too many listeners out there. Lady Mother," he turned to the Larga, "you're in charge here until I get back. Don't look so worried, lady mother. Yes, Richard probably had a hand in this. He hopes I'll do something before my oath-feast to disgust my vassals. But he won't interfere personally. Kingsland wouldn't stand for it."

The Larga smiled shakily. Karne kissed her cheek, sprinted to a fighter, jumped onto its wing, and slid into the pilot's seat. When he looked out the side to be sure all the spectators were now behind blast shields, he saw Egil, watching him with a grin from behind the passenger seat. Egil uncoiled and crammed himself in the too-small chair.

"After your speech the other night about safety, I decided not to ask if I could come with you. Your fight's my fight, Karne."

Karne looked into the deep blue eyes. He could argue, but he might as well argue with the moon. And there was not the slightest possibility that he could throw Egil out of the fighter bodily. "Would it do any good to order you out?"

"No good at all. I didn't come here to skip all the excitement."

No, he would not come to miss the excitement. His ancestors had explored Earth, then much of the galaxy, all in search of excitement. Karne looked at his control panel. The green go light began blinking.

"Ready when you are, milord." The voice of the com-center tech filled the small compartment.

The go light held a steady green. Karne lifted the fighter up and out into the gray, wind-whipped dawn. He felt fierce exultation, as he always did when a flier he piloted leaped for the sky. This time, a deep, burning anger fed on the exultation. Zicker had defied him, and Karne was sure Richard was spreading the news judiciously among the Houses.

Four hours later they reached Farm 3. Karne saw the troop shelter domes below on a level plain, broken here and there by enormous, upright black rocks. He circled the area once, then landed so close to the command dome that the wake of his passage bent in one side of it. He jumped from the flier's wing and hit the ground running, loosening the flap that held down his beamer as he ran. The other four fighter pilots were running, too, and the transport was settling gently onto the wind-packed snow. With Egil at his heels, Karne burst through the windlock into the command dome, beamer in hand. General Zicker and his aides whirled and gasped. They had been playing Deeps and Fliers, and pieces knocked over in their surprise rolled across the playing board. The faint *wip...wip... wip...* noise seemed loud.

An aide inched toward a com unit. Karne fired a beamer bolt between the man and his goal. The aide jerked his hand back, cursing, and the plasti wall beyond him melted. Snow blew against the hot hole and sizzled.

"Look what you've done!" the general began.

"You won't need the shelter anymore, General," Karne snarled at him. "You're dismissed, in disgrace, for mutiny."

Gregg ducked through the doorway, followed by the other three fighter pilots, Nik, and a troop of Blues from the transport. The men spread out around the edges of the dome. The general's aides froze in position. Karne fixed his eyes on one of the aides, a slender young man with a reddish tinge to his hair and large, capable hands.

"You there, do you have any communication with the farm?"

The aide nodded nervously.

"Do the slaves have a leader? Do you have a line to him?"

The aide nodded both times.

"Then why are you still here!" Karne roared at the general.

"You are interfering with a commander in the field, my lord. I have matters well in hand. Your—"

"General Zicker, you will return to the manor now with Pilot—"

Karne looked at the man to his left.

"Jenkins, milord."

"—with Pilot Jenkins. You may go unbound if you give your oath. No, you were my sire's man too long. I can't trust your word. Egil, tie his hands behind him. There's utility cord in the third pocket from the right on his accessory belt."

Egil stalked toward General Zicker. The general leaped to his feet.

"Spare me the humiliation, my lord!" General Zicker sounded more outraged than pleading. The general turned slightly, his right hand dropping into his pocket.

Egil lunged and twisted the general's right hand until the man opened his fingers, gasping with pain. A tiny dart pistol fell onto the game table. Karne stared at it. Death. From one of his Family's own officers.

"Thanks, brother. I didn't..." Karne paused, waiting for the icy numbness to fade. When he looked at the general again, his yellow eyes were as hard and cold as a cat's. "I've lived too long on a world where a human's word could be trusted and an officer's loyalty to his commander never wavered." Karne looked toward the waiting Blues. "You, prefet, take this traitor outside and shoot him. Leave his body for the bears."

"Sooooo." Zicker let the sounds out in a low, malignant hiss. "The woman of the Halareks thinks to rule in truth. You'll never be a fraction the Lharr your sire was!" The words stung and the general knew it. "You and your dam, with her soft-hearted, foreign ways—"

"TAKE HIM OUT!"

Joining the prefet, Jenkins and several Blues hurried the general out.

"In front of your men!" Egil's face and voice both showed his amazement.

"It's a common belief, fostered by my own sire," Karne answered with bitterness. He looked at the pilots. "One of you take over the com unit. I want all the centens in camp here immediately. Von Schuss, you check every barracks-dome and put on the transport every man with frostbite or snow-fever, then report to me how many are left. You," Karne indicated the Blues' troopleader, "see the general's aides are disarmed and then lock them up securely in the transport. Post a guard."

The aides went white and one of them sagged against the game table. More game pieces clittered over. "My lord, we knew nothing of the general's plan—" "We obeyed legal orders, milord—" "Lord Karne, have mercy!"

"You can prove your loyalty some other time," Karne snapped. "Right now, I'm not in a mood for taking chances with the lot of you. Where's the map of the farm entrances?"

One of the aides, his color returning, pointed to a roll lying against the dome wall. "Thank you for our lives, lord. Your sire would not have given us a second chance."

Karne turned his back as if he had not heard and went to the maproll. He pushed it up against the dome frame and held it open with the clips attached to the frame. "We're here?" He stabbed a finger on a spot on the map.

The aide who had spoken nodded.

"Right beside one of the entrances?"

The aide nodded again. "The general didn't want to walk very far in the snow with his gout and all."

"Then why, in the Guardians' names, didn't he use it?"

"It only goes to the ponics sheds, lord, and that's controlled by the slaves. There are two others, to the deeper levels, still open, my lord."

"Then why did he pick this entrance?"

"It wasn't then controlled by the rebels, milord."

Karne swore feelingly in three languages. His soldiers looked at him in amazement for a moment, then broke into grins. That stopped Karne in mid-word. "What's the matter?"

The men's grins widened. Then Karne grinned, too.

"Those aren't the words the 'woman' of the Family would know, are they?" Karne laughed and the soldiers laughed with him. Karne turned to the pilot at the com set. "Are the centens coming?"

"Aye, milord. The sound of the general's execution did nothing to slow them, either."

"See if you can reach the farmhouse."

The com operator turned back to the set.

Karne beckoned to the aide who had shown him the map. "Your name?"

"Obren, lord."

"Show me where the rebels are known to be."

The young officer pointed to sheds and buildings on the map. The rebels completely encircled the farmhouse. Karne did not turn from studying the map when he heard the windlock open and shut several times.

"Where are the entrances that are open?"

The aide pointed.

"How many levels down?"

"Stairs down nine levels, lord. The lift just outside is for freight and goes only to the ponics shed. Rebel ground, as I said before."

Karne turned around and studied the clump of centens who had just entered. They were all near his sire's age. Three of them looked rumpled and heavy-eyed. Two whispered to each other while clenching and unclenching their hands; their faces were pale and shiny with sweat. The last of the group, a thin, grizzled officer of about fifty winters, stood a little apart from the others, watching them with a slight twist to his lips that might indicate amusement.

"Where are the others? There were eight."

The grizzled officer took a step forward and saluted. "Centen Wynter, milord. I just put them on the transport. They've been nursing their men and caught the snowfever themselves. Centen Roth looks near death, milord."

"Thank you, Wynter. What have the rest of you been doing? Sleeping?" The three rumpled officers flushed and would not meet Karne's eyes. "And you two? Well?"

"They were just leaving, milord," Wynter said after silence had stretched itself thin. "Urgent business in a warm inn in the freecity of Loch, I believe." Wynter's tone was very dry. "Zicker had warned them once about leaving their men, but Zicker wasn't around to stop them this time."

The two nervous officers turned red. They glared at Wynter, but they did not deny what he had said.

"Who was the duty officer?"

One rumpled centen pointed to the taller of the two nervous officers. "*He* was."

The accused man stammered something about medical supplies and frostbitten toes.

"You're a prisoner. You'll be executed if a court-martial finds the charges against you true. The duty officer! *You* there, prefet, take this man to the transport and put him in solitary confinement."

Karne turned to the other of the two. "You are dismissed. Be off the Holding by daybreak. An officer belongs with his men until his commander orders him away." Karne stared fiercely at the remaining centens. "Lay down your arms now." He waited until they had dropped their weapons to the ground. "You, excepting Wynter, will take the transport back to Ontar and there you'll nurse the casualties of this—this fiasco until they all are discharged from the clinic. We'll consider at that time whether you keep your commissions or not. Move!"

The centens scurried out. Karne motioned three Blues near the door to follow them.

"Where were you, Wynter?"

"As I said, lord, I'd just put Centens Martin and Roth on the transport. Before that I'd been putting my own Century's casualties aboard, lord." Wynter slammed his fist into his palm. "This damnable sitting did it! Barracks-domes weren't made for sieges nearing Uhl, lord!"

"How many of your men?"

"Thirty percent, lord, mostly frostbite."

Karne whistled. "The other Centuries about the same?"

"Mostly worse, milord. I set my domes in the lee of some of those big rocks."

Karne nodded. "Good thinking. Call up your able-bodied men. You're going to help us break this siege." Karne turned to the com operator. "Did you contact the farmhouse?"

"No answer, milord."

"I hope we aren't too late. Are the rebels on the air, Obren?"

The aide nodded and named the wavelength.

"See if you can raise them, then, Pilot. The rest of you take a look at this map." He jabbed the paper. "We use the two deep entrances. If they're blocked with snow by now, use fighter exhaust to clear them. We spread out in the lowest corridor and come up on the rebels—"

"The rebels, milord, they have the farm manager hostage." The pilot did not look up from his unit when he spoke.

"Turn up the sound," Karne ordered.

The rumble and muttering of an angry crowd filled the dome. Karne took a deep breath and wished for a tri-d. *Tactics I've learned, and psychology, and negotiation, but negotiation is much easier when I can see my opponent's face.* Karne cleared his throat, wiped his sweating hands against his thighs, and picked up the remote. "Move half your men down now, Wynter, under your best troopleader. Pilot von Schuss, who's the best troopleader in G Century, Roth's command?"

"Karsen or Waltt, milord."

"Pick one and send him down the other way with fifty men. Have them hold channel 26 open for orders."

Wynter and von Schuss saluted and left.

Karne turned on the remote. "Command dome here. I am Lharr Karne. This rebellion has gone on long enough. We end it today. General Zicker is dead. Give up now and save a lot of blood-spilling."

"We know about blood-spilling." The deep, harsh voice vibrated the com's speakers. "It's ours that'll flow if we give up now. We'll die in a good fight, not lined up for execution."

Karne heard the rebels muttering agreement with the speaker. "Who speaks there?"

"Anse-the-smith. You're the new Lharr, then?"

"Aye."

"They've sent a boy to do an army's work?" the smith jibed.

"I send myself. Release the manager and there'll be no executions."

There was no response from below.

"There'll be no executions if you release the manager and go back to work," Karne repeated.

"'No executions'!" A harsh, grating laugh followed. "There's no word-keeping between your kind and mine. No, the farm'll crack and we'll dig in. You'll never get us out."

Karne saw Wynter had returned. He walked his fingers downward and questioned with his eyes and brows. Wynter shook his head and held up five fingers.

Got to talk some more. "We can starve you out, just like you're starving the farmhouse."

"Take years, my fine lord. We've got the ponics techs. And you have Uhl."

The man's thinking. Karne looked at Wynter, who nodded. "You haven't a chance against trained fighting men. Give up the manager and the techs. They have no part in this."

"'No part.' You can say 'no part'? You, who get the taxes beaten out of us? You, whose fees for food go up monthly? We must buy our clothing now, and when we got the charges for our sleeping quarters and increases in work hours— Our families are *starving* because of your manager's fees and you say he has no part!"

Karne shot a glance at von Schuss, who shrugged and gave a tiny shake of his head. Such arrangements for slaves were not usual, then. Karne's brain raced. Was this simple greed on the manager's part? Or was there something more in this situation? Gharr habits of survival, long un-used, stirred to life in Karne. The timing of the revolt was too neat, too close to the oath-feast, too good an opportunity for Karne to publicly humili-ate himself or even get himself killed. To foil that intent, to save himself and his House, he would have to take action considered out of the realm of possibility for one of the Nine. He must choose a path a man of the Gharr, raised on Starker IV, would never see. Karne clicked off the remote and turned to his men. He studied their faces, his thoughts spinning through the actions he might take. At last he saw what to do. He set his face and voice, a show of authority House officers would not argue with, remembering his sire's way with arguers. "I'm going down to talk to the smith face-to-face." The horror he had expected distorted his officers' faces, but, also as he expected, they said nothing. "We need this farm to last the winter and we have to end the revolt right now if we expect to get home. Flying weather can't last much longer. I can end the revolt, probably without more casual-ties, if I speak to the smith face-to-face. They know how easy lies are from a distance. I want Wynter, von Schuss, Egil, Jenkins, you, you, you of the Blues, and you, Pilot—?"

"Willem, lord. Yan Willem, House Justin."

Karne gave him a quick, grateful smile of welcome, betraying none of the anger he held out of sight: No one had told him House Justin's men had arrived. He turned on the remote again. "I'm coming down to talk and I'm bringing eight men, but I leave my personal weapons here." Karne thought over what he remembered of slaves and weapons. It was likely their main weapon was numbers, but some farm tools could be vicious. "I'm new at this job, smith. Give me a chance." Karne had the com turned off before the slave could answer. He adjusted the hood of his survival suit and started toward the windlock. His men protested.

"Milord, you weren't serious!"

"You don't have a chance."

"Let the men on level one take care of them."

Karne whirled on the young Blues officer who made this suggestion, his anger flying free at the hapless man. "And if surprise doesn't give them victory, what? They're dead. All of them. Dead! We've had enough casualties here already, stupid, stupid casualties! The rebels have eight levels to ambush, blockade—" Karne shook his head and lowered his voice. "No, I'll give the men on level one a better chance by dividing the slaves' attention. When I sent them down I expected to do better negotiating from here." Karne hung his weapons belt on a rack by the windlock.

Von Schuss put his good hand on Karne's arm. "Let some of us go ahead, my lord. Don't risk yourself unnecessarily."

Karne nodded. "You won't be one of those, Pilot. Your House is no better off for heirs than mine."

Karne motioned Willem, Jenkins, and two of the

Blues to precede them. They stepped out into snow knee-deep. It had drifted almost to the top of the rectangular box that housed the lift, but it did not yet cover the lift gate. One of the Blues jumped onto the box and opened the cover. "Clear here, lord, if the controls haven't been jammed," he called up.

The men escorting Karne jumped onto the edge of the box, then dropped down into the square freight lift. Karne sprang down after them. Light green powder, spilled from some container, mixed on the lift floor with melting snow from the men's boots, leaving darker green puddles on the gray metal. The vapor from those puddles smelled dark and pungent, like a newly cleaned sanitary.

"Disinfectant," said Egil through his translit, wrinkling his nose.

"They use that stuff on your world, too?" said von Schuss.

Egil nodded and they both laughed. Karne punched the controls and the lift dropped, rapidly. Several men clutched the walls for support.

"Not meant for humans," Nik explained to Egil in Sternlangue. "In winter the Gild can send one of their heavy robo-freighters in above the weather and just drop supplies through the hatch. The impact of however many M-tons the trigger's set for turns on the lift and down it goes. Blam! there it is, just outside the ponics shed freight door."

The lift stopped abruptly. Almost everyone tumbled over. The door slammed open and a squat, muscular slave, backed by at least fifty others, glared into the lift. Karne and Egil stood, legs still braced against the impact, waiting for the others to get up. Karne thought he caught a gleam of respect in the squat slave's eyes.

"Which of you be the Lharr?"

Karne stepped forward a pace. "I am. You're Anse-the-smith?"

"Aye. You be much younger even than I'd thought. Be you coming out?"

"I feel safer here," Karne answered. "I don't know how much you control your men. Mine won't fire unless attacked." He held his arms away from his body. "See, I have no weapons."

Anse-the-smith grunted. "That's not much, seein' your men be armed and you be protected on three sides. But you *did* keep your word," he added grudgingly. "*That* one wouldn't have." He jerked his head toward a quivering mound of brown cloth huddled against the wall near the lift. "Thought he'd escape like a parcel, he did. Left his family to us, the moment he heard soldiers were coming." The smith grinned wolfishly, baring broad, uneven yellow teeth. "Only his family be locked up safe and he's with us." He kicked the mound of cloth. "Stand up."

The cloth heap moaned.

"Stand up or I'll kick your teeth in."

The mound straightened slowly, holding onto the smooth shed wall for support. The man finally raised his head and Karne saw a sharp face with darting eyes and a narrow mustache.

"My lord, have mercy," the trembling manager whined.

"Did you charge these people for their food?"

The man's hands twisted in the folds of his robe.

"Did you charge for food?" Karne roared.

"My—my lord. Y-yes, my lord."

Karne's face was grim, but his voice was controlled. "You charged them for clothes and sleeping quarters?"

"Yes, my lord. I did, my lord. I have to live, too, my lord."

Karne counted to thirty in Galac, slowly, twice. He forced himself to speak slowly, quietly. "We pay managers well. We provide for our slaves. We have never charged them for what they need. Your charges are illegal. They are inhuman!" Karne shut his eyes and took several deep breaths. "House Halarek has always provided well for its slaves and it has never had trouble with them. *You* throw an entire farm into revolt with your greed. *You* caused several hundred military casualties."

The manager looked stunned. "But, my lord, the House has always allowed a little extra on the taxes, a little extra work for the manager—"

"A *little* extra work, a *little* extra tax. But not fees for necessities. There are hundreds of soldiers on the surface, sick or injured *by your greed!*"

"But, Lord Karne, someone called from Ontar manor and suggested the new fees. He said many other Houses operated so and that the new Lharr—"

Karne's fingers dug into the man's arm. "Who said this?"

"He—he didn't give a name, lord."

"And you didn't think that strange?"

"I—I didn't think, lord."

"Too good a chance for profit to think it out, right?" Karne felt like kicking the man himself. Instead, he turned to the smith. "I want the farm family here, and safe."

"That be beyond your powers, lord."

"You'll have a new, honest manager within three days."

"We're hungry here, lord. Promises fill no stomachs."

The mob behind Anse-the-smith shoved closer, muttering.

"I keep my promises."

"We'll have to see that, lord."

"What do you want?"

"Pardons, lord. And the manager there, to do with as we see fit." The smith jabbed a finger in the manager's side and the man squawked and trembled.

Karne felt a little sick. Had the man no pride? How could he cringe like that? "Pardons you have, smith. The provocation was extreme."

The men behind Karne shifted their feet and made disagreeing noises.

"Your sire wouldn't say so, young lord."

"My sire's dead, smith."

"You soon may be, too."

"You're not stupid, smith. Kill me and House Halarek goes into trusteeship. That means into the hands of the strongest Families—Harlan, Odonnel, Justin..."

The smith looked thoughtful. "Not good, that, lord. Lost four toes to the Odonnels' axman. So I wouldn't run away again. Then I was sold here." He turned away and conferred with a huddle of men. When he turned back, the whole group pressed forward. "They don't trust your promises,

lord. They don't like that bunch of soldiers hidin'
below us. They don't want that—that filth," he
poked the cowering manager again, "to get away.
You didn't say you were sending soldiers up from
below, lord."

"I made you no promises, except about myself. I
had to insure my life."

Something above made a loud *snick*. Karne
looked up, then looked questioningly at the smith.

"We're just insuring *our* lives, lord. The lift can
go up by hand-pulling, or you can walk to a stair
and up, but the power cable's been cut."

Chapter Seven

———◆———

ONE OF THE men in the lift gasped. Some of the
slaves behind the smith brandished hayforks and
docking knives. The mob surged forward, shoving
the smith into the lift.

"Back!" the smith roared.

The slaves scrambled backward.

"We're even again, lord," the smith told Karne
with a grim smile.

Karne stared at the slave while weighing his al-
ternatives. Surprise was gone, it did not matter
how, and the soldiers below would be waylaid on
every level if he and Wynter called them up.
Enough might live to kill or capture all the slaves

in the ponics shed, but by that time everyone in
the lift would be dead.

Behind the smith, slaves were waving fists or
banging weapons against the walls. Some toward
the back of the mob were jumping up and down to
see what was happening and shouting with frustration. One of these, a boy of twelve or so,
climbed onto a neighbor's shoulders and began
yelling a report of what he saw. Along one wall a
scuffle started. The smith watched Karne with a
wry twist to his mouth. "Think hard, young lord. I
wasn't always a slave and know well the crafty
ways of the nobility."

"I've promised you pardons. If I die here—"

A gnarled old man in a ragged sark shoved
closer. "Pardons is easy here, lord," he snarled,
"but what's to say we still have them when you
reach the surface?"

Karne stiffened. "I keep my word."

"Says you," the old man jeered.

"I've kept my word with you so far."

"No weapons ain't the same as no executions."

Wynter pushed out of the lift and grabbed the
old slave by one arm. "This is the Lharr. No one
talks to him like that!"

Karne caught the centen's eye. "Peace, Wynter.
The old man's words don't hurt me. No one's died
and I want to keep it that way."

Wynter's lips tightened and he frowned, but he
also let go and stepped back into the lift.

"Back of me, Enoch. I do the talking." The smith
firmly pushed the old man into the center of the
mob. His powerful shoulders strained the cloth of
his sark and the muscles of his arms bulged as he

shoved aside men as if they were snowflakes.
"Keep him there," Anse-the-smith said to the old
man's neighbors. "I don't want him stirrin' people
up." He came back to the lift door. "My control of
them be near its end. They've waited long. We have
to trust each other. Now, lord."

"I offer freedom."

The smith spat just beyond the open lift gate.
"What do they care about freedom? They want
something concrete."

"And you?"

"I was free once, was one of the old Kingsland's
accountants. He sold me into slavery for a gambling debt, said handling money would be too
much temptation for a gambler. Well, I'm gambling now, lord, that you'll do as you say. Freedom'd suit me, but they," he jerked his head over
his shoulder, "they need something they can touch.
The manager. His life for yours and some of those
soldiers below."

Karne looked at the cringing pile of brown cloth.
He's earned it, Karne thought savagely, whatever
they do to him. Balder's ideas of justice could not
survive here. Here people believe a man's victims
give him the most fitting punishment. He nodded
once abruptly, agreeing, then said, "Bring his family to me."

The smith turned to a gaunt youth. "Bring the
family and cousins here, Nile." Anse stripped off
the wide studded belt that tightened his sark.
"Your proof you be my messenger. Make 'em run
back. It ain't far and we're in a hurry."

Karne's neck and shoulders ached with tension
and his leg muscles felt knotted. He tried to make

himself loosen up to prepare for the final steps of the bargaining, but his mind would not be diverted from the problem facing him now. The smith was smart, clearly a leader, and he was therefore dangerous as long as he was a slave. Trev Halarek would have arranged an accident as soon as possible after Trev himself was safe. That would leave the slaves leaderless and therefore docile, for a while, but all Anse-the-smith's natural ability would be wasted. Karne had to do something about the smith as soon as the trade was done. There must be some way to earn his loyalty, to use his brains and his power over other men.

A child wailed in the corridor outside the shed and women's sobbing ran under that sound, a chorus of fear and despair. The door opened and the mob inside the shed parted to let a group of about fifteen pass through.

"This be all?" the smith asked.

The gaunt youth nodded. "Two grown women, six children, and nine cousins, Uncle."

"He had *two* wives?" Karne asked in amazement. He had no stomach to ask the quaking, shivering coward huddled against the wall.

The smith nodded. "Aye, and a slave leman, lord."

Three women, the man has three women! Karne thought, burning with rage. So few women since the Sickness that many minor lords die without direct heirs, and this—this insignificant son of an insignificant House takes *three!*

Karne stepped out of the lift and motioned the family in. "Get them up to the surface, Anse-the-smith," he said in a tight voice.

"Our bargaining isn't done, lord."

"I'll stay here. Get his 'family' out of sight of him."

"Don't be a fool, Lord Karne!" snapped Wynter.

"I'm staying with you." Egil pushed his way out of the lift.

"Three is better than two," Nik von Schuss said. "I'll stay, too."

"You're the last heir of your House. You can't take the risk, Nik."

"You're the last of yours."

"These are my slaves. This is my farm. This is my problem."

Von Schuss set his mouth stubbornly and would not look at Karne at all. Willem unsnapped his beamer cover and moved out behind von Schuss. Wynter followed him.

"Guard these people till we come up," Wynter ordered the three Blues in the lift. The three unsheathed their stunners.

Karne jerked his thumb toward the lift. "Hurry up," he told the huddled family, "time is running out for all of us. Move!"

They roused themselves and shuffled into the lift. Anse-the-smith spoke two quiet words into the shed's intercom, then shut the lift gate. "I have men below on the winch."

The lift rose slowly out of sight. No one spoke until the level indicator showed that the lift had reached the surface and was on its way back down. When it arrived again at the shed, Karne pushed open the gate and prodded the quivering bundle of cloth beside it. "Get up."

The manager squeaked and tried to make himself even smaller.

Karne choked on his anger and disgust and had to pause to swallow it down. "Our lives and the soldiers' below and an end to the revolt for us, the manager's life for the others and freedom for you? Is that a bargain, Anse-the-smith?"

The smith turned to the mob and repeated Karne's offer. "Is it a bargain?"

"YES!" roared the mob. It rushed forward, absorbed the manager, and dragged him, screaming, into the corridor. There, the tone of the man's screams changed and Karne steeled himself against them. He made himself concentrate on the room and the people in it. Other than the smith, only a few slaves remained, and these were crowded around the doorway, watching and listening to what happened outside. The manager's screams grew weaker and fainter. The smith's face revealed nothing about his thoughts.

"I have proven I keep my word, smith. I need a guarantee that the revolt stops now."

The smith shrugged his shoulders and spread his hands. "What's the word of a slave, my lord?"

"It's not your word I want, smith, it's you. A hostage for your promise. Tell your winchmen you go with us unhurt and will stay unhurt as long as this farm works as it should." Karne saw the smith's body tighten and he reached for his missing beamer.

Egil sprang forward and landed beside the smith in a partial crouch. He smiled a chilling smile. "I've been hoping for a chance to take you on,

Anse-the-smith. Do you dare take on a Drinn wrestler?"

The smith whistled softly. "You're one of them!" he said in Galac. "I be not willing to fight you for harm, young foreigner. We'll fight for fun sometime." He turned to speak the code words into the intercom, spun, and rushed Egil. Egil dodged aside and back in fast, catching and twisting the smith's arm and forcing him to stand still.

The smith laughed. "I thought you'd be good. Another day I'll more than test you. We'll see how much good your skill and youth are when I'm not letting myself be caught." The smith continued to smile and made no attempt to call to the men at the door for help.

Egil held him, just the same, until the other men in the lift had him in their sights. The smith walked into the lift by himself, chuckling, and Egil and Karne followed him.

The lift crawled up its cables. When Egil reached high and opened the gate, snow slid down onto the passengers. Karne sprang out and over the edge of the box, landing lightly in the snow. He was surprised to find day almost gone; the wind of evening was rising, bringing fresh snow with it. Heavy, gray clouds, bulging with snow, hung overhead. An early Uhl storm was coming but, for the moment, the thought of the gathering storm did not bother him. He lifted his face to the bite of the wind and the icy sting of the snow it drove ahead of it. He took deep breaths, savoring air unscented by human sweat and fear, rejoicing in being still alive to feel and smell.

"Wynter, how was the transport when you saw it?"

Wynter dropped from the lift box to the snow beside Karne. "Nearly full, milord. The casualties of eight Centuries..."

"Fill it with as many more wounded as will fit. Von Schuss, collect the able-bodied men and send them down to Karsen and Waltt. You and the Blues can then escort the farm 'family'—" Karne paused to swallow his disgust at the farm manager's greed, "—escort the farm family to the transport. You can return to Ontar when ready."

"Lord Karne, may I speak to you alone?"

Karne tried to read von Schuss's intention from his face and could not. He walked to the far side of the lift with him. The wind roared around the lift, tearing at the men's survival suits and pushing them away from their original positions. For several minutes, snow blotted out all their surroundings. Even the brilliant ground lights of the transport disappeared.

"Karne, come on the transport," Nik said urgently. "It's the only flier that should take off tonight. The rest are too light and too risky in a storm like we're going to have in just a little bit."

"Both of us, on one ship? Wouldn't *that* be a coup for Richard!"

"What chance is there of Harlan attacking here, at night, on 35 Narn?"

"What chance would you have said he had of getting someone at Ontar to feed that manager the idea of fees?"

"You know he could do that from anywhere. To get the transport, Richard has to have at least heavy guns, here, on Farm 3. Gild pix would have shown that. It would be known."

Karne sighed. "Maybe I'm fighting shadows. Guardians, Nik! A traitor in the House somewhere, a slave revolt that isn't yet entirely taken care of, and an oath-feast tomorrow—" He watched Wynter and Obren take advantage of a lull in the wind to walk the smith toward the transport. "From not suspicious enough, maybe I've gone to being too suspicious." He looked back at his friend. "I want to live, Nik. I want to save my House, but I don't want to die doing it."

Nik put one hand on Karne's shoulder. In silence, they watched Wynter and Willem return.

"Wynter," Karne said, "I know you've had a hard three days, but I need more work from you. I'm leaving you in charge here. Have the men on level one check the entire farm. I want all slave gatherings broken up and the slaves sent to their quarters and kept there for the duration of this storm. Nik thinks the storm should blow itself out by midday tomorrow and we can send the transport back for you and the men. The slaves should stay peaceful, at least for awhile, after they calm down. You can have a week off back at Ontar."

Wynter saluted and trudged off through the snow to the nearest escape-stair shelter. Karne and Nik joined Egil, who waited on the opposite side of the lift, and they all walked through the blowing snow to the transport.

Hours later, the transport reached Ontar. Karne personally supervised the unloading of casualties, assigned the centens their nursing shifts, and saw Anse-the-smith confined to comfortable political prisoner "guest" quarters. Karne ordered bread, meat, and beer for all able to eat it, listened with relief to the Larga's report of an uneventful day, then he and the other able-bodied soldiers separated to get a few hours' sleep. Alone in his cold, stark room, Karne sprawled across the big bed and was asleep before he could pull a blanket over himself.

It seemed his head had just touched the pillow when impatient hands drumming on his door awakened him. "Get up, sluggard! It's your big day! Your vassals are waiting." Egil's voice boomed into the room.

Karne rolled over and stared up at the stone ceiling. The ceiling was so gray. The entire manor was so gray. How pleasant, Karne thought sleepily, to have ceilings painted blue, like the summer sky, edged with tall grass and wildflowers like the rim of the world. Maybe then winter would not seem so long.

Egil pounded louder. "Aren't you awake yet? Come on! Orkonan's waiting for you to look at a chart of your vassals and their duties."

Karne sat up slowly, groggily, swung his legs over the edge of the bed, and stretched. At least winter meant safety—no sieges, no duels, not likely an assassin, either—for at least 160 days. He groaned. *"That's* what didn't get done this past week. Oath-feast work." He pushed himself up and off the bed and stumbled to the sanitary.

A few minutes later he came back into his room, toweling dry his hair. "Come on in, Egil. Sorry I'm so slow—big day? Vassals? Guardians!"

Egil roared with laughter. "You should see your

face! Yes, vassals. They've been waiting a couple hours now. You slept far overtime. No one could wake you. The Larga finally sent your sister in to try."

Karne shuddered dramatically. "I slept through *that?* I didn't know anyone could sleep through Kit's wake-up routine." He looked at his chrono and his mouth twisted ruefully. "I'll have to put my ceremonial clothes on now, looks like."

The clothes had been laid on the rok-hide chest at the foot of the bed. Karne put on a pair of close-fitting, Halarek-blue trousers trimmed with a narrow strip of short brown fur down each leg, a loose, tan shirt with full sleeves and embroidered edges, a velvet vest of Halarek blue trimmed with narrow bands of green, a floppy wom-skin hat, and a knee-length blue cape lined with white and trimmed with the same narrow green bands as his vest. He fastened the cape so it hung over his right shoulder, then took a long, leather-wrapped package from inside the chest. Egil came closer to see. Karne laid the package on the bed and unwrapped it reverently. Inside was a much-used sword with a jeweled hilt, from which several of the jewels were missing, and a stained and battered scabbard. Karne belted the sword around his waist so the scabbard hung on his left hip. In one smooth motion, he drew the sword and flourished it.

"This is the sword that won Halarek Holding five hundred Gildyears ago. We're a young House." Karne posed, legs braced, sword point against the floor between his feet, hands crossed on the knob of the hilt. "How do I look?"

Egil walked slowly around him. He stood in

front of Karne a moment, hands on hips, head to one side. "Quaint."

Karne's smile flashed. "We are very traditional here."

Egil laughed, then pointed to the sword. "Do you still use those things here?"

"Only for formal duels." Karne sheathed the sword and turned Egil bodily toward the door. "Let's eat before Orkonan and his chart find me. Or my duties as host, for that matter. I seem to have missed a lot of meals in the last few days."

But there was no time for that. Orkonan met the two in the hall and immediately began talking to Karne of vassals and liege lords and oaths. Too soon, he thought, Karne stood in the midst of his official retinue at the door of the Great Hall, waiting for the Larga. People packed the Hall and the galleries. Wide banners of different colors, each with the wide band of dark blue flanked by narrow bands of green that was the Halarek mark, hung from the columns under the galleries. Flaming torches sent trails of black smoke toward the vaulted ceiling. Scented smoke drifted over the heads of the crowd from ceremonial censers waved by blue-robed boys.

Friends, Family, allies, and vassals—the gathering shifted and moved like a lake in a breeze. Everyone wore bright holiday clothes. Here and there Karne saw an especially vivid splash of purple or green or red or even gold, each splash the delicate floor-length veil of some noblewoman's tall conical hat. "Sun" glowed through the clerestory windows, making the tiny panes of colored glass glow and setting the jewels in the crowd

glinting and sparkling. At the other end of the
Hall, was Lharr's dais. High above it hung an im-
mense wooden cross. Under that cross Karne
would take his oath when he was officially installed as the Lharr on 10 Aden next. Today, after
the vassals had taken their oaths of fealty, the
Lharr's table would be set on the dais for the feast.

The Larga's personal Lifesguardsmen opened a
path for her. The Larga hurried up to Karne. "I'm
sorry I'm late, Son." She adjusted her tall, pointed
hat a fraction. "How do I look?" She turned slowly.
The Halarek-blue gown, made of some fleecy mate-
rial, contrasted strikingly with her gold coloring.

"Fine, my lady. Fine."

"That's just what your sire would have said."
The Larga sighed. "Oh, well, it's not the worst
thing you could've learned from him. He paid attention, after his fashion." She slipped her hand
into the recesses of her skirt. "Here, you'll need
these." She dropped the heavy beaded necklace of
House administrator into Karne's hand.

Karne poked the ends of the necklace under his
sword belt, then adjusted his floppy hat. "Our
guests are waiting. If you're ready, Lady Mother?"

She took his arm and they walked toward the
dais, the Larga's guard and some of the household
Blues opening a path. Murmurs of recognition, low
comments about their clothes or bearing, asides
followed by laughter, and the heavy scents of per-
fume, incense, and sweat surrounded them. Somewhere in the crowd a dog yelped. Karne and the
Larga reached the low platform and climbed the
steps onto it. The serfs of the household staff, gath-

ered under the galleries, surged forward crying, "The Lharr! The Lharr!" and knelt around the dais.

Karne responded with the words tradition demanded. "My thanks, good people. I value your loyalty. Go with God's blessing."

The serfs filed out. Karne looked out over the brilliant, glittering crowd. He dreaded the next step in the ritual. How much had his sire's contempt for him influenced that moving, whispering mass of people? What will they do? Karne wondered. Will I alone cry the words? He swallowed, then shot his clenched fist above his head. "The Lharr is dead. Halarek lives!"

Without hesitation, the crowd roared back, "Halarek lives! Halarek lives!"

For just a moment Karne felt giddy with relief. *They didn't deny me!* Then he remembered the next step, so carefully drilled into him. He beckoned Tane Orkonan, who stood in the front ranks of the crowd, to come to him. "Family, lords and ladies, friends of House Halarek, this day we install our new House administrator, Tane Orkonan, son of House Konnor."

Orkonan knelt at the edge of the dais. Karne bent and slipped the necklace of office over his head. "Tane Orkonan, will you strive in all your duties to act and speak for the best interests of House Halarek?"

"I will, so God aid me."

"Rise, then, and may God and his Four Guardians go with you." Orkonan stood. Karne put his hands on Orkonan's shoulders and kissed him on both cheeks.

When Orkonan had taken a place beside the

Larga, with his stylus and pad poised to record oaths and gifts, and Gareth had taken his place on Karne's left, beside a long table spread with packages, the Larga Alysha walked to the edge of the dais.

"Now I call all loyal vassals of House Halarek to come forward to renew the vows taken by their grandsires in ancient days and renewed at the Lharr's pleasure. I, regent in House Halarek, do declare Karne Halarek Lharr in all but age. Do you make your oaths to him." Her mellow voice had surprising power, for the first vassals to come forward came from the rear of the Hall.

Four men in scarlet-and-gold robes came to the edge of the dais. The oldest of them bowed and saluted Karne by removing his cloak. "We are aldermen of the freecity of Ontar, my lord. Though a freecity, we acknowledge our dependence on Ontar manor and Halarek Holding for protection and financial support. Therefore, we owe Halarek our loyalty and support. Freemen's customary neutrality will not lessen this loyalty, Lord Karne."

The men all bowed and backed away ten steps before they turned and went back to their places. Aldermen of the freecities of Treen and Frieden followed, acknowledging their obligation for land and for the orak stone or silica used in their crafthalls. Such acknowledgment was all tradition required and the aldermen returned to their places with promises of aid or loyalty. Orkonan finished his notation for the freecities and announced, at full volume, that the freecities had given their due.

Karne took from Gareth a pair of shoes and a bolt of cloth. He held them up for all to see. "Every

Halarek serf in these cities receives this day new shoes for himself and his children, and cloth enough for sark and hosen for each member of his family."

Although this, too, was a tradition, the crowd celebrated the gift with shouting and cheers. The Larga stepped to the edge of the dais and lifted her head a little, proudly. "Now do I call the noble Houses. Come forward as custom has set the order."

The first representative of the Houses, a spare, gray man, came forward, knelt, and placed his two hands between Karne's. "I, Paul III Druma, by the grace of God Duke of Druma, will, from this hour forth, be faithful to Karne, Lharr of House Halarek, and his successors. I shall not cause by word, deed, consent, or counsel that they lose life or limbs or be taken captive. I shall cause harm to be removed if I am able and will tell about it if I am not. I will keep Halarek secrets. I will aid, to the best of my ability, the holding and defending against all men of the patrimony of Karne Halarek. May God and his Four Guardians aid me."

Karne bent, kissed Druma on both cheeks, raised him to his feet, and gave him a large box, elaborately wrapped. "Go with God," he said.

Druma was the only member of the Nine Families owing fealty to House Halarek. After the Duke, the lords of the minor Houses of Konnor, Labar, Durlin, and Nomer came forward, gave the same oath, received the same kisses, gift, and blessing. Halarek cousins who held land from the Lharr followed and gave their oaths. Last to swear fealty were younger sons of minor Houses who held factories or mines from Halarek for a share in the profits. These men received a bonus in Gild currency instead of a gift.

"Go with God," Karne said to the last man, then beckoned to the chaplain of The Way, who had been sitting in a chair under the gallery, waiting for his moment.

The old man hobbled forward, raised his arms in benediction, and rushed through an inaudible prayer. When he had hobbled back to his chair, the crowd in the Hall was free to stay or go. The Larga signaled the minstrels to begin, then slipped away herself. Tambourines clashed, pipes piped, tumblers flipped across the floor in front of the dais. A juggler moved into the crowd, tossing silver knives in a circle above his head. The spectators began to laugh, shout, talk to each other. Dogs were unleashed. One began yapping at the tumblers and running alongside them as they flipped from one side of the Hall to the other. Somewhere in the galleries a small baby squalled. Some people filtered out into the corridors, making gaps in the shifting crowd, but most stayed, waiting with a tense expectancy. Karne looked sharply toward Orkonan.

"What are they waiting for?"

"You forgot the announcement that all the noble vassals had completed their duties, my lord." He held up a hand as Karne opened his mouth to speak. "It's just as well, lord. Roul, Nerut, and Melevan did not come. What do you want done, Lord Karne?"

Karne swore under his breath. "That's why they're waiting out there. They've counted and they're waiting to see what I'll do." Karne looked out over the crowd. He knew its expectant silence was not a friendly one.

They're waiting for me to show myself the weakling my sire taught them to expect. He stared down at the expectant, almost eager faces and, for a moment, hated them.

"Do you want me to call the regent back, milord?"

"What?"

"Do you want me to have the regent called back, milord."

"That would just confirm their poor opinion of me, Tane. Announce that— No. I can't let someone else speak for me." He lifted his head with arrogance and spoke in a cold, hard voice. "Lords and ladies, people of my House, I interrupt your pleasure to make a serious announcement. The ceremony of fealty is not complete. Three vassals have refused to make their oath as they are sworn to do. Nerut, Melevan, and Roul are now named oath-breakers and disobedient vassals. They will all three be punished for forsaking their duties." He spun away before anyone could ask him how. "Meet me in the library," he told Orkonan quietly, and left the Hall.

When Orkonan reached the library, Karne was leaning back against the stones of the fireplace with his hands in his trouser pockets, drawing a wandering pattern on the stone floor with the toe of one white ceremonial boot. He stood erect as Orkonan came toward him, took his hands out of his pockets, and straightened his shoulders with effort. "Advise me. I must make the right decision the first time," he said without preamble. "I'll have no second chance, not with my Family, not with the three vassals, not with Richard Harlan." Karne turned, slapped the flat of his hand against the stones, and stared down at the hearth. "Be my Sire's Blood, those three would never have tried this with him! I'll wager they think Uhl will stop the Halarek 'women' from taking any action."

Orkonan settled into the chair at the worktable and waited. Karne pushed away from the fireplace and paced the distance to the opposite wall and back. The soft boots made faint *pat, pat* sounds against the stone floor. Karne spun around at the fireplace and headed back across the room. He stopped pacing even with Orkonan's chair.

"My sire would've packed up his army in transports and beaten his vassals to their knees, Uhl or not, and those three know it! By all that's holy, why is killing the first thought on this world! I have more than one hundred men downstairs in the clinic and bedded in the corridors, all frostbite or snowfever, and that will be a fault in my enemies' eyes, that there are no dead, yet, no wounded. And no dead slaves. I'm already hearing sneers and insults for not slaughtering the slaves." Karne's shoulders drooped and he sank into a chair across from Orkonan. He met the older man's dark eyes. "You're one of five people on this entire world I can trust, and two of those can be no political help to me except as brides to cement an alliance. Guardians! Who are my allies, really?" Karne spread his hands and pretended a deep interest in them for a time. He let his hands fall to his lap and looked up, his face grim.

Orkonan looked down at the younger man with

sympathy in his eyes, then he turned to his desk and began ruffling pointlessly through the papers there. "Your firm allies are Druma, Justin, and von Schuss, lord. Kingsland is a fair man, but impartial, and far too slow-witted to keep up with the Harlan Heir."

"I'm going to need a lot of help deciding what is the right thing to do." Karne shoved himself out of the chair suddenly. "I saved my House more casualties, I avoided the frightening expense of replacing half a hundred dead slaves, Farm 3 is working again, and all I hear is cousins and more cousins, all accusing me of weakness and stupidity!" He stopped pacing and stared at Orkonan, his eyes blazing, his body tensed as if he were about to smash something. Orkonan backed away a step and the movement brought Karne out of his fury. His shoulders slumped, his eyes fell. "Call in Egil and Nik, then, Tane. My lady mother, too. She knows nothing of tactics, but she is regent and legal details are more important than lives and futures to the Gharr, I think. Farm 3 was a mistake, as far as my Family is concerned. I should have taken command myself from the first. And made sure a lot of men were killed in the fighting," he added bitterly. "I can't afford another mistake, even though *I* still can't see that I made a mistake. I thought I brought this House out of that mess amazingly well. Balder's thinking. Oh, why was I sent away so long, Tane? Why!" Here, with his friend, Karne did not try to hide his feelings. The time for hiding would come again soon enough.

"You know why you were sent away," Orkonan said calmly. "You told me yourself the day you learned it. But your sire's dead and what he thought and did don't matter anymore. He's beyond hurting you. *You* are the Lharr now. This House runs as *you* decide."

Karne sat down in a dark silence, lost in his thoughts. Orkonan pressed the panel in the side of the table. Gareth came almost at once and Tane sent him to the Great Hall with Karne's message. The two men sat in silence, waiting.

Nik escorted the Larga through the door, with Egil close behind. The Larga would not sit down. "This is your oath-feast, Karne," she said irritably. "The food will be ready in minutes! What can be so important that you and I must be absent from our guests?"

"Rebellion, Lady Mother. Did you not notice Roul, Nerut, and Melevan did not come?"

Chapter Eight

———◆———

THE LARGA SAT with a sigh in the chair Nik had pushed forward. "I don't know why I didn't notice those three weren't making oath. I expected trouble from Roul. He's been stubborn and rude since your sire died."

"You could attack their manor houses as soon as possible with as many men as possible," Orkonan suggested.

"What would the casualties be?" Egil asked. "I've heard about your winter."

Nik looked thoughtful. He glanced at Orkonan, who shrugged. "They'd be high, probably," Nik said. "The entrances would be heavily defended, which would leave men on the surface a long time, longer than at Farm 3. Then, too, the storms get worse as Uhl advances, so you could expect to lose troop and supply transports to storms. Yes, losses could be high."

"Ignore the rebels, then," Egil advised. "What harm can they do before spring, I mean Thaw-time? They'll be confined to their homes like everyone else. In spring, if you must punish them, your casualties will be from fighting, not the weather. No commander sends men out to die of snowfever or frozen limbs."

"Balder's rules," Karne put in harshly.

"That plan would cause such a loss of honor our House would never recover," the Larga added more gently. "Ignoring rebellion is cowardice, and a reputation for cowardice would lose us what political power we have. Going down to make peace with slaves may have been foolish in the eyes of the Families, an exhibition of weakness, but no one says it was a cowardly thing. It took much courage."

"Houses survive on honor almost as much as fighting ability, Egil," Nik explained. "Karne made the best decision for Farm 3 and his House, but it wasn't a traditional one. You must already see how important tradition is here. Karne *has* to punish those vassals now, Uhl or not. If he doesn't, his other vassals may abandon Halarek and what they see as its weakness for the protection of a stronger House. Some might even deal with Harlan to get a piece of this Holding."

Karne dropped his head into his hands. He shook it slowly side to side several times. "There must be some way other than a surface attack. There *must* be." He looked up, his face haggard. "Egil, the Academy taught that every problem has three or more solutions. What else is there?"

The Larga's hands twisted in her skirt. She did not look at any of the men. She began, hesitantly, to speak. "We could—we could settle with them. Give them the land around their manors, or the mine, in Melevan's case, in return for recognition of Karne's Lharrship."

Nik shook his head. "No, Larga, they already hold the land in return for fealty. The land couldn't be cut out of the Holding legally and, even if it could, Halarek wouldn't want patches of disloyalty within its boundaries." He turned to Karne. "Even if you confiscate the land, you'll still wear the name 'coward' unless you take the land back by force."

Karne sighed. "Somewhere in this universe there are problems that include desirable solutions." He stared for a time at his spread hands. He closed them suddenly. "By the Four Guardians! There has to be a solution with a lower cost!"

No one said anything for a long time. The ventilator fans whirred softly and once in a while Orkonan, who had a head cold, sniffed. Then Karne's gloom fell away. The words rushed out. "We cut off all their fuel and raw materials. Tane, can we purchase from the Gild all fuel allocated to that sector of the Holding for Uhl and Arhast?"

"If the Gild will take short-term mortgages for it."

Nik picked up the idea excitedly. "No light, no ventilation, no power for the mine—I doubt they'd hold out a day after they figured out what turning off the fuel pipe would mean. It'd be the shortest rebellion in history!" He paused and the glow faded from his face. "It will also do you, personally, no good, Karne. Heads-of-House always make their names, their reputations, in battle. No man earns position and power by diplomacy."

Egil snorted his contempt for such rules.

Karne flinched and turned to the regent. "Lady Mother?"

The Larga met his eyes squarely. "It's your decision, Karne. Just remember, the expense would be heavy and your oath-feast has already put a strain on our resources." She stood briskly. "I'm returning to our guests. If you need a signature for any legal document, you know where to find me." She swept gracefully out of the room.

"Tane, how will our accounts look if I buy the fuel?"

"Besides the mortgages to the Gild? Until you bring those men into line you get no income from the mine or from Roul's blown glass works. The combination of mortgages and those losses and the expense of the feast might bring your House down, Karne, if your vassals hold more than the usual reserve of fuel."

Karne blew out a resigned breath that stirred his forelock. "If I let vassals rebel without punishment, this House falls. If I send my armies out into Uhl, most of the men won't come back. If they hold a season's fuel, Halarek falls, bankrupt, into the hands of whoever can pay off the debts. Tane, what do I do?"

"It's not my place—"

"You've been my friend for years. What do you mean 'place'?"

"This House has always been very strict about rank, my lord."

"This House is less strict now. About the fuel idea, Tane."

Orkonan looked down and shuffled through some of the papers on the table in front of him. "Check with your officers, Karne. My skill is numbers, not tactics."

"I don't trust them. They're my sire's men. I'm beginning to understand why a Lharr usually dismisses or executes his predecessor's officers." Karne looked grim. He glanced at Egil and Nik. "What do you two think?"

Egil nodded thoughtfully. "It could work."

Nik shook his head. "I don't know...It goes against all tradition, Karne, and you've damaged yourself, at least in the short run, by the way you've handled Farm 3."

"Wait till Family and enemies hear what I still must do with Farm 3," Karne muttered.

Nik went on as if he had not been interrupted. "On the other hand, if you lose a lot of men on the surface fighting your vassals, you won't be able to hold off Harlan when he figures a way around his trustee. It's your future. *You* had to decide."

It was true, and Karne had known it. In the end,

all House decisions were his. It's natural to want to share a burden like this, he told himself. I'm not soft because I don't spring to attack. But his sire's ghost hung over his shoulder, laughing at him. Karne licked his lips. "You can go back to the feast, Egil. Off-worlders can't be part of a military discussion. Thanks for your advice."

Karne ordered his officers, including General Shen, to join him. He kept his face and emotions under rigid control as he explained his plan. They opposed the plan to a man. They presented tactical objections, traditional objections, political objections. They offered the usual and unusual ways to penetrate to the living levels of a small-holding. They argued that not using the army would ruin the army's morale. They sneered at the fuel embargo as a "tradesman's trick." They brushed aside Karne's repeated objections to the very high casualities of their solutions. At last, frustrated, tired, and hungry, Karne ended the meeting with an order. "All of you are assigned to the clinic, in a rotation of one day shift and one night shift, to tend the wounded from Farm 3. Dr. Othneil and the centens already down there can show you what to do. You, General Shen, as commander of the Holding forces, do one rotation a day." Karne spun away from the officers and headed for the door, adding curtly as he went, "Those of you not on duty may report to the great Hall for whatever's left of my oath-feast."

Wynter and von Schuss caught up with him in the hall.

"You, Wynter, you can't support my plan at all?"

"In all my years in the service and in my sire's

tales of his, no one has brought a vassal into line or ended a rebellion without killing. Your House keeps an army to use it, milord."

"I must send men to die in Uhl because of that?"

They had reached the servants' door under the Hall gallery.

Wynter appeared to consider the question seriously. He cleared his throat. "A man, or a lord, proves himself in battle, milord. There are some you won't convince until you do that." Then Wynter shrugged. "However, the Lharrs Halarek have always done as *they* wished with their vasals. Excuse me now, lord. I'm on duty."

Karne watched Wynter's straight, spare figure march away. That was an officer he could rely on, but he was now sure he was going to have to get rid of most of the others. The question was, how to weed out the reluctant and the downright disloyal? Another problem.

He and Nik entered the Hall together. The servants had set up a long table on the dais and had filled the floor of the Great Hall with more tables. The Larga, Kit, and Egil sat on the dais at the Lharr's table. The feast was well along. Karne mounted the steps, motioned Nik to follow him, and slid into the Lharr's chair, with its high, carved back and very hard seat. Egil, who shared a long platter with Kit, looked up from the drumstick he was eating. "The meeting with the army went badly."

Karne nodded. "We can't talk about it here." He reminded himself this was his oath-feast and should be a celebration. He brightened with effort and asked in a teasing tone, "Did you leave anything for Nik and me to eat?"

Egil waved grandly and a line of servants in Halarek livery appeared with platters of roast young pig and broiled rok haunches, tureens of gravy with bread for dipping, meat pies, vegetables of many kinds arranged in animal- or bird-shaped piles, jellies, and salads. "These are just the leftovers," Egil said, laughing. "You two should have seen the supply when we started."

Karne looked at the crowded platter he was to share with his mother and his churning stomach flinched at the thought of food, but he stabbed a slice of rok and bit into it. The dark, rich meat was tasteless to him. He was hardly aware of it at all, his mind on the decisions ahead of him. Tradition or no, he would *not* send men to die in the wind and cold of Uhl without trying almost everything else first. He knew the Gharr held it a matter of honor to send soliders to the surface to fight during a siege, if your opponent would let you send them up. He also knew no one fought in winter. No one. Weather conditions became deadly very quickly. Which meant his promise to Farm 3, of a new manager and freedom for the slaves, must be taken care of quickly, somehow, within days.

A serving maid filled Karne's mug with wine. Karne lifted the drink to his lips and looked out over the colorful crowd of guests while he sipped. The wine begin to relax his taut nerves. Surely, Karne told himself, an experienced ruler doesn't feel this tremor in his knees, this churning in his stomach when faced with a vital decision. They'll

go away when I'm more sure of what I'm doing. I
hope.

Somewhere near the front of the Hall, a hawk
changed position on her master's wrist and her
bells tinkled. The Hall itself was very quiet, except
for the scrape of utensils on platters, the thunk of
mugs on the wood tables, and a low buzz of conversation. Once a hungry baby squalled and its
mother carried it out. Now and then a child
choked and was patted, cried and was silenced.

"It's time for The Pie, Karne," the Larga whispered.

Karne looked up in dismay. The Pie signaled the
end of the meal and he was just beginning. Then
he laughed at himself. He was Lharr. He could eat
when and where and as long as he liked. He motioned to the heralds fidgeting under the edge of
the gallery. The four boys stepped forward briskly,
lifted long trumpets, and blew a flourish. Four
kitchen serfs rolled a cart carrying a giant pie to
the Lharr's table. The Family cook followed,
bowed to the Lharr and Larga, and handed Karne
a big knife. Karne stood, bowed ceremoniously to
the cook, and walked to the pie. He heard rustling
in the Hall and low, tinkling sounds as guests un-
hooded their hawks. The crust of the pie quivered.
He hesitated. He had everyone's attention. Should
he tell the Family now what he was going to do to
the rebels? No, this was not the time; he must not
appear to ask permission or even approval of his
decision. And there might be, probably were, spies
out there, who would carry the plan to the rebels,
or to Harlan. No, he would announce the fuel cutoff after he had accomplished it.

Karne slid the knife carefully through the pastry and opened it from side to side. The crust exploded upward and a cloud of yellow birds burst from the pie. Five or ten dogs rushed out from under tables, barking and leaping. Children shrieked with glee and some of them jumped up on their tables to try to catch one of the birds: Five Gildcredits went to any child who caught one. Overhead hawks screamed and stooped and, at the tables, hawk owners shouted wagers across the room. Karne remembered the excitement he had felt when he was young enough to catch a bird. Now the scene in the Hall looked barbaric and slightly repulsive. He glanced at Egil. Karne had gone with him to a wedding feast on Balder. There the guests left their pets and small children at home. They had not gamed and fought and finally passed out in drunkenness. *That* part of this banquet was yet to come.

Egil did not look disgusted. His big blond head swung from side to side eagerly. "This is fascinating, Karne! Are all your feasts like this?"

"Just big Family occasions like coming-of-age, weddings, oath-feasts."

"The food! The colors! The Pie! How, by Heimdal, did the birds stay alive?" Egil's eyes sparkled and danced. "I'd like to be here for your coming-of-age."

"If I live to my coming-of-age." Karne stood abruptly and pounded on the table with the hilt of his ceremonial sword. It was some time before the human uproar diminished enough that Karne could be heard.

"Friends and Family. As I'm sure you noticed, Nerut, Melevan, and Roul did not renew their oaths. I promise that in less than two Gildweeks, these Houses will renew their oaths, and pay compensation for the delay."

The Hall rang with shouts of approval. Karne acknowledged them with a nod and sat down. The Larga looked worried. "Sixteen days, Karne? Was that wise? How can you promise that?"

Karne leaned close to her and spoke very quietly. "With no fuel there's no ventilation, Lady Mother. Say nothing about this until the fuel is mine. Tell no one."

The Larga nodded, then straightened and rang a small bell. A page set a bowl of cheese and fruit in front of Karne.

"The bell's the signal for the entertainers," Karne told Egil. "If you liked the feast, you'll really like this."

The juggler entered the Hall, balls a blur above his head. The tumblers bounced, flipped, and rolled into the center of the Hall, where they began pushing tables back to make room for some barrels and a springboard. Before they finished, a fat, black-beared man strutted into their cleared space, towing a large, black Zinn bear on a chain. The crowd gasped, both at the bear's immensity and at having such a notoriously dangerous brute so close. At a command, the bear stood on its hind legs and began to shuffle in a circle. The tumblers' red, contorted faces told their anger, but they dared not risk attacking the man because of his bear. They would have to wait until the pair finished and collected the money thrown to them. The tumblers would now have second place and the money thrown would be less.

Karne watched the tumblers lose the silent struggle. He turned to Egil. "Our guests will watch and drink, Egil, and then the fights will start. If it weren't for this emergency, I'd have to sit here and watch until the last drunken lord fell under his table." Karne rose and turned to the Larga. "Lady Mother, I'm leaving to talk to the Gild's First Merchant."

The negotiation with the First Merchant ran into the early morning, but it ended well. House Halarek now owned all the fuel for the rebel sector, fuel which would be held by the Gild till Halarek wanted it. Karne went to bed satisfied his plan would work, slept late, and woke groggy. He swung his legs over the edge of the bed and sat there, assembling his wits, he..ing the muffled beat of a Blues patrol go by and the quiet whirr of the fans. He dressed and headed downstairs.

The stairwell smelled of hot, fresh bread. Karne's stomach reminded him it had been empty a long time. He had been going to the tri-d room, but the enticing smell detoured him toward the Great Hall. A Halarek cousin, perhaps five years older and twenty kilos heavier than Karne, met him on the level 4 landing and blocked it with his body. Karne looked up at him coolly.

"I hear you're trying to 'persuade' our rebel vassals to keep oath, Karne."

Karne stiffened at the hostility in the man's voice. "Military plans are supposed to be secret." His voice was icy.

The cousin's mouth twisted down at the corners. "You can't keep a bird-witted plan like yours secret," he sneered. "There's nothing 'military' about it. Afraid to fight, Karne?"

"I don't know you. I don't even know why you're living in this manor. Why should I tell you anything?"

"Cutting off their fuel is a stupid idea!" The cousin's mouth turned down even more. "Power is all that sort understand, the power of Halarek soldiers. "I'm—"

"You're volunteering to fly over Nerut's smallholding in Uhl, Cousin?" Karne's voice was deceptively low and silky.

"Me? I have a family. Which I would take back to our own manor if it weren't too late in the year. I'm ashamed to be connected to such a coward. I certainly won't eat with one. My family will eat in its quarters from now on." The cousin turned to go.

Karne grabbed the man's arm in steely fingers and spun him around. "You eat in the Great Hall with the rest of the Family or you don't eat and if you speak with disloyalty to anyone else, I'll send your personal family home in a flitter no matter what the weather. You're the coward of us, Cousin. You'd send other men, who also have families, into weather you yourself are afraid of." Karne flung the man's arm away. "My sire didn't warn me against traitors in my own House!"

The cousin looked down at Karne, remembering briefly, perhaps, that he was the Lharr. Then he lunged. Karne stepped to one side, his arms and feet flashed in several quick movements, and the cousin lay on his back, one arm bent at an unpleasant angle. "Don't make that mistake again, Cousin," Karne said conversationally. "I may be smaller than you, but I can't be bullied and I won't be so gentle with you a second time. Get that arm set, then pack your family's goods and leave. By tomorrow. You!" Karne stepped into the corridor and stopped one of the prefects in a passing patrol. "Take this man to his quarters and watch him. He's to pack and be ready to leave here in the morning. I'll tell the duty officer your orders."

Karne stalked on down the corridor to the tri-d room, left his message by com with the duty officers, ordered up a quick meal of fresh bread and klag, had a com-tech call Roul, cleared the tri-d room of all but the essential operators, and waited impatiently for Roul to appear. When the picture cleared, it was not Roul Karne saw, but the Lady Elisabeth, his wife, as close and real as if she were in the same room. Karne's whole body tightened and he glanced quickly at the techs. Their faces were stiff with horror. A vassal had refused to even face his lord, sending a *woman* to do his talking. Karne wished he could dispense with the techs entirely, but he could not run the equipment himself.

"Peace be on your House, Lady of Roul," he said tightly, rigid inside with an insult so extreme that even his years on Balder could not shield him from it.

The Lady Elisabeth lifted her head proudly and faced Karne squarely, but he noticed her eyes were red-rimmed and her hands were shaking. Her voice, too, shook as she lifted a paper and began reading it. She neglected to respond to the ritual greeting and Karne was quite sure that, too, was on instructions from her husband. "There is no negotiation between a man and a woman, Karne of Halarek, so I have

sent my woman to deal with you." She spoke so
softly Karne had difficulty hearing her. Her voice
caught and her eyes flicked up from the words. Two
gleaming tears slipped out. "My lord," she said, almost in a whisper, "this is not my will. He is wrong,
dreadfully wrong to defy you so, but he is the lord of
this House and I must obey him." She looked down
at the paper again. "Council will, in time, see the
error of its ways. Until it does, Roul is a free House,
entitled to seek a liege lord where it will, if it will. I
swear no allegiance to Halarek, a Family without a
Head. There is no strength or honor in a person who
dickers with slaves." In Gharr, the non-gender of
"person" was, in itself, a gross insult. Karne needed
no coaching to remember that; it was bred in the
bone of every Gharr from the moment of learning to
talk. Roul was provoking his lord, taunting him.
Karne sucked in his breath and fought down the
blind rage that struck without warning.

You have dealt with insults before, he reminded
himself. It's just that none of them were aimed at
the feelings bred into you; they were the fighting
words of other cultures. Keep your head. Say what
you have to say and be done.

Karne counted, slowly, backwards, from twenty
in Galac. Some of the red fury left him. He cut any
further reading from the paper off with a slice of
his hand. "You have said too much already, my
lady," he warned very quietly. "Oath-breaking is a
very serious offense. Your lord is twice the fool to
add fighting insults and open rebellion to his
crime. I will not risk men's lives for a fool. Tell
your lord he has two Gildweeks to make his oath.
After that, there will be no need for Roul to swear,

for there will be no Roul." The Lady Elisabeth's face went white. "Nay, lady," Karne said gently, for the fault was not hers, "I will not have to touch your Holding. Roul himself will have condemned you all. No fuel has flowed to Roul since this morning. None will until oath is made." Before she could say anything, Karne had the connection cut.

Calls to Melevan and Nerut followed. The insults were less extreme, but both lords clearly thought to win independence of the "woman" of the Halarek clan. Melevan stated plainly he would never swear fealty to a "woman," leaving Karne to decide if he meant the regent or Karne himself by that remark, and Nerut said only that he and Melevan were neighbors and in-laws, he would stand with Melevan. Karne left them with the same curt demand— their oath in return for the fuel to maintain their Holdings. The tri-d techs looked at him with new respect; it had not taken them long to figure out what happened to a Holding deprived of fuel. Karne hoped his vassals were as quick of mind.

He went slowly down the stairs of the Great Hall, forgetting he had ordered his meal brought to the tri-d room, listened impatiently to another cousin's complaint about his handling of Farm 3, then ordered his meal brought to him and joined Orkonan in the administrator's office. He sat on a bench near Orkonan's desk and slumped back against the welcome support of the room's wall. "I needed someplace to hide for a time," he explained to Orkonan somewhat sheepishly. "My method of dealing with vassals won't be liked by the Family any more than Farm 3 was; in fact, one cousin has already gotten violent about it. And I thought at least military planning was secure."

Orkonan's eyes ran over him. "*You* don't look ruffled by the encounter with the violent cousin. I don't suppose the same can be said of the cousin."

Karne's mouth twisted up at one corner, reluctantly. "He's probably in the clinic now, getting an arm set."

Orkonan smiled a little. "I thought something like that. You were easy on him." Orkonan came to stand before Karne. He set a hand on the young lord's shoulder. Karne looked up. "Think, Karne. Not of the rigid minds in your House but of the lives you're saving. Your vassals have to yield or die. I think none of them are suicidal. These rebellions will be settled."

"Will they?"

"Having doubts already? Your intuition has been trained, Karne. How long will Melevan hold out?"

Karne's eyes narrowed. Orkonan knew already he had called his vassals. Could any act or decision be kept quiet? Orkonan nodded his head toward the tray with food on it. "No spies, my lord, just a page who got here faster than you did."

Karne grimaced at his suspicions, knowing both that suspecting everyone meant survival on this world and that such wariness could destroy the few friendships he had among the Gharr. "How could I not have doubts? I know nothing about ruling other than what I observed my sire do when I was a child and what I read in books at the Academy. And those two sources had very different ideas and methods. I was trained to make *peace*, Tane. Here I can't do that. Not in one lifetime. Instead, I'm expected to make clan war skillfully and beat vassals to their knees in short order. And my efforts to save lives are met with condemnation and contempt. Guardians!"

"Those lords won't wait until the lights go out and the fans go off. House Nerut has only one escape stair. Is Nerut going to wait until he has to evacuate hundreds of people up that one stair? Into the storms of Uhl?"

"I pray not."

"And Roul—Roul is stubborn, Karne, but he's not stupid. Melevan, well, we'll see." Orkonan poked through some of the papers on his desk. "Not all of the Gharr are rockbound and blind. Do you the matters with the Gild and those vassals on paper or reeltape, lord?"

"Either. Use your own judgment."

"I'll do both, then, to be double safe." Orkonan slid a flat recorder out of a drawer, laid it on the desk top, and began speaking into it.

Karne sat in Orkonan's office, staring at the wall and listening to his own thoughts whirling in his head, until his stomach loudly demanded food again. He gritted his teeth and went out to face his outraged Family. He was in time to eat midday but he was not to eat in peace. He had just sat down when Berta Longtress, another cousin, planted himself in front of him, hands on hips. "Say it isn't true, Karne. You aren't really letting Roul and Nerut and Melevan get away with this. You wouldn't disgrace the Family like that."

"No. I wouldn't disgrace the Family. I expect the rebels to surrender, on my terms, in eight or nine days." Karne began cutting a piece of rok meat into bites, though his appetite had suddenly left him. Berta did not leave. Karne looked up, holding his temper in rein with considerable effort. "If you have more to say, Cousin, say it. I don't like to be stared at while I eat."

"George tells me the army is still in barracks."

"George is afraid to talk to me himself, he? Poor George." Berta flushed at the mock-pity in Karne's tone. Karne chided himself for such a childish blow. "Get to your esteemed husband's point, Berta," he snapped.

"If there are no soldiers to make them, why should your vassals yield? I see no action against them. Taking no action dirties the Family's honor."

Karne set his fork on his platter wearily. "Is it fighting you want, Berta, or these three oaths?"

Berta's forehead crinkled. "You can't get one without the other."

"Can't I?" Karne speared a piece of meat and ate it.

Berta's frown deepened. "George says you have some fool plan to stop their fuel. What will that do? Even in the worst days of Arhast and Koort, the manors are warm without fuel. You know that."

Karne chewed his meat thoroughly before answering. "You and your fine husband haven't thought this out, Berta, and I'm not going to take your fun away by explaining it to you."

Berta flushed and threw back her head until her long, black braid almost brushed the floor. The braid switched like a cat's tail. "Your soldiers are sitting and you won't lead them." Her voice got louder. "You haven't chosen a *man's* way to deal with this, Karne. Your sire was right about you.

Only women use words instead of weapons." Berta spun away and stalked off, braid still switching.

Heads turned in the Hall to watch Karne's reaction. The insult stung, especially since Berta had delivered it in the hearing of much of the Hall, but Karne bit his tongue on a retort. Answering her back could not help, it could only make the matter worse. He had no personal doubts about his masculinity, but he was well aware how great the insult was to Gharr eyes. Cowardly George, who sent his woman, knowing a man's life would be in danger after such words. Karne wished fiercely that George had delivered his own message. He watched Berta flounce the rest of the way back to her seat. He tasted the warm salt of blood in his mouth. His right hand and arm had tightened until they hurt. He slowly raised his right hand to his lip. The fingertips came away bloody. *The pacification officer does not show his feelings. Emotional displays often influence the outcome of an issue.* The words raced through his mind again and again, but rage and hurt and frustration were pressing very hard against Karne's wall of control. He sat in the Lharr's chair long enough to kill any suspicion that Berta had driven him away, then he stood and went to his quarters. He did not run, as he would have liked to do. He did not slam the door behind him, though that would have felt good. He did lock it.

It's too much, he wanted to shout aloud. It's too much for any person to stand! He leaned against the back of his leather chair. I control my feelings until I want to burst! Crisis after crisis piles up and I have neither training nor experience to handle them. I'm blundering where I need to move skillfully. I have skills, but they aren't the skills my House needs now. I had my life planned. I *wanted* a Navy career. I *wanted* to be based on Balder. I *wanted* to space out as a Navy negotiator. Maybe with time and experience I could've been—but that's past. I'm here, in the thick of a clan war and I'm being pushed to start another war, of the very kind Altair trained me to prevent. Guardians, help me!

He remembered times his sire had teased him to rage and forbidden him to show it and how he had gone to his room to this chair and beaten it in frustration. He needed that relief now. He did not want even Egil to see how incompetent and overwhelmed he felt. He pounded the rolled top edge of his leather chair until his fists were bruised and his arms ached. Drained, he slid over the chair's arm into the cushioned seat and sagged against the padded back. He dozed.

Soft paws awakened him. Karne hugged Wiki, then set the little animal on his shoulder. He knew he would have to keep busy to maintain outward control of himself through the waiting to come.

Three interminable days passed. Karne endured the anger and ridicule of the Family with what patience he could muster. He visited the clinic every few hours to check on the men there and to be sure the officers were doing their rotations of nursing duty. He made surprise visits in the middle of the night and the small hours of morning. In the first two days Karne dismissed more than half the oldest officers for disobeying the nursing order and sent them out of Ontar manor to live in the city. General Shen fulfilled his duties to the letter and no more. Karne wanted to dismiss him, too, but he had no senior officers with even close to as much experience and he needed an experienced leader should Harlan attack again, so Karne set Wynter and the pilot Jenkins to watch Shen. Any hint of disloyalty or betrayal and Karne would do without the general's experience. The general's attitude toward his new duties was obvious. Of the other men's, Karne could not tell. He wondered whether the duty had any value except as an indicator of potentially dangerous officers. Then he saw one of the remaining older officers rush to the sanitary after changing the dressings on a young soldier's severely frostbitten feet. On another visit he saw an officer pass out when Dr. Othneil told him one of the patients he was nursing had died.

These men, at least, will remember the human cost of Zicker's decisions, or lack of them, he told himself. But uncertainty plagued him. Would clinic duty make the centens and other officers consider the cost of tactical decisions? Had he been right to make them nurse their men? He had been right about negotiating with the slaves. Hadn't he? Or had that encouraged Roul and the others to rebel? If turning off their fuel failed . . .

The slaves! he thought in dismay. Dear God, I forgot to free those slaves. This will be the final stupidity in the Family's eyes, to "reward" the slaves for their revolt. But I promised.

A part of Karne cringed from the effect his promise would have on his already difficult life in the manor. But he had promised, and the slaves were keeping their side of the bargain: The conveyer tubes from Farm 3 were bringing the farm's quota of vegetables and fruit to the manor again. Karne left the clinic and walked toward the com center.

He passed the kitchens, which occupied the large central core of clinic level, and he passed the political "guest" quarters, where Anse-the-smith was confined. He stopped and went back to the smith's door. He looked at the plain black knob, thinking. He set his hand to the knob but did not turn it. I'm already gambling the future of my House, he told himself, what harm can one more small risk do? Anse-the-smith has abilities I shouldn't waste.

He touched the unlock code into the holes ringing the knob and entered the smith's room. The smith lay on the bed-ledge, propped up on one elbow, gnawing a knuckle bone. He looked up as Karne entered, but did not stop eating.

"Get up, Anse-the-smith. You're going back to Farm 3. As the new manager I promised."

"Lord?" The smith's face showed deep skepticism.

"I'm not playing with you. I mean it."

The smith sat up with surprising speed for a man of his bulk. "You won't regret it, lord."

Karne smiled. "I don't think I will, either. Take whatever you want from here and get to the flitter pad. The weather's clear right now and I want you at the farm as soon as possible. I'll go ahead of you to the com center and send word to the farm that you're returning and that they're all now free men."

The smith nodded and began dressing for outside. Karne liked the way the man took the news, as something that was his due, and made no noisy thanks or professions of gratitude. Karne left him to pack his few possessions and went on down the corridor to the com center, punched the code on the entry lock, and pushed the door.

"My lord!" The surprised tech recovered himself quickly and went down on one knee.

"Up, man. I want a narrow-beam transmission to Farm 3."

Narrow-beam was supposed to keep outsiders from hearing House communications, but Karne learned within hours that the beam had not been narrow enough. Baron von Schuss called by tri-d. A page informed Karne of the call just as he was sitting down in the library with Orkonan and Nik to look at manor defenses and supplies.

When Karne entered the tri-d room, just down the corridor from the library, the tech had already fine-tuned the image on the tri-d screen. The baron sat in a deeply padded brown chair, one side of a fire in a fireplace visible behind him. Every detail was as real as if the baron had been in the Halarek tri-d room. Even the napped upholstery of the chair looked real enough to touch. Karne glanced at the hard surfaces and unconcealed technical equipment in his sending room. There was no chair of any kind to sit on, no fireplace or bright tapestries for a warm appearance. A "man" needed no such "frills," according to Trev Halarek.

"Ahem."

Karne brought his attention back to the baron. Von Schuss's round face looked concerned. "Peace be on your House, Karne Halarek."

"And on yours grace, and peace, Baron."

"Have you in truth freed the slaves on one of your farms, Karne? Richard Harlan has been talking to his allies about such on the broadest band he could

manage, planning with them what to do when the
slave revolts you've caused begin. He says no slave
will work for a master once freed. He also says
you've begun to 'reap the fruits' of your stupidity at
Farm 3, citing the rebellion of Roul, Nerut, and
Melevan. Half of Starker IV must have heard it
by now, from Harlan directly, or by listening in."

Karne sighed. The effect of his promise to Farm
3 was going to be far worse than he had imagined.
He met the baron's eyes. "Yes, Baron. Freedom was
the condition for releasing the farm family and returning the farm to production." Karne went on to
explain the manager's greed, urged on by someone
from the manor claiming to speak for Karne. "As
to slave revolts, Farm 3 has been sending its quota
and sometimes a little more ever since. That
doesn't sound like revolt to me."

The baron listened, sucking on a porcelain pipe.
He neither praised nor blamed, but he looked less
upset. He nodded slowly after Karne finished his
explanation. "Needed to know the truth, Halarek.
Can't let this kind of news keep going if it's false,
you know. Don't know how Harlan thought he'd
get away with this."

Karne's mouth tightened. "He doesn't have to get
away with it long, Baron. He appeals to ancient
prejudices, then, no matter how Farm 3 works out,
the men who believe slaves must always be slaves
will find dire consequences in it. They'll see what
they need to see to continue believing as they do."
Saying the words brought to Karne how frighten-
ingly true they were, and he burned with a savage
anger against Richard Harlan and the blind lords
who would believe this trouble-making.

"Von Schuss is with you, Halarek. All the way. Do what I can to cut through Harlan's hints and inneundos." The baron cleared his throat and fingered the large medallion on his ample chest. "Nik around? Like to talk to the rascal as long as I'm 'here,' so to speak."

Karne nodded, grateful for the baron's support, had Nik paged, conversed socially until Nik arrived, then left the tri-d room. He turned toward the back stair, so he could go to the Great Hall without passing Family guest rooms or the quarters of resident Family. He did not want to face any more scorn. I only have to take it twelve more days, he reminded himself. Only twelve days. They surely can't hold out past 12 Uhl with the fuel turned off.

A junior officer passed Karne without looking at him or saluting.

"Troopleader!"

The young officer kept walking.

"Troopleader, halt!"

The officer stopped but did not turn. Karne was very briefly grateful not to have the embarrassment of running after one of his own officers to discipline him. He strode to the man and whirled him around. The officer, though young, was older than Karne by two or three years. He looked at Karne with contempt.

"I'm your commander, soldier. You didn't salute."

"A commander commands, 'my lord.' He doesn't sit on his tail and wait for Thawtime."

Karne, goaded almost beyond bearing, raised his fist to smash the sneer on the other's face. He stopped himself, lowered his hand, and took one step closer to the troopleader. He was shaking with the effort of restraining himself. The officer's eyes widened in surprise. He took a quick step backward.

"I won't strike you," Karne said very quietly. "Be glad I'm not my sire. *He* would have had you *executed!*"

The troopleader's face paled at the tone and his lower lip quivered. He tucked his chin tight against his neck to make the quivering stop. He had enough good sense to say nothing more.

"Execution's what you deserve," Karne went on, "but I'm only going to kick you all the way down to subprefet. You'll have your things out of your quarters and into prefets' barracks within one hour and you'll work in the scullery until Thawtime." Karne stepped to one side so he could reach the intercom buttons without taking his eyes off the troopleader. "Captain Rad, to level 4, barracks side, now!"

"You don't even have the nerve to order an execution." The former officer was regaining his nerve.

Karne looked at him coldly for a long moment. "Would you rather die than wash dishes and peel vegetables?"

The man did not answer.

"Don't tempt me, sub. I'm not as fond of blood as my sire, but if there's a second time you'll get my sire's sentence, beginning with being flayed alive in front of your men to show them authority must be treated respectfully."

The man turned white and said nothing more, not even after Captain Rad arrived. Karne charged Rad with seeing that the soldier followed his orders and watched Rad and the former troopleader march down the hall and around the corner. He rubbed his hands across his forehead and down the side of his face, then turned and detoured to his own quarters.

The room was not empty. Egil lounged in the leather chair and Gareth perched on the foot of the bed. Gareth opened his mouth, then closed it. He would not meet Karne's eyes.

"Go ahead. Tell him," Egil ordered.

Gareth cleared his throat and picked at the knee of his hosen. He still did not look up. "I bring a message, milord, from Richard Harlan. This one," he waved a hand in Egil's direction, "had me bring it here and wait for you. He didn't say it was urgent. My lord of Harlan, I mean. I copied it out—Tane is in Ontar—and was going to ..." The rest of his sentence was just a mumble.

"I heard the first part of the transmission clear out in the hall," Egil added. "Harlan claims to have overheard a declaration of freedom for your slaves broadcast and wondered if you made it or if someone in this House is talking in your name."

"'Wondered.' I'll bet he 'wondered.' He knows my voice. He called on a wide band, too, in his 'concern,' didn't he?" Gareth nodded miserably. "He's been talking to his allies on the widest band about the slave revolts that will surely come through my stupidity. Now everyone who was tuned to that band knows he called me, too. He put in the part about someone talking in my name to get a reaction from me, I think, to see if I know someone here stirred up Farm 3 for him. By my Sire's Blood!" Karne took a deep, unsteady breath. "I sent that delcaration to Farm 3 by narrow band. Harlan must have a listening post somewhere, monitoring our com-bands. Give me the transcript of what he said."

Karne skimmed the page, then spat a string of original and inventive curses on the entire Harlan clan and their trouble-making.

When Karne stopped for breath, Egil raised an eyebrow. "That's all well and good. But what are you going to do now?"

"Do? Do?" Karne sank onto the edge of the bed and spread his hands hopelessly. "There's nothing more I can do until I hear from my rebel vassals. If I hear from them."

Chapter Nine

———◆———

UHL WAS EIGHT days old when an excited page called Karne from midday. "It's Cyril of Melevan, my lord. He says he begs interview with you. *Begs,* my lord!"

"Melevan!" Karne's eyes flashed. "Come, regent, this may be our game at last." Karne dashed out of the Hall and up the stairs, wishing as he went that the tri-d room weren't the farthest room from either stairway. Outside the tri-d door he stopped to tug his tunic into order and to wipe his mouth, just to be sure no undignified crumbs were left there. He thought of the authority and power of a Lharr and drew on that authority like a cloak, then he walked in front of the broadcast camera. Melevan

wore his ceremonial robes and a glistening layer of
sweat. He dabbed his forehead with a large handkerchief. Karne saw Melevan's wife and children in
the background, fanning themselves with scarves
and thin books.

"Peace be on your house, Karne Halarek." Melevan sounded like he was choking on the words.

"And on yours grace, and peace, Cyril of Melevan. You asked to speak to me?" Karne felt a little
proud of the icy tone of his voice.

Melevan flushed and sputtered. Karne could see
his hands shaking. "I—I—" Melevan choked and
turned his head away. "I—"

Lady Melevan came forward and tugged at her
husband's arm. "Say it, Cyril. Must we die for your
pride?"

Melevan stuffed the handkerchief into his belt
and faced Karne squarely. "I—I beg forgiveness,
my lord. I made a—a stupid error. I owe you fealty
and I promise to renew my oath wh-when travel is
again safe. We'll suffocate here, milord, if you
don't allow us fuel. We've cut power, but ... We
must have more fuel, Lord Karne, now. We've—
I've learned we can't live with the fans at half-
power and the mine is closed down completely. I
throw myself and my personal family on your
mercy, my lord."

Karne heard the rustle of the Larga Alysha's
skirts but did not look away from Melevan.
"Mercy," he said softly. "You expect mercy after humiliating me and House Halarek in the presence of
Family and guests from the rest of the Nine?
Would you show mercy to a vassal who refused
fealty, Cyril of Melevan?"

Sweat dripped in bright streaks down the sides of Melevan's face. He put his hand on his handkerchief, then changed his mind. He said nothing.

Karne read the man's fear and humiliation. He kept his face stern and cold. "I will be merciful, Melevan. This time only. My terms are these: your two eldest sons and both your daughters as hostage for your word, plus three thousand decacredits; when the hostages arrive here, I will release to you enough fuel to run manor and mine for the winter, but none for fliers of any kind; you will pay me for the fuel, of course, and for storage costs, with an added fee of one thousand decacredits per M-ton as penalty. Do you accept those terms?"

Melevan threw an anguished glance toward his wife. "My lord, so many of my children—"

"I will have them, here, before I release any fuel to you," Karne said implacably, then added, "You're a lucky man to have two daughters survive the Sickness. They'll be very valuable to you when they reach marriageable age." Karne paused. "I'll treat them as part of my personal family," he promised in a gentler voice.

"Take me hostage for my family, lord." Melevan held himself stiffly.

Karne could see how much it cost the man to plead, and how much Melevan valued his children. He felt a brief flash of jealousy, which he suppressed instantly. "You're needed there to run the mine. I'll take the best care of your children."

Melevan swallowed visibly. "But, Lord Karne, Uhl has begun."

Karne stiffened. He must not weaken, even in the face of a father's love. The time for mercy was past. "The risk of Uhl is yours, as the choice to rebel was yours. The oath-feast was in Narn, safe traveling time. No hostages, no fuel, Melevan. And I won't have to attack you if you refuse. In less than a week, according to my ponics techs, your ponics sheds will have to shut down. If you still have air by that time. The choice is yours, Melevan."

"Some time to consider..."

"You had time to 'consider' before my oath-feast."

Melevan turned his back for a moment, then turned again toward the camera and Karne. "You win, Lord Karne. May I have two days' grace in hope of better flying weather?"

The Larga Alysha laid her hand lightly on Karne's arm. She looked up at him questioningly.

Karne nodded the tiniest amount. "You have two days, Melevan. I expect the hostages no later than 11 Uhl, before fast-breaking."

The Larga turned her back to the camera and smiled her approval at Karne, then left the room. Karne nodded curtly to Melevan and followed her. He heard a burst of talking and crying among the Melevans before they broke connection. Karne leaned against the wall outside the tri-d room door and let relief flood through him. *One down, two to go, and Nerut hangs with Melevan.* "Page!"

A small page came running.

"Find Frem Weisman. I want him here."

The boy ran off and disappeared through the nearest library door. In moments Weisman came out and hurried toward Karne, the page close behind.

Weisman sketched a bow. "My lord?"

Karne stood away from the wall. "Melevan has surrendered and is sending hostages. Order Family rooms prepared for them—two girls and two boys. Perhaps the boys would like to berth with the pilots. Then call Nerut. Then call Roul. Tell them about Melevan and if either of them wishes to surrender, call me. I'm going to finish my midday."

Karne strolled back to the Great Hall. A weight had been removed from his shoulders, and another would be before evening, he was sure. He hummed a tune, very quietly, because Lharrs did not make music in public.

The Great Hall was empty. Karne carried the remains of his meal to the small private dining room of the Lharr's personal family, rarely used. He ate without the many interruptions from scornful or angry relatives that had plagued the last twelve days. He licked the last of a berry tart from his fingers, leaned back in his chair, and stretched his legs out in front of him. At the touch of his finger on a silent bell, a quiet serf cleared away his dishes. Karne let his eyes roam over the painted scenes of the walls and ceiling. Herdsmen watched hairy uleks grazing the low mountain pastures in summer. Boys of the Nine and their falconers climbed stark cliffs to get the nestlings for Family mews. The "horses" of Starker IV raced across a browned autumn plain. A sleek, black Dur cat lay in the sun along a barren, sand-colored ledge, watching hunters on the plain far below with slitted yellow eyes, its litter of three kits tumbling over and around it. The very barrenness of the mountain landscape made Karne think of the brilliant skies and open air of Balder. He heard again the clear bubbling song of the skylark and the whisper of wind in Balder's tall, lush grass. Shalim ran toward him, leaving a wake of bent grass behind her...

Someone was shaking him very politely. Karne opened his eyes and saw Weisman.

"Nerut would speak with you now, my lord. He didn't need long to think after he heard Melevan had already given in. Roul, now, Roul turned off his transmitter, milord."

"Roul will have to pay higher penalities then, won't he?" Karne levered himself out of the chair and followed Weisman to the tri-d room.

Nerut accepted much the same terms as Melevan, but, since he had no living daughters, Karne required he send all three of his younger sons and his only niece. "There will be no fuel delivered until the hostages arrive at Ontar manor," Karne reminded Nerut.

Nerut looked horrified. "My lord, it is Uhl!"

"I see you didn't think I meant what I said." Karne's eyes narrowed. He fixed the man with an icy look. "What lord can keep his vassals in order by letting them walk on him? Nay, it was your choice to wait so long, so on you are the consequences."

"My boys—"

Karne's mouth thinned. "You have two days' grace to pick good weather, no more. I've already risked too much of the honor of my House on you." He bowed stiffly and cut the connection. He looked at Weisman. "Only Roul left, Frem Weisman. He'll probably hold out as long as he can, and that probably means he'll lose all his hostages to Uhl. Damn his stubbornness! He'll find I won't give in."

Weisman lifted his brows in surprise, but said nothing.

"Waiting, waiting, and more waiting," Karne added under his breath. "Well, the waiting is almost over." He stared at the empty tri-d screen for a moment, shook his head angrily, and left the room. He took a lift to level 6, hesitated a moment outside the pilots' barracks, then knocked. Pilot Jenkins opened the door. His face brightened with welcome, he saluted, and opened the door wide. "A pleasure, my lord."

Karne heard a sudden flurry of movement. He strode into the room. The officers present were already standing or getting up. "My lord Karne," they said.

He returned a quick salute and nodded recognition to each of those present in turn. "Pilots von Schuss, Willem, Jenkins, Phillipson. Another Willem? Good. Egil. Troopleader Gregg. I'm celebrating the surrender of Nerut and Melevan, gentlemen."

The young officers crowded close to pump Karne's hand and slap his shoulder. Karne flushed with pleasure. It had been too long since he'd had such companionship.

Egil pushed through the others and gave Karne a thump that staggered him. As a matter of habit, Egil shot out his other hand to steady Karne. "Sorry, Karne." Egil laughed, a little sheepishly. "I got carried away again. This is good news! The Academy taught you some tactics that Gharr didn't know about. You'll make an impression on Starker IV yet."

"The impression I wanted to make just now is with skills matches," Karne said dryly, rubbing his aching shoulder. "Anyone here interested?"

"Aye, Lord Karne."

"I'll come."

"Me, too."

"Count me in."

The chorus of excited voices pleased Karne. He had been alone and working for weeks it seemed. It was past time to do some playing. Egil draped one arm across Karne's shoulders and Karne pretended to sink under the weight of it. Egil grinned down at his friend. "What are skills matches?"

Karne laughed. "You'll see. Come on down to the arena with us."

Only Phillipson, who had to go on duty soon, stayed behind. By intercom Karne told the armorer what they would need, so when they reached the arena, the sword dummy stood ready with swords and padded jackets. Other padded jackets and fencing foils lay against the arena wall a little away from the dummy, and six beamers with boxes of light-cartridges and metallized target jackets had been arranged in a precise row on a narrow table at the opposite side of the arena. Jenkins and Dennen Willem went immediately to the beamers.

Egil walked around the dummy, studying it from all angles. "What does it do?"

"It fights." Gregg put on a padded jacket, fitted one of the battle-swords into the dummy's grip, and picked the other up for himself. He hefted it.

"Seems a little light." He walked behind the dummy, followed by Egil, and turned the dial on the dummy's back to "7—advanced."

"Out of the raked circle, quick!" Gregg snapped, and leaped backward himself.

The dummy whirled, raised its sword and slid toward Gregg. "Limited range," Gregg said, parrying a blow. "I can escape outside the circle anytime. Trick is to stay close and give it a 'mortal' wound." Then Gregg had no more time for talking because the dummy had homed in on his body heat and movement. Gregg parried, struck, ducked in under the dummy's guard, backed away, grunted when the dummy's sword reached him.

"The fight ends," von Schuss explained to Egil, "when the swordsman strikes a blow that registers electrically as 'mortal' or 'disabling' or the dummy does. The only other way to end the fight is to leave the circle and unplug it. It doesn't get tired. I usually can beat it in '6,' at '7' a draw's the best I can do. How 'bout you, Lord Karne?"

"I used to best it three times out of five at '7,' but that was six years ago. I beat it at '8' the other day," he gave Nik a significant look, "but that was a fluke. I haven't practiced much since I left here; the Altarian Navy doesn't fight with swords anymore."

The dummy went *blat*, its red eyes flashed, and it stopped moving. Gregg leaned on his sword, panting. "That was—close. Glad it wasn't—a real man." He wiped sweat from his forehead and sat down on the sand.

"I've heard Richard can draw a dummy at '10,'"

Jenkins said from across the floor, hefting a beamer for balance.

"Maybe, but the Harlans are known to overstate their abilities." Dennen Willem looked directly at Karne. "However, don't ever take a chance that Harlan's just bragging, milord. Never."

Karne made a wry grimace. "Thanks. I won't chance him if I can help it." He looked at the other men. "What will it be now? Beamers at fifty paces? Fencing?"

"Beamers!" Jenkins and Yan Willem cried together.

Karne looked at the others. They nodded and began putting on the metallized target jackets, all except von Schuss, who could not get his cast through a sleeve.

"I'll referee," Nik offered.

The others laughed, since the jackets themselves were the referees. Karne held out a jacket toward Egil.

"Look. The red areas are mortal wounds, the blue disabling, the yellow slight wounds. Three slight wounds equal one disabling wound and you're counted out. If the light beam from the cartridge touches one of the target areas, the color will glow. The team with the last man on the field wins."

Egil looked at the jacket doubtfully. "How about wrestling instead?"

Karne laughed. "None of us would have a chance. Look," he opened a box of cartridges, "these don't look anything like actual ammunition. No one could load a beam-cartridge by mistake. It will be Dennen Willem, Olafson, and Halarek against Yan Willem, Gregg, and Jenkins."

Egil slid the jacket on—the armorer had found one big enough to fit him somewhere—still looking doubtful. He soon caught the spirit of the contest, but he did not have as much practice as twisting and dodging beams as the others and was the first man out, with a "mortal" wound. He shrugged and moved down the arena to try his luck against the dummy. By the time he finally scored a mortal hit, the other five men were sitting or lying flat on the ground around von Schuss's feet. Egil dropped his sword and walked over to the others.

"Who won?"

Karne and Dennen each raised an arm. "Halarek and Willem." They laughed and let their arms droop limply back onto the sand.

Gregg looked wearily up at Egil. "As long as you're up, Olafson, com us some beer."

"Why not you, Gregg?" Egil asked, wiping sweat out of his eyes.

"You're on your feet and I'm lying down."

Egil prodded Gregg with his toe. "I'm a guest here, remember?"

Gregg laughed. "Aye, off-worlder. We of the Gharr make servants of the likes of puny people like you."

With his foot Egil shoved Gregg over onto his stomach, then went to the com in the wall and ordered down fourteen beers. He settled himself comfortably on the sand near Karne then asked with a puzzled frown, "Don't you ever drink milk here?"

"Milk? What's milk?" Yan responded mockingly.

"Funny man," Egil snapped. "All mammals know what milk is."

"This friend of yours has sure gotten uppity since he cut loose from the translits, Lord Karne." Jenkins sat up and tipped his head back to look at Egil. "Our uleks, the milk animals, are up on the surface, Olafson. We won't see any milk until Thawtime." He flopped back onto the sand as if exhausted by his explanation.

They were still waiting for beer when Kathryn burst in. "Karne! Karne! There's just been a Council alert from Breven. Asten Harlan is dead!"

The men sprang to their feet and ran for the lift.

"Wait for me!" Kathryn wailed.

No one stopped. She looked both directions, then hiked her skirt up to her knees and ran. Von Schuss let her catch up, then hurried her along with his good hand under her elbow. They slid into the lift as the gate began to close.

"Tush, Kathryn, you're a scandal, you are," Karne whispered in her ear.

"Oh, Karne!" Kit brushed her skirt into order again. "Don't tease. I would've had to wait for you to go up and the lift come down. I might've missed the broadcast."

"What do females need to hear such news for? They—"

"Karne! You're just copying Lady Agnes, stuffy old—"

Karne grinned and hugged his sister with one arm. "You know I don't mean it, Kit. You're as good as any boy as far as I'm concerned."

She glared at him. The lift jolted to a stop and

the gate opened. "I won't tell Mother how bad you were. The others won't either, right?" Karne looked at the others in the little group.

The six men nodded solemnly. Kathryn took one look at their dancing eyes, stuck out her lower lip in a mock pout, and flounced out of the lift. She was only halfway to the tri-d room when impatience got the better of her. She hiked her skirts again and ran almost to the door, skidded to a stop, and entered the room at a sedate, lady's pace. The hall echoed with the officers' laughter. The Lady Kathryn poked her head back around the door frame and stuck out her tongue. Karne caught Nik looking speculatively down the hall. "Nik? Is something the matter?"

"What? Oh—no, nothing. Let's catch the broadcast."

The tri-d room was already full when they reached it. Space appeared the moment Karne said, "Let me through, please," and the five officers and Egil walked behind him to the front of the room. Karne stood beside the Larga's chair. The others sat on the floor around it.

"Rank has some benefits," Egil whispered loudly to Nik. "You can get a front-row seat with it."

Karne looked down at Egil and grinned. Kit, who was standing behind the Larga, giggled. Lady Alysha turned and shot her a quelling look. The tri-d screen glowed white and the crowd in the room quieted. The deacon of Breven appeared against a background of ancient books, looking as if he were close enough to touch.

"God's peace, Nine Families and minor Houses. One of you has left this world for another..."

"A much hotter one," Kit whispered.

"Shhh!" said the Larga. "He'll hear you."

The deacon folded his hand and gazed at the camera.

"Does he have a wall full of monitors?"

"Hush, Kathryn!"

The deacon ignored the whispers in the background, whispers from more Houses than Halarek. "Asten Harlan departed this life after many days of almost complete paralysis. There is already a rumor that he died by his own hand. This is obviously impossible, since he could not use his hands even to—"

"Have done, old man," a harsh voice cut in. "We have important business to finish."

The deacon winced, but he dropped his hands to his sides and spoke faster. "Since transporting the body home before Thawtime is clearly impossible, we will hold the last service for Lord Asten here at Breven tomorrow at midday. You will be able to watch the last words being—"

The harsh voice cut in again. "I say the last words, old man. The words are, 'Halarek dies!'"

The deacon turned, bewildered, looking for the voice. "Who is that?"

"Richard Harlan, Duke of Harlan."

"Duke-designate, Lord Richard, as long as people are interrupting—I, Davin Reed, remind everyone that House Harlan is under trusteeship until the Thawtime Council decides to end it or until Gild findings aboard the *Aldefara* exempt House Harlan from the charges of illegal assassins and siege."

The deacon threw up his hands and waved the camera away. "I yield to Frem Reed."

"What have the Freemen to do with this?" Lord Richard's voice was so distorted by rage or grief, it sounded little like him.

"The law has been set, Harlan, and we, the Freemen, will, for our own protection, see it is obeyed. Kingsland, as trustee, speaks for Harlan now."

There was a slamming noise. "I speak for my House and its grief! My father is dead, a direct result of Halarek lies in Council. Show my face, damn you!"

Reed waved the camera away and the transmission from Harlan manor took the screen. Richard Harlan stood, legs braced, hands on hips, handsome face flushed with anger, glaring at the camera. It looked like much of his Family had joined him, for the room was jammed with men and a few women, all dressed in black. Quiet weeping made background for his words.

"My sire died of a stroke directly caused by Karne Halarek and the shame of imprisonment. I will clear his name by wiping the slate clean with the blood of Karne Halarek. I vow now, before the Nine Great Houses and all the minor Houses, that I will destroy House Halarek to the last stone and distant cousin. I will ruin that House and then I will grind it to dust! The Four Guardians be my witnesses!"

A great gasp filled the tri-d rooms of all the Houses and the sound of the horror of so many others strengthened the feeling of it. No one had ever taken such a bloody oath, then called on the peaceful Guardians as witnesses.

The fine bones of the Larga's hands stood out in hard lines as she clutched the arms of her chair. "He'll do it, I feel it in my bones. He'll kill us all, Karne."

Chapter Ten

———◆———

KARNE'S MOUTH TIGHTENED, but he did not answer his mother. He spun away and ordered the officers with him to collect the senior officers of the Halarek army and of the Blues and bring them to the Great Hall. Karne himself went to the com center on level 2, Egil right on his heels. Karne stopped outside the center's door. "Egil, this is Gharr business. It's against the law for you to listen. I'll see you upstairs."

Egil looked down at Karne. His face set stubbornly. "If I can't go in, I'll stay right here. I'm not moving from this door, Karne. If the Lharrs Halarek have never had personal guards, now's the time to start."

Karne reared back his head, releasing on his friend the anger he had been holding in so long. "The Lharrs Halarek have never had personal guards! Never! The 'woman' of my father's sons cannot change that. Not and hope to seem a man in the eyes of other Houses." He flung out an arm in the direction he wanted Egil to go and started to turn away to enter the room.

Egil clamped his hands on Karne's shoulders painfully hard, preventing movement, and stared down at him fiercely. "Turn off the Gharr in your head, Karne, and turn on the pacification officer! You've just been threatened, most sincerely, by an enemy you already know won't act by tradition or law. You also know someone in this manor acted for Richard in the matter of Farm 3. Think, Karne!" Egil communicated his urgency without ever raising his voice.

The powerful grip and sharp, logical words penetrated Karne's anger. His eyes slid away, ashamed of his loss of control. He sighed. "You're right. I know in my head you're right, but the Gharr part of me would rather die than take on the protection only women need."

"Die is exactly what you will do if you don't protect yourself!" Egil gave Karne a sharp shake, released his grip, and stepped back. "Do what you must inside. I'll guard the door. No one will go in, and no one will come out unless you personally tell me it's all right." Egil's eyes took on a glint of mischief. "You know you can't stop me once you're inside. You can pretend you know nothing about it. Just the crazy off-worlder's idea of what's right. And so on." He sobered. "I'm going to stick to you like glue, Karne."

Karne nodded and went into the com center.

When he came out more than an hour later, he looked drained. "Just as I suspected. There's a secret com link to the outside, to somewhere in the foothills to the northwest. A coded message came over it just a little while ago. That's how we found it. The com chief's cut the connection and is tracing the link inside the manor. We should know by tonight where the traitor's working, at least." He turned away so Egil could not see how deeply this additional bad news had disturbed him. "I'm going to my quarters to hide for awhile. Do you intend to guard me there, too?"

"I intend to stick to you like a shadow until you appoint some Lifesguardsmen to your own protection."

Karne cleared his throat. "Thanks, brother. You're letting yourself in for rough duty, because I absolutely cannot have personal guards."

The two men walked to the Lharr's quarters in silence. The door was slightly ajar. Newly cautious, Karne stood to one side and, with his toe, shoved the door the rest of the way open. The room looked empty.

Egil stopped any further movement with his hand. "Stay here. I'm going to check the next room." Egil searched the sitting room, the sleeping room, and checked the iron stair. "Clear," he said curtly, and sat on the edge of the bed.

Karne entered and sank into the old leather chair. He stared at the stone floor, his mind spinning with memories of what had happened in the last weeks—Richard's threat, the vassals' rebellion, the contempt of Family and allies. He could not bring order to his thoughts. Eventually, as he stared at the floor, his eye caught sight of a patch of pink fluff lying just where the edge of the bed's cover touched the floor. Karne at first dismissed it as a bit of rag left by the cleaning serfs, but something made him look again. He slipped from the chair to the floor and reached toward the small pink mound, hesitantly, unwillingly. The fluff was damp and came out easily, leaving streaks of red behind it. Karne stared down in shock at the mutilated body of the uhl-uhl. "Wiki!" he cried. He took the tiny animal into his lap and turned it over gently. It had been hideously tortured. There was not a spot left on it not tinted with blood, not a bone unbroken, and it had been recently done, for the little body was still soft and warm.

Karne stroked the damp, matted fur. "Wiki, old friend, why?" he whispered. Then Karne saw the tag of yellow paper beside the place where Wiki had been tossed. He picked it up and unfolded it slowly. On it was scrawled, "This is the fate of all Halarek." Karne stared at the thick, bold letters.

"Father of All! Has Richard been here himself? It's Uhl!" His voice was hushed and trembled a little. Karne looked down at the tiny, mutilated body. "I'm sorry, old friend. I'd planned for you to have a quiet, comfortable old age. Instead you die in terror and agony, because of me." Karne cradled the small body in the crook of one arm.

"Karne?" Egil sounded worried.

Karne looked up, his face girm. "It's my fault. I never thought anyone would—" Karne choked and turned his face away so Egil would not see the tears that hovered in his eyes. He could not hide the roughnesss in his voice. "You were obviously right about the danger. But you will have to guard me without appearing to. I've done enough to encourage talk of cowardice already." He looked down at Wiki again. "I must take care of Wiki. Tell

Tane to tell Wynter to begin the officers' meeting."
Karne nearly choked on the frustration of such
roundabout orders, yet Egil, an off-worlder, could
not legally speak to Wynter himself about military
matters. "Have Wynter start by checking out our
readiness for siege, then have him find out if the
men Konnor and von Schuss promised have arrived. If not, whether or not we can still expect
them. I should be down by the time he gets to that
point."

Egil quickly located Orkonan by com, forcibly
blocking Karne from leaving his quarters until the
message had been given. "You'll not leave without
me!" Egil said fiercely when Karne tried to brush
past him. "I meant what I said to the letter: I'm
going with you everywhere, absolutely everywhere, even to sleeping in your room, unless you'll
give your word you'll lock all your doors."

"Then I might as well have called Tane myself,"
Karne snarled.

"Aye, that you might," Egil retorted good-hu-
moredly, "but it's done now. Shall we go wherever
you were going?"

Karne bent his head over the limp ball of fluff
and walked silently to the nearest lift. With Egil
beside him every step of the way, he carried the
small body to the crematorium and did not stay to
see Wiki disposed of.

Two hours later, Karne came out of the conference with his remaining officers, sure that House
Halarek was as prepared as it could be for either
attack or siege and that the House could probably
defend itself without House Justin and House
Freeson—Freeson had withdrawn its offer of sup-

port because Karne had negotiated with slaves,
Justin had withdrawn for Karne's "cowardice" in
dealing with his rebellious vassals. "I cannot appear to condone such tactics as yours, young man,"
Allet Justin had said in a recorded message. "The
young rascals already with you may stay, but there
will be no more. Cowardice sticks to all who asso-
ciate with it."

Karne paced slowly down a corridor, he was not
even sure which one, maintaining an outward
calm in spite of the grief and rage tearing him
apart inside. He wanted to scream his grief, to
shred the men who would let his House fall before
accepting nontraditional solutions to the problems
that had faced him, but he had made mistakes
enough already. He cast about for an acceptable
way to rid himself of that violent energy before he
lost control of it and committed some irredeem-
able folly in the eyes of the Gharr. He needed violent, draining action, immediately. He thought
then of Brenden. Karne looked up to get his bearings and turned immediately toward the stable
area on level 2 and the stall of his favorite "horse,"
a shaggy bay. Egil and the two Lifesguardsmen
Egil had publicly requested for his protection at
the opening of the conference accompanied him
closely.

The moment the men stepped off the lift, the
harsh ammonia odor of the midden-room pinched
Karne's nose and made his eyes water. The soft un-
derscents of dried grasses and oiled leather took
longer to come to awareness. There was a quiet-
ness in the stable area that immediately began to
do him good. He entered Brenden's stall and

reached toward the "horse." The animal bent its long, shaggy neck and snuffled Karne's pockets. Karne wanted to bury his face in the animal's thick fur and cry. The wanting tore at him but, with Egil and Egil's two guards watching, he could do no more than run his hand over the animal's soft nose and up its face to the hard ridge between its horns.

"I saw true horses on Balder, you know," Karne whispered to the animal. "You're a horse only because you have four legs, a long face, and a mane." Karne scratched behind the horn-ridge and the horse whuffled its pleasure. Karne pulled the stall door open, swung onto the horse's back with only a grip on its thick, curly fur for help, and sent the horse out of its stall and into the arena with a nudge of his heels. Egil would set watch on the arena doors. Egil and the men with him then slipped from Karne's awareness.

"You don't get an easy winter down here away from the wind just for breeding," he told the animal. He dug his heels hard into Brenden's sides. The animal leaped into a run, straight down the center of the arena. Small puffs of the chemically bonded sand flew up beside Brenden's feet. Karne directed the horse in sharp turns, sliding stops, and in the sideways leaps so necessary for avoiding beamers in battle. Karne rode through every tactic for avoiding attack again and again and again until horse and rider both dripped sweat. He then rode the horse many times around the arena slowly to cool him, dismounted, and held onto Brenden's fur until his own wobbly legs steadied.

"Too little practice, boy. I'm out of shape," he

panted in the animal's ear. He patted the horse's
cheek, took a firm grip on its mane, and walked it
around and around the arena some more, stopping
for a moment in front of the battered sword
dummy to push a piece of stuffing back inside the
dummy's cloth body. "Come on, Brenden, it's time
for cleaning up."

He refused a Lifesguardsman's offer to put the
horse away and picked up the grooming brush
himself. He worked quickly and hard. While he
watered and brushed the horse, Karne could forget
Wiki and Roul and the hostages flying into Uhl
and the men Justin and Freeson had promised. He
let the rhythm of the brushing absorb him. He
brushed long after the horse was clean. When he
stopped, Brenden's coat was fluffy with static and
as shiny as a winter coat could be. He checked the
animal's food and water again, slapped it on the
rump, and left the stall, bolting the door behind
him. He felt better. The rage and feeling of betrayal were still there, but they had no power left
to damage him.

Back in the lift, Karne looked down at himself.
He bristled with bay fur, the edges of his sleeves
were gray from the brushing, his palms were almost black, and the front of his tunic was blotched
with blood. Wiki's blood.

The lift stopped. Karne looked out into the hall.
Kit stood by the door to the Larga's quarters, staring at the floor, her cheeks shiny with tears. He
had sent a message to her of Wiki's death, but he
knew he could not deal with her grief, too, just
now. He pressed '6,' the lift door slid closed again,
and the lift went on up to the conservatory,

Karne's refuge of last resort. He left Egil outside as guard and went in alone, shutting the door and backing against it. The soft smells of damp earth, green leaves, and wet air surrounded him. He looked up at the domed skylight. Somehow, the day had run away from him and now it was night, with snow drifting against the skylight's curving sides and rattling against its thermal glass. He noted the skylight's vulnerability, then shoved away the thoughts accompanying that one. There would be time enough for them later.

He walked into the center of the greenery, pulled out a reed bench, and sat in the darkness, smelling the plants, feeling the warm dampness of their breathing, almost tasting the heavy fragrance of the imported tam-tam trees in tall pots directly under the skylight. The violent anger he had worked away, but the fierce, rending grief remained. The only sounds in the room were those of the snow against the glass and his own breathing. Slowly, the silence and the soft, green-smelling air quieted Karne's spirit and healed the rawest places in his heart.

On the evening of 10 Uhl, flitters from Nerut and Melevan delivered hostages and decacredits as promised. For the three girls, quarters near Kathryn's were ready, as well as serf-women trained to serve as ladies-in-waiting and noble-women for chaperones. The young men were bunked with and were treated the same as the bachelor officers.

Roul held out until 15 Uhl, when he began losing

slaves on his lower levels to suffocation. A page wakened Karne very late on the fifteenth to receive Roul's surrender. Karne threw a salk-fur robe around himself and stumbled to the tri-d room one level down, stubbing his toes in corners as the stairs turned at the landing and bumping into walls in the manor's "night" lighting. He stopped outside the tri-d room to rub his face vigorously, then walked into the brightly lighted room. The portly Roul was standing tensely beside an ancient wood desk. He wore the lightest of clothes. Sharp lines creased his cheeks and forehead, but he held his head high. "I surrender, Lord Karne, Lharr of House Halarek. You're far cleverer than I thought. What are your terms?" The man's eyes did not waver.

Karne admired the courage that kind of pride required. The terms could not be lessened, however, no matter how brave the man. Karne straightened until he stood stiff and proud before the camera. "My terms are: your oath of fealty given when we meet; yourself and all your children but the two males eldest born as hostages; the cost of the fuel I deliver; and a tax of ten thousand decacredits per M-ton as penalty. No fuel leaves the Gild depot until the hostages arrive."

"Those are harsh terms, my lord." Roul's voice was rough with strain.

"Oath-breaking is a harsh act, and usually its terms are death. You made oath to my sire to be faithful to him and to his successors. I am his successor and you refused me homage."

"The storms of Uhl have begun."

"The storms of Uhl are severe," Karne agreed

calmly. "You knew that. You've known that since you were a child. It's true you run a great risk flying in Uhl. However, the timing of your rebellion was your choice. Holding out for nineteen days was your choice. Even now I can't guarantee successful fuel delivery because of the weather. The pipes may have frozen from nonuse, Benjamin Roul. You may have waited too long."

Roul paled and swallowed hard. "How long do I have left at home?"

"Until first clearing. Early tomorrow, from what I've been told."

Roul groaned, turned away, and cut the connection.

The next morning Lady Elisabeth Roul, her face swollen and red-splotched with crying, tri-ded confirmation of a small transport's departure with the hostages. House Halarek waited. Karne waited.

The transport was one hour overdue at Ontar. When it was two, the com chief sent out all-band homing signals. Nik von Schuss took a flitter out to the top of the pad shaft and brought it back down. He walked very slowly across the pad to where Karne stood, looking out the com-center observation window. "There's no visibility at all out there," Nik reported, "and the wind is high enough to blow a troop transport into the mountains. Roul wasn't bringing anything that heavy."

"Guardians, protect them," whispered one of the com-techs, watching a remote wind-speed indicator.

"That's the only help they'll get until the storm blows past," Nik snarled. He turned abruptly and

stared out at his flitter. "The fool!" he muttered.
"Six children lost, all for pride!"

Four hours later, near dawn, the worst of the
storm passed and House Halarek asked the Gild
for a satellite fix on any downed flier on the Holding. The House received a positive infrared fix fifteen kilometers away, in the high pass over the
mountains. When the com-tech shoved the plat direct from Gild computers into Karne's hands,
Karne could only stare at it. The distance was
nearly impossible in the aftermath of the storm.

"They can't get here from that far away. If anyone survived the coming down." Karne looked at
Nik's stricken face. "I've killed them, Nik. All those
children. I've killed them."

Nik set a hand on Karne's shoulder, awkward
with emotion. "Karne, their deaths aren't your responsibility. Roul knew the risks. He knew the
penalties the others had paid. He gambled he
could hold out until he found another source of
fuel. He lost. Whatever happens is his responsibility."

Karne ran one hand roughly through his hair
and sighed. "Whoever is responsible, there are six
children out there. Prefet!"

The soldier Karne looked at stepped forward.
"Get Flight Instructor Kranz down to the flitter
pad," Karne ordered. "And soldier," the young
man, who had started to leave, turned back, "are
my sire's Specials still a unit?"

"Aye, lord."

"Their commander?"

"Centen Roth, lord."

"Good man! Get Kranz right away."

The prefet saluted and marched away. Karne paged Centen Roth from the nearest com. In a few minutes a hoarse voice responded. "Roth here, Lord Karne."

"I want your Specials on line in fifteen minutes, Centen. Roul's transport crashed in the pass."

"Gregg will line them up for you, milord." Roth coughed, deep and racking. "I'm still abed in the clinic, lord."

"Gregg is of the Specials?"

"Usually, lord. Your sire detailed him to manor duty with the household Blues shortly before—it was only a small infraction of your sire's dress standards, milord." Roth began to cough again.

"That's enough, whoever you are," a waspish voice snapped. "This is Dr. Othneil and I order you to leave this man alone. He's still in serious condition."

Karne gulped down a laugh; the doctor was dressing down his lord and did not know it. "Yessir! I'll stop right now, sir!"

"Don't sass your betters, soldier." The doctor turned off his speaker.

The laughter faded slowly from Karne's face. "Guardians, I needed that! Nothing funny's happened to me for weeks."

Nik's mouth twisted in rueful understanding.

Gregg arrived and halted with his men outside the com center. Karne went out. Kit and the Larga stood at the back of the group of soldiers. Gregg snapped a salute and his men, already dressed in survival gear and carrying medkits, lined up in five neat rows behind him. "Two decades of the Second Century on line, sir!"

"Roul's flier came down in the high pass, Troop-leader." Karne kept his tone crisp, without any shade of the emotions he was feeling. "If there are any survivors, I want them here, quickly. The dead can stay with the flier until Thawtime."

Gregg bent his head in acknowledgment. "As you command, Lord Karne. I took the liberty of having the horses from the stable sent to the surface, assuming you'd want them. Our fliers would have no better luck in the pass than Roul's. Do you approve, lord?"

Karne nodded. "Sounds like good thinking to me. How long will it take?"

"Three days, lord, four if there are many survivors, or any badly hurt ones."

"Good luck." Karne saluted the Specials and watched them until the lift carried them out of sight, wondering if he had just sent two decades out to die.

Kit, who had been sidling closer and closer as the men talked, slid one arm around Karne's waist and pressed the fingers of her other hand against the deep lines between Karne's brows. "This is the way Starker is, Karne. You made your best decision. You can't keep feeling guilty about it. Think how many more people would've died if you'd attacked those three manors." She stood on tiptoe and kissed his ear. "You're a better ruler already than our sire ever was. You care about people."

"Kathryn!"

"He's my brother, Lady Mother. It's not as if he were Egil Olafson or somebody like that."

Kit freed her arm and walked away down the

hall. Nik excused himself a moment later and followed her.

The Larga came to Karne's side and stood looking after Kit. "She needs a man to quiet her down. I don't know from one moment to the next what scandalous thing she'll do."

Karne looked down at his mother, perplexed. "She seems well-behaved to me. Not so well-behaved that she's dull, though, like some of our female cousins."

"You've been away too long, son, in places where females expose their limbs and middles and talk freely with men and walk about without chaperones." The Larga turned with a swirl of soft blue fabric and walked away. Her pace was ladylike, her motions graceful.

"No, I don't think Kit's ever going to be like that," Karne said softly. "Kit sheds sparks when she's angry." He reentered the com center, pulled up an empty chair to the side of a com unit, and settled down for a long wait.

The Specials kept in contact. They reported high winds and treacherous ice, but no injuries. The Gild satellite helped them find the wreckage the second day out. They reported only two survivors, Roul himself and his two-winters daughter.

The Roul the Specials brought to Ontar manor was not the lord who had refused fealty to the Halarek "woman," but a broken man who muttered constantly to himself, "I killed my boys, my stubbornness killed my boys." No one could console him, not his wife, not his surviving elder sons, not his small daughter, Mikette. After two weeks, during which Roul wasted to a shadow of himself, Dr.

Othneil ordered him taken to the staff clinic for force-feeding and sedation.

Shaking his head sadly, Karne watched two Lifesguardsmen half lead, half carry the stumbling Roul to the lift, then Karne joined the Larga and her women in the Larga's sitting room. The five women made a peaceful scene, sitting on low stools and bright cushions, their heads bent demurely over needlework of one variety or another. Karne thought of sitting quietly with them for a time; he needed a few quiet moments. Kit, peeking up at him slyly through her dark, curly curtain of hair, winked. One of the hostages, a girl about Kit's age, watched him from the corner of her eye no matter where he moved in the room, and that made him nervous. Then he thought of the tri-d call he had just made to Lady Elisabeth to tell her of her husband's condition and saw how very unpeaceful his own feelings were.

By my Sire's Blood! Karne thought savagely, I wish there were some private way to talk to Lady Elisabeth about Roul! It'll soon be all over Starker IV that Halarek tortured Roul until he lost his mind.

Karne grimaced. Paul of Druma had already reported hearing just such a rumor and he lived half the world away. Spying and tricks had always been part of the Families' lives, but Karne had never been enough a part of his Family to know it. Now he was learning the uncertainty of life among the Nine with a vengeance. Treachery, spying, betrayal—Karne knew he desperately needed time to get his bearings and his balance, but events were not allowing him that time and, if Richard Harlan had his way, he would never find it. Well, at least he had a group of friends now that he could rely on.

Karne went to his mother and touched her lightly on the shoulder. "Lady Mother, I think I'll find Egil." Karne spun and left the room.

He found Egil, Nik, Gregg, Jenkins, and the two Willem brothers sitting in the Great Hall with the remains of their nightmeal. Karne swung a leg over a bench and sat down with them. In the past weeks, the seven of them had talked and practiced weaponry, played games of an evening, exercised by the army's book, flirted with the ladies-in-waiting, and, when the Larga was not looking, had teased Kit and the two female hostages nearest Kit's age. These men had come close to Karne, in spite of his sire's relentless drumming to trust no one. He told them about the torture story Harlan was spreading.

Dennen Willem shrugged. "That kind of story can't hurt you, milord. Many men will think better of you if they believe it's true."

Karne sighed. "You're likely right, Dennen." He slumped into glum silence, his chin in his hand.

After a long pause, Gregg ruffled through a much-used deck. "Cards?"

Egil stood and stretched. Yan Willem gave him a friendly punch in the belt.

"Sit down, giant, you're throwing a shadow on my cake."

"I'm going to see if there's more of that hot bread," said Egil, sniffing loudly and following his nose toward the door.

"Me, too," several of the others chorused.

Benches scraped back. There was some jostling to be first out the door, then the group pelted down the stair to the kitchen.

"I'll look the place over," said Gregg, and peeked around the side kitchen door. "Bread's on a table on the other side and there's only one person in there, a man in the scullery."

The group crept around to the other side of the kitchen. "As if the Lharr couldn't eat whatever he wanted," Nik commented wryly.

The bread was just the right temperature. They tore a loaf into chunks and leaned against the counter to eat it.

"Good bread!" said Yan through a mouthful of tender crust.

The others added their comments. "Nice idea, Olafson." "Why haven't we done this before?" "Let's do some beamer practice while we're down here."

Egil pushed a last chunk of bread into his mouth and stood away from the counter. "You could show me how that horse of yours works with beamers, Karne."

Jenkins checked his chrono. "Count me out. I go on duty in a few minutes. Let me know how the horse does, Olafson." Jenkins crossed the kitchen swiftly, then paused to look hard at the man in the scullery. "Say, aren't you one of the duty officers at the com center?"

The man did not answer, but began stacking pots and griddles into cabinets with amazing speed and noise.

Jenkins beckoned to von Schuss. "Nik?"

Nik strode close to the man. "You were a com officer. I remember your face."

The man turned to face the other two as if cornered. "I was. Until Lord Be-Kind-to-His-Enemies broke me to subprefet." The man shot a look at Karne, then darted out the kitchen door.

Jenkins shrugged and left. Nik looked at Karne questioningly.

"He was unbelievably insolent. I never even learned his name. Captain Rad took care of the punishment. I would've broken him out of the army completely, only it was Uhl and I didn't want to risk a good officer taking a bad one off the Holding. I probably should've raised it. Nerut and Melevan made it." He shrugged. "No one's right all the time."

The men wiped crumbs from their mouths and went on to the arena, Karne leading. He disappeared with Egil into the stable area while the others went directly to the practice area. The horse, Brenden, was restive and hard to handle. Karne talked to him and stroked his neck fur, but the horse would not be soothed. By the time the two of them were in the arena, they were both sweating. Something had set the horse off, Karne was sure. He checked the bridle and under the riding pad. If someone had tampered, he was cleverer than Karne. Karne mounted. Brenden pranced and tossed his head. "Easy, boy!" Karne warned sharply. "You almost gored me that time. What's the matter?" Karne looked across the arena to the other men, who were wearing beamers and beamer jackets. "Ready down there?"

The five men loaded their light-cartridges and

took firing positions imitating an infantry attack. Nik, of necessity, was shooting left-handed. Karne took a deep breath. This exercise always felt like he imagined a real battle would. His stomach knotted, his heart beat faster, his hands grew slippery on the reins. He took another deep breath. "Shoot when ready. Only two at a time, please. Brenden and I need some chance."

Brenden's ears twitched.

"Go, boy!" Karne kicked the horse into a lope.

For the next ten minutes the pair put on a brilliant show of sudden stops, abrupt sideways leaps, and quick changes of speed or direction. Karne glanced down at his jacket. Two yellow patches glowed. One more and he was "dead." Brenden jerked forward and spun around in the same moment. A light beam passed harmlessly. Nik and Gregg fired on intersecting courses. Brenden evaded both. A second later Karne thought he heard three weapons fire. Then his back felt bathed in fire. He screamed in agony.

"Heimdal! A real one!" Egil cried.

Chapter Eleven

———◆———

KARNE HEARD THE hiss of another beam. Another shot would kill. He jerked at Brenden's head as if in a spasm of pain and fell to the sand. He lay just as he had fallen, one arm twisted painfully under him. There were only the six of them in the arena and one of them had shot him. He was betrayed. The word echoed in his head—betrayed, betrayed, betrayed—beating time with the throbbing pain. He lay very still and hoped the traitor would think him dead.

After the first shock, pain seemed to sharpen his senses. Boots scrunched on sand. Karne held his breath. Someone was breathing quickly and very loudly nearby. Coming back for one last shot? Karne could not risk a look.

"Get him!" Nik shouted from somewhere across the arena.

Despair swept Karne. Nik? Not Nik? Boots scrunched quickly closer. Karne tried to prepare himself for the final searing shot. A large hand slid under the collar of his tunic and gently touched the pulse in his throat.

"Alive, thank God," Egil called to the others. "Don't move, Karne," he added softly. "There are men coming from the clinic with a litter. The Willems are on your other side. We think the man's gone, but we don't want to give him a chance for another shot. Nik and Gregg have gone after him. Don't move." Egil lifted away the burned edges of Karne's beamer jacket and began to swear, fiercely and very quietly.

There was no other sound in the arena. Karne tried again to ease the arm he had fallen on, but that pulled the muscles in his burned back. Karne heard himself whimper, then he blacked out. He came to, briefly, when he was put on a clinic litter.

"Set it for 'hover only,'" he heard one of the

techs say. "We can push it faster than it will move by itself."

"His quarters, Troopleader?" another tech asked.

"Main clinic," Gregg answered curtly. "He's got to have help fast."

Then darkness closed in again. When Karne next opened his eyes, he was in a small, bare room lit by a nightlight near the floor. The air smelled slightly stinging, medicinal. He was lying face-down, strapped to a man-shaped frame. He strained against the straps, trying to lift his head enough to see something more than the floor. The movement made the skin on his back feel like it was crinkling up and it hurt incredibly. Karne put his head back down on the forehead and chin supports with a moan. This did not look like the clinic. He'd had an intimate acquaintance with the clinic since Farm 3.

He fought off panic. Where am I? How long have I been like this? He tried to twist his head to see to the sides, but only succeeded in hurting his back again. He bit his lip hard to prevent a scream of pain. Despair washed over him. His House was still in great danger and he was weaker than a baby. Karne heard a door opening slowly and saw the rectangle of light from outside get longer and longer until it lay yellow on the floor beneath his chest. Shoes went *snap, snap,* on the polished floor. Karne twisted his neck to see who it was and the twisting hurt.

"Nay, lord. Don't move." A man's hand with a loose, black sleeve touched his arm gently. The man moved closer, but the light was so dim that all Karne could see was his dark robe. The man took Karne's pulse. "Orderly, the lights."

A dark shape outside the door moved, the lights came on, and the man in the black robe crouched beside the bed, level with Karne's eyes.

"Othneil!" Karne had not recognized the gentle, concerned voice as that of the harsh, sharp-tongued man he thought he knew well.

"Aye. Who else would it be?" The acid was back in the doctor's tongue. Othneil studied Karne's face. "You've been having nightmares, lord. You struggle with them so much you break open your back again and again. You were very lucky. Your metallized jacket reflected enough heat that you have only a middle-degree burn and your friends got you here at once. Your entire back is burned." The doctor looked down at the polished floor for a moment and his voice was lower, rougher, when he continued. "We thought for a time you were going to die, lord."

"Where am I?"

"Well, my lord," the doctor drawled, "I know the Family always gets treated in Family quarters, but I couldn't have gotten the equipment upstairs, even if there'd been time to do it. Here." Othneil stood, leaned hard on one side of the frame, and Karne found himself faceup, resting against the straps and slings that had held him down. Othneil patted Karne's arm. "There, that's better, isn't it. Easier for you. Easier for me. When a man has fifty winters, his knees aren't what they used to be. Now, where was I? Oh, where you are. Well, actually this used to be a supply closet. I had it cleared and disinfected while you were getting emergency treatment."

Karne blew out a slow sigh of relief. "I was afraid at first I'd been captured..."

"Captured, Lord Karne? In your own house?"

Karne looked away, ashamed now of his suspicions. "I didn't recognize this place. There are a lot of men in the manor from other Houses, there's at least one traitor living here, and I—I suspected my friends."

"It wasn't reasonable, but it wasn't surprising, either, considering how you were raised. Before any of you were born, lord, your sire had two friends try to turn him over to the Harlans. He never got over it. And your great-grandsire, of course, was a friend to the Harlan of his generation—until he shamed the Duke by Sealing the woman the Duke expected to wed." The doctor shook his head, as if, even after all the generations between, he still could not believe a man would do such a thing to a friend. "Right on the Black Ship he did it—"

"Was it one of my friends? No one can load a beam-cartridge for a light-cartridge by mistake."

"Like I told you, milord, those five saved your life. The off-world giant and the Willems shielded you from another attack while Pilot von Schuss commed me and then, with Gregg, chased the assassin down. The man had been a com officer until you broke him from service. Your friends 'convinced' him to talk; he said Lord Richard had heard of his breaking to the ranks and offered him money and a chance to get back at you. He took it. Troopleader Gregg found decacredits in his pockets, far more than a com officer could save in years. Unfortunately, he broke away from Pilot von Schuss, who should not have been indulging in such business with his arm in a cast anyway, and was stun-killed as he tried to escape through the conservatory skylight. Your friends assume he was the one who set up the secret com link, also the one who tortured Wiki to death." Othneil laid a hand on one of Karne's in sympathy. "I was sorry to hear that, lord. The little beast had been here longer than I. I shall miss him."

Karne bit back grief. "I'd hoped he was the only one—a com officer could have talked to Farm 3 and to Harlan's listening post, could have laid the secret line into the manor—but to have cash money..." He shook his head and grimaced and was silent from the pain for a moment. "No one from outside has been here since Council. Richard still has someone in this House."

"That seems likely, lord."

Talking seemed to consume a lot of energy. Karne lay silent a time, then said huskily, "I suspected my friends. When they had done nothing to deserve it, I listened to my sire's lying voice and suspected them!" In spite of himself, a tear slipped down Karne's cheek. He bit hard on his lip to prevent any more escaping, but it was no use. He had lost the strength to resist. He turned his head away so the doctor would not see.

Dr. Othneil produced a large handkerchief and patted up the tears. "Do not feel shame, young lord," he said gruffly. "In times after great pain, while the body and will are still weak, tears are all right, unavoidable often. I've seen them in older, less-hurt men than you." Othneil moved toward the door. "There's a buzzer under your left hand if you need anything. Go back to sleep. I'll come again in the morning." He turned out the lights.

"Doctor?"

Othneil paused in the doorway, a silhouette against the light from the hall.

"What day is it?"

"5 Arhast, late, milord."

"How long will I be—when will I be all right again?"

"Depends. Three to four weeks, usually."

"Guardians! That long?"

"Your whole back is burned. Yes, as long as that. Longer if you aren't careful after we take you off the man-frame."

"That's 5 Koort!"

"Aye, lord. Goodnight, my lord." Othneil went the rest of the way out and shut the door.

Karne lay awake for a time, staring at the faint shadow of the man-frame that the night light made on the ceiling, feeling the damp tracks tears left on his face and neck. But the effort of talking and the earlier struggle against the straps had left him very tired and he was soon asleep.

Karne spent the next two weeks on the man-frame, being turned "like a griddle cake," as he called it. He had so many Family visitors, Dr. Othneil finally limited visiting hours. Kit and the two older female hostages visited often, properly chaperoned by Lady Agnes, a tall, dour woman of uncertain age, or the Larga. The young women played Deeps and Fliers with him or retold the ancient legends of the Gharr.

"That's courting behavior," Karne complained to the Larga one afternoon when they were alone. "I'm tied and helpless and two young females come courting. Nerut's niece is the only female of age, and she's so colorless I can't even remember her name more than an hour at a time."

"Marienne."

"I don't care what her name is! It's embarrassing to be courted by someone I don't even like." The subject of Marienne made Karne want to turn his back and walk away, but the bonds of the manframe made even a small movement of rejection impossible. "Besides," he muttered, "the man's supposed to do the wooing."

Larga Alysha laughed. "So rumor has it, but except for the Black Ship brides, you'll find that rumor isn't really true. Watch Kathryn when she's near young von Schuss, for instance."

"Kit? Nik? Good! I hope she catches him."

"I thought you didn't like females to do the wooing."

"Kit's special."

"Were the girls on Balder 'special,' too? From Egil's stories, you didn't object to their wooing."

"It's different there." For a moment he saw Shalim— long arms and legs and curly red hair—and Nadia—petite and dark, with slanting eyes and ridiculously long lashes. "The same behavior was just friendship there. There was no—seriousness in being with a female. We enjoyed their company without thinking of marriage and appropriate

Family alliances. On Balder people marry for love or friendship."

"Ridiculous!" the Larga snorted, "and dangerous. Only carefully planned alliances hold society together. Love is for children like Kathryn and young von Schuss."

"They're both of marrying age, Lady Mother."

"They both know we don't need a marriage to tie our Houses closer. No, they'll marry elsewhere, both of them."

"What about me? Are there women of suitable rank for me among the Families? This Mariette is the only female of proper age I've met and she's intolerable. Do I marry a Freewoman?"

"Her name's Marienne. And don't be absurd. Even if the Family would permit it, the Freemen would never let you marry into them. They won't risk their precious neutrality by marrying into Houses." The Larga paused, looking thoughtful. "We could afford a Black Ship in five or six years' time, if all goes well. Maybe you and Nik and some of the Justin boys could get together and—"

"The Justins are Nik's friends, not mine. Allet Justin has refused the help he promised at Council, remember."

The Larga drew back a little, offended. "You don't need to snarl at me. The Justins protected you at Council, didn't they? What I'm trying to say is, House Halarek desperately needs another heir. Kerel's boys are south of the equator with their mother and there they'll stay, at least until our House is safe. You must think of marrying, soon, and a Black Ship bride would bring such prestige to our House."

"Five or six years is soon? Kerel's oldest will be eight or nine by then, old enough to rule through a regent."

"Humph!" The Larga tossed her head disdainfully. "If those boys are raised completely by that woman Kerel married, they're not likely to have a brain in their heads."

"She came from House Durlin, didn't she?" Karne could not help the snide insinuation in his tone.

The Larga stiffened. "I didn't say any female from the Houses would be suitable. Netta is a bewitching little thing. I suppose she can't help it if she has no brains and Kerel didn't mind." The Larga stood gracefully and smoothed the wrinkles from her skirt. "We've talked enough and I have manor business to see to. I'll be most glad when you can take the reins completely, Son." She swept out the door.

Karne smiled at the grandeur with which the tiny woman moved, but the humor faded quickly. His nose itched and he could not scratch it. His neck ached and he would have to call someone to turn him over. He needed a bedpan and that was the most humiliating part of the entirely unpleasant man-frame experience. He grimaced and sighed and pressed the call button.

After twenty-five days, Dr. Othneil freed Karne from the man-frame. "No strenuous exercise," the doctor ordered sternly, "no stretching those back muscles, no lifting, not so much as a beamer. Nothing heavier than a fork for another week, at least. I'll change your dressings in your quarters every day. Plan on it."

"Yessir, Doctor sir." Karne snapped a salute. And winced.

Othneil gave him a sour smile. "Serves you right, young man. Up five minutes and sassy already. Go on, get out of here."

Since von Schuss's cast was removed about the time Karne was released, the two men worked back to their former combat-ready physical condition together. In spite of the training, in spite of his improving physical condition, Karne knew Richard Harlan could best him in any weapons match, and he had powerful doubts about his own ability to meet and counter any move Richard, through his trustee, would make against Halarek. He knew, come Thawtime, Richard Harlan would do something toward the fulfillment of his terrible vow as soon as he could move men and equipment, and Karne had no one to lead Halarek against him. He did not want to use General Shen, because he felt strongly General Shen would not obey any orders different from what Trev Halarek would have commanded in a similar situation. Yet Karne had no equally experienced senior officer. As a result, Karne spent the remainder of Arhast and all of Koort with a sense of doom hanging over him.

He was worrying the problem as he watched the soldiers from Konnor, McNeece, and von Schuss training daily with the Blues; the men of the two minor Houses had been unable to return home after the oath-feast because of the weather and had been granted permission to fight with

Halarek. Karne reminded himself grimly that such permission came only because no House would feed extra men for the winter if those men would not fight for that House. Without such a promise, Trev would have sent all two hundred away, to let the storms of Uhl do what they would. He worried the problem each day after military drills when he went over and over the lists of men and supplies that would be needed to successfully fight off a siege. Each time Karne went over the lists, he looked for an officer to replace General Shen. There was no one of comparable experience, no one. Every time he got to this point in his thinking, the process stalled, because Karne had to face the thought that he, as Head-of-House, would have to lead the fight against Harlan himself, armed only with book knowledge. The thought frightened and appalled him. He had already done what he thought was best for Halarek in dealing with Farm 3 and with the rebellious vassals. Each time, the Gharr had condemned him for cowardice. Each time he had lost supporters, and the loss of Justin was a disaster that could not be mended except with a decisive win over Harlan in the next encounter.

In addition, there was the strong possibility that, since Asten Harlan was dead, Thawtime Council could end the Harlan trusteeship at once and, with Harlan allies in the majority, it probably would. Council could even decide to remove the Larga as regent, install some other regent, or remove Karne and replace him as Lharr in Halarek, just because he would not be of age until a month after the Council meeting.

As a result, Karne learned to live with disaster hanging over his shoulder. For the rest of the Family, the winter passed in its usual fashion—taking inventories, making weekly trips to chapel for First Day services, visiting by tri-d with friends and vassals, and reading or playing games for hours. Egil was bored and fussy before Koort was half gone.

"How can you stand this?" he demanded plaintively of Karne in a private corner of the library. "Everyone sits around playing and gossiping—" Egil paused to watch Nik and Kit, with the chaperone, leave, and his eyes gleamed speculatively. "Nik, now, has something interesting to think about."

"It's just baby-love. They'll get over it."

"Hmmm," was all Egil answered. He stood and stretched until his joints cracked. "I want to do something. At home, we ski, race ice-boats—"

"'At home' the wind wouldn't blow you from here to the equator," Karne snorted. "You'd arrive there frozen solid. Nobody goes out in Koort, even for an emergency. We were lucky to get all our Specials back the day of Roul's crash."

"Give me something to do with my hands, then, Karne. I feel like I could crawl out of my skin."

Karne looked at his friend and his mouth twisted thoughtfully. He chewed his lower lip. "You did some portraits of Nadia once, and the big picture of the Academy's mall that blew up with my cabin on the *Aldefara*. Paint me something on the bare wall across from my bed, something to remember you by when you've gone home. Some of the crafthalls in Ontar can supply you with materials."

Egil started for the door at once. He touched Karne's shoulder on his way past. "Thanks, brother. Maybe my skin and I will still be together come Thawtime."

"Can you find your way?" Karne called after him.

"You know me. I can find my way out of a labyrinth blindfolded."

Karne smiled to himself. It was true; Egil had an uncanny sense of direction.

Egil settled into his new project immediately. "Heimdal at the gates of Aasgard in the evening of the old gods, scenery from Balder," he told everyone who asked what he was doing and many who did not, told them at length, and in glowing detail.

On 8 Nemb, the Gild broadcast to all members of the World Council that Gild and Patrol officials had finished the investigation of the *Aldefara* affair, that the trial had begun, and that it should be concluded by 1 Verdain, ten days before the Thawtime Council. Like everyone else on Starker IV, the Halareks gathered to watch the tri-d cast.

"Why has it taken them so long, Karne?" Kit asked when the announcement ended and the picture of the First Merchant's office disappeared.

"The Patrol ship nearest Starker was three Gild-weeks away. When the Patrol arrived, the crew and the three surviving passengers had to be questioned, evidence found and analyzed. Then the Patrol had to find a jury of peers on Telek's home

world and conduct a trial over monitors. All the
while, someone from Gild or Patrol had to pacify
the governments of the passenger witnesses, explaining why free citizens were being held in protective custody above a backwater world instead
of going about their business elsewhere. The trial
process is very expensive and maybe the Gild had
to borrow money from another Gild sector to help
pay for it. In the Federation, the common govern-
ment pays for such long-distance trials. Here, the
Gild must spend its own profits to protect its reputation, and that does not make the directors of the
Gild at all happy."

Karne looked thoughtfully at the now-blank
tri-d screen. The surface blurred and disappeared
as his mind turned inward, to the consequences of
the trial for Halarek and Starker IV. He continued
speaking to Kit without taking his eyes from the
screen. "The First Merchant told me this morning
that, as of this day, the Gild will never again carry
a Family passenger anywhere. From now on we're
trapped in our own system. No more pleasure
trips." Karne took a shuddering breath, then continued with a bitter edge to his words. "The Black
Ships are all other worlds will know of us now—
kidnapping and terror, and killing sometimes…
Guardians! The Gild protects its profits at Starker
IV's cost! How can our world become more like
Federated worlds if no one can visit them? Starker
will stagnate, then rot in its traditions and barba-
risms!"

Kit put out a comforting hand. Karne flung it off
and bolted from the room. Kit found him again,
much later, sitting cross-legged on his bed, staring

at Heimdal, already painted in his place at the end of the Rainbow Bridge with his horn to his lips and black thunderheads piling high above the mountains of Jotunheim.

"I didn't realize until now that I look at our world like that, Kit. I hate the cruelty here and the senseless traditions, traditions kept only because they've always been kept. If the Gild shuts us out and the Freemen keep themselves apart, the Jotuns of Starker IV will take over." Karne stared at his hands, knotted together on his knees.

"Our side hasn't lost yet, Karne." Kit's voice was soft, almost a whisper.

Karne wriggled his back. "No? I was lucky with the beamer. The next time—"

Kit flung her arms around him and squeezed hard. "Oh, Karne, I don't want to lose you!"

Karne smoothed her soft brown hair. "It's the way of our world, little sister, as you told me not many months ago. How many of the last ten Lharrs lived more than thirty winters?"

"Four."

"More than forty winters?"

"One."

"I have to look that in the face and learn to accept it, Kit, and it's hard, oh, it's hard!" Karne put his arms around her and rocked side to side, his face in her warm hair, feeling her tears on his neck. "I love life and I love my family. I want to have children and grandchildren. I want to be old. Oh, Kit, I wanted to stay on Balder!" There was a long silence, then Karne lifted his head and tipped Kit's back so she looked up at him. "I didn't want you to know that, Kit. I haven't told anyone else."

Kit buried her damp face in his neck again and held him fiercely tight. They were still that way when Gareth called from outside the door. "Council Chairman deVree requires your presence in the tri-d room, milord."

"Can't it wait?"

"Nay, lord. He says now. Council rules, something like that."

Karne set Kit away, brushed the tears from her cheeks, kissed her, and got up. He changed his wet and wrinkled tunic for a dry one, then told Kit, "You can stay here until you feel better."

In the tri-d room, the Larga, Orkonan, Weisman, and General Shen stood waiting. On the screen, Chairman deVree looked up from some papers he was reading.

"Ah, Halarek. You look like you recovered well from your burn."

"Well enough, milord. What does the Council want of me?"

"It is Council law that any House intending to besiege another give forty days public notice, so that neutrals in the dispute and noncombatants may leave the siege area." DeVree cleared his throat. "The Earl of Kingsland, as trustee for House Harlan, announces a siege of Ontar manor and city, Halarek Holding, to begin forty days from this or 8 Kerensten of the new year."

"No noncombatant can possibly leave before 20 Kerensten! You know the weather in Thawtime, milord!"

"Sorry, Halarek. The law says nothing about delays for weather. Kingsland and Harlan have fulfilled the law. Prepare for siege." DeVree abruptly broke the connection and his image disappeared.

Chapter Twelve

———◆———

KARNE STARED AT the tri-d screen, stunned. "How can Council permit it?" he whispered. "It's the letter of the law but my entire Family could be wiped out if no one can leave. Technician, get Kingsland." Karne stood tensely in front of the Larga's empty chair, waiting. After several minutes, a stark tri-d room appeared on the screen, and in a few minutes more, a lean, sharp-featured man in his early twenties walked into the room. He looked coolly out at Karne. "You wanted to see me, Halarek?"

"I wanted to see the Earl."

"I am the Earl. My sire had an unfortunate accident in late Koort. Did you have business with Kingsland, or with my sire?"

Karne knew panic. He kept it from showing, but only just. This was not the man he had thought to reason into withholding siege until after 20 Kerensten. This man had no justice in his face. This face was harsh, willful, violent. Karne suddenly understood how Harlan had acquired his trustee's consent for siege. An "accident" had brought to power a more pliable lord. Karne willed his hands to stop shaking and saluted the new lord of Kingsland. "Peace be on your House, my lord."

"What is your business, Halarek?" The new lord stared at Karne with hard, unfriendly eyes.

Karne stiffened a little. "I ask you to allow time for my noncombatants to leave the manor."

"You have the time. You have the legal forty days, Halarek."

Frustration and anger warred with the Academy's training in Karne. The Academy's training won. Karne took a deep, unobtrusive breath and spoke to the Earl in a level voice. "You know as well as I do that flying isn't safe until after 20 Kerensten."

"It's as safe as the weather in mid-Uhl, when your vassals had to send their hostages to you." Kingsland paused for his meaning to sink in. "Do you still complain of the timing, my lord?" The Earl's voice was smooth and very, very pleasant.

Karne permitted no sign of his anger and despair to show on his face. "I grieve for your sire's untimely death, my lord," he said quietly and cut the connection.

Karne waved the techs out of the room and sat slowly in the Larga's chair. Ingold Kingsland had allied with Harlan, perhaps had hurried Earl Nellis's end to allow a new trustee to give consent to siege, something the old Earl would never have done, not in early Kerensten. A new problem, before the previous ones were solved. Siege meant Karne could no longer put off a decision about General Shen. There would be other officers who followed General Shen. The midst of battle or siege was not the time to find that a general or some of his officers were not going to follow orders. Karne's mouth thinned to a hard line. He would do something about those officers immediately.

He called a general-staff meeting in the Great Hall. While he waited for the officers to come, he paced back and forth in front of the dais, raking his hands through his hair and planning how to trap any officers not completely loyal to him into admitting it. Then he would have to make whatever officers remained want to follow him. Centen Roth and his Specials entered the Hall, followed by Centen Wynter and his five troopleaders. The others came quickly after. Karne looked out at the tense, expectant faces. He began abruptly, for the shock effect. "Harlan has declared siege, to begin 8 Kerensten." He stopped and waited for the uproar of surprise and outrage to quiet. "We have forty days to reinventory our supplies of food, weapons, and ammunition; to strengthen our position on the surface, if possible; and to prepare evacuation of the Family to their own small-holdings as soon as possible."

"Siege is truly set for 8 Kerensten?" an officer toward the front asked Karne, unbelieving.

"Yes. We're here to plan for that and for preparing the Family for a very difficult escape, perhaps an impossible one. You heard Harlan's vow. This is how he plans to crush our House."

General Shen stood. "Excuse me, young lord, but I don't think we'll need evacuation. We're invulnerable here. We can—"

"I didn't ask anyone's opinion about whether or

not to evacuate, General," Karne interrupted sharply. "I've thought about our options since Narn. In Thawtime, we can be ruined by a long siege. Our supplies are low and will get lower until Gild freighters can fly again early in Kerensten, just when Harlan sets up his siege force. Do you think he'll let our freight lifts operate? Do you think he'll leave the stair exits unblocked for us to retrieve misdropped shipments?"

General Shen's feelings were visibly ruffled. "Young man, I was practicing tactics on the battlefield while you were practicing standing up!"

The crowd of officers murmured uneasily.

Karne fixed the general with a fierce look that brought a thin sheen of sweat to the man's face. "Insubordination is a serious offense anytime, General," Karne said in a quiet tone, "but when the House is under attack, it's treason."

The general paled, then pulled himself together. His bearing said plainly, "This was only Trev's third son, after all." He turned to the officers. "Here's how we should proceed. If we leave the surface pad-gate open, even in a power cutoff the enemy can't—"

"General Shen," Karne interrupted in a deceptively calm voice, "who are your favorite staff officers?"

Shen looked nonplussed for a moment, then named a dozen men. Karne called Centens Roth, Wynter, and Martin to him.

"Select loyal men from this room, search these twelve officers, and confine them to quarters until the siege is over. General Shen will be confined, alone, in a secured cell until such time as I decide what to do with him."

The centens began immediately to obey.

"M-M-My lord, what have I done?" General Shen looked and sounded genuinely bewildered.

"You treat me as if I were still a boy, General, as if I were the boy my sire thought me. I am the Lharr, and I rule here. Your attempt to take over the planning just now was your last act as a Halarek officer." Karne ripped the general-rank insignia from Shen's tunic. "It is only because I am not my sire that I didn't draw my stunner and kill you right here." Karne nodded curtly at Wynter. "Take him away."

Whispering swept through the remaining officers like a wind and like wind it died away. Karne stood straighter and watched Wynter step up to the general and disarm him. He looked out over the room. "If there are other officers whose first loyalty is to Trev Halarek or to one of the thirteen officers now dismissed, leave now. You'll go pension-paid for your honesty and will receive free quarters in Ontar until you can leave the Holding. This House needs officers who will put the House first."

A very young troopleader near the back of the group stood. "General Shen is my uncle, lord. I go with him." His voice trembled.

Karne looked at the young man's white face and frightened eyes. "I'm not Trev Halarek, to terrify you so," he chided the troopleader. "I commend your courage for speaking out and I'll keep my word with you. Are there others?"

Seven other troopleaders, one centen, three captains, two pilots, and four squadleaders left from loyalty to the arrested officers. Karne waited a few minutes, to be sure no one else was going to leave, ordered the thirteen arrested officers taken to their secured quarters, then began talking about preparations. "The ironmongers have already been called in to make a grate for the conservatory skylight, our most vulnerable point. We'll construct heavy walls around the flitter pad-gate and all three surface exits. The exit stairs must not be taken, no matter what the cost. Is that clear?"

The officers nodded and murmured agreement. Karne thought a quick prayer of thanks that bombs and grenades were unknown on Starker IV. Family code required hand-to-hand fighting, one-to-one. "We'll leave the freight lifts as they are," he continued, "but shut off the power to them and to the lift that goes up to the manor garden. Captain Rad, direct two of your engineers to check the circuits. If other power draws from those three circuits, we have time to get them changed."

Rad nodded and wrote the instructions on his order pad.

"Centens Roth, Wynter, and Martin back yet?"

"Here, lord."

"How many of your Century are still in the clinic, Martin?"

"Twelve, lord."

"Wynter, of yours?"

"Just one, my lord."

"Roth?"

"More than twenty, lord."

"Then your Century will be backup for the ones on the surface." Karne looked Roth over carefully;

the man was pale and still very thin. "You haven't recovered completely yourself, from what Dr. Othneil says. I do want one troop of your Specials up top with Wynter, though." Karne paused to check his own quick notes of what he had said. "These officers will move to new commands: Captain Rad, take the Fourth Century as soon as you get your engineers started; Troopleader Gregg, take the engineers; Troopleaders Karsen and Waltt, move up to captaincy. Jenkins, Phillipson, von Schuss, Yan Willem, Dennen Willem—take troopleader spots."

"But we're pilots, Lord Karne," they said, almost as one man.

"Pilots we can't use now, troopleaders we need. This will be ground fighting in rough weather. The two open pilot positions will stay open until the siege is over. There are still four troops and four squads without leaders. Centens, you know your officers. If you have an opening, fill it with the best man you've got. Have I covered everything?"

"How about Olafson? Where does he fight?" a young squadleader at the edge of the crowd shouted.

"He's off-world. To use him would be treason against Starker IV. You know that."

A captain in the back stood. "He says he's your brother-by-choice, that you have the same blood. If that's so, then he's not really off-world."

Karne held up his right arm and pulled back the sleeve so the livid scar on his wrist was clearly visible.

"A brother! A brother!" and "My troop! Put him in my troop!" the officers roared.

When the noise downed, Karne raised a hand to finish the quieting. "What's so special about Egil?"

Yan Willem stood to answer. "If you were a manor dog going out to fight a pack of wolves, would you want a friendly Zinn bear to help? He has the size of two men and the strength of three."

"But if he's my brother and acceptable to fight, he goes with me. He's my brother."

After the laughter died away, Waltt stood. "I don't wish to share the general's fate, my lord, but why will there be ground fighting? Ontar has out-lasted winter sieges before."

"Those were in early winter. Uhl drove the at-tackers off. This is Thawtime, before our freight drops, as I said at the beginning. We can be starved out. That's why we're going to attack Harlan from out of the foothills. We're going to build shelters hidden in the pines, weather giving us any chance at all, and attack Harlan's rear. We have to drive Harlan off or we're his."

"What are our chances, lord?"

"Better than if we sit down here. How much bet-ter—?" Karne shrugged. "The Academy trained me to stop wars, not fight them. But I was also taught tactics, I've ended rebellions by slaves and vassals in record time, no matter what outsiders say about how I did those things, and I know the value of surprise. Lord Richard thought to surprise us with a very early siege. Gentlemen, we'll give him a much bigger surprise."

The officers cheered the thought.

Karne raised his hands for quiet and lifted his head proudly. "Most important, I'm ready to die for my House if necessary. I don't plan for it to be necessary."

Someone in the back started it. Soon the cry rang through the Great Hall. "Halarek lives! Halarek lives!"

The waiting began. Karne appointed Roth commander in the manor, with von Schuss under him; Wynter commander of the surface defenders of the manor; and an older troopleader named Kyle and himself to lead the two attacks from the foothills. Since soldiers on both sides would be wearing white survival suits, Karne ordered reversible collars made for his men so they could reverse the collars to Halarek blue in close fighting and distinguish friend from enemy. House von Schuss promised more troops if the weather cleared enough to fly transports in. Only the few soldiers chosen to be part of the secret force knew about the attack on Harlan's rear from the foothills.

The first small thaw of Kerensten, the Day of the New Year, came and went, uncelebrated. All the New Year meant this year was decent weather for the engineers to build shelters in the hills. On 5 Kerensten, Kyle, Karne, and their troops set off for their shelters. Kyle went east, to a shelter built among the sentinel rocks near Zinn. Karne, Egil, and Yan Willem took Willem's troop to the shelter below Dur Peak, north of the manor, at the foot of the high pass. Each man in each troop carried a pack with two weeks' supplies of thermo-fuel and dried food, plus a nightbag. Willem also carried the troop's medpak.

They reached their shelter in half a day, near evening. The shelter had been built of bluepine logs and camouflaged with branches the engineers had trimmed off. Snow on the roof glistened in the sunlight and the shelter's eaves dripped quietly. Karne hoped that when Harlan's pilots flew over, none of them would notice the new-cut stumps. The men filed into the shelter and dropped their packs on the floor. Karne set an observer on the tall boulder flanking the building. Willem appointed two cooks, who began preparing an early nightmeal.

During the first night, a storm came howling down the pass. The bluepines roared like a waterfall as the wind whipped their tops from side to side as if they were blades of grass. Icy air seeped through cracks between the shelter wall's logs. The night guard set up six extra thermoes to keep the room temperature above the danger point. Karne did not sleep, only partly from the cold, for now he was out and away from the manor, his plan seemed thin and weak and without a chance of succeeding. He imagined their shelter discovered immediately, attacked, and overrun by superior numbers. He pictured his men, Egil and Willem especially, dying in a hopeless fight.

He was up as soon as the wind quit screaming around the building and was outside at first light. In the cold, trees were popping with sharp, cracking sounds. Huge snowflakes floated through the air, powdering the trees, blurring the view of the manor grounds, settling into and filling up the tracks the troop of men had made. Karne felt a little of his tension ease. They could not now be tracked, and the large snowflakes told him the upper air was warmer; there would be another thaw along soon. Other men came out, too, to see what, if anything, was happening. Some of them swore at the cold.

"Lord Karne! A fighter, coming low. There. To the west!"

Karne stopped at the foot of the observation rock and looked. The soldier who shouted had been on his way to the lookout post on top of the rock. He silently handed Karne the observer's distance glass. The craft was definitely a fighter, marked with the black-and-white Odonnel checks. Everyone except the observer ducked into the shelter, out of sight. The observer flattened himself against the boulder until the fighter could no longer see him, then climbed up the rock.

"I thought they'd be early," Willem remarked sourly from his place in the doorway.

Karne stepped past him and watched through the glass. "Transports and fighters from Harlan and Odonnel have landed on the plain south and west of the manor grounds," he reported. "They're unloading about nine Centuries. They must have risked flying above the storm," he added conversationally to the men in the shelter, "just to escape being seen by any of the Holdings they passed over. Richard must be sure no one's going to live to report this second violation to Council. Those transports also mean he's had our coms jammed— no, look!" He pointed across the plain to one of the Halarek com dishes. A lone man in Harlan green ducked under the rim of the dish and out again, then the rest of a troop attacked the dish with

pipes and stunner butts until it hung shattered
and unusable. "He's had the wires cut, then his
men disable the dish, just in case we send anyone
up to try to fix the wires." Karne made no attempt
to conceal his rage. "By my Sire's Blood! I'll wager
the manor had no time to send a protest. Perhaps
no one yet knows the siege is set." Karne swore
feelingly, then turned to his men. "Harlan seems to
be assuming no one in the manor will survive to
inform on him. Some of us must survive to tell
Council what happened here, no matter what happens to the rest of us. Egil," he called, "come out
here a minute, will you, bring a couple of nightbags for our watcher. That rock has to be cold."

Egil came, ducking his head to avoid hitting the
lintel. He backed far enough from the shelter that
he could see the man lying on the rock and then
hurl two nightbags up to him. The soldier immediately unrolled one and lay down on it.

Karne climbed partway up and handed the soldier the distance glass. "Put the other bag on top of
you. Insulation." Karne then steered Egil to a spot
in the lee of a clump of bluepines. He put an arm
across Egil's shoulders, as if they were talking
merely about friendship matters, and spoke very
quietly. "Harlan's three days early, with about nine
Centuries. I think Richard plans to batter his way
in and take the manor before anyone off-Holding
learns what's happening. What do you think?"

Egil looked down at his boots, his mouth pursed
thoughtfully. "Sounds likely. They can't mean to
feed that many men for long and, from what you
say about Kerensten, he can't rely on being able to
fly food in."

Karne sensed his friend was giving him support but no advice. He was the Lharr, the decision had to be his, and he did not want it. The weight of his inexperience pressed on him. Below on the plain, the besiegers were setting up barracks-domes in a circle around the manor garden.

"Maybe they plan to forage." Egil's mouth twisted to one side. He stroked his chin thoughtfully. "Heimdal only knows what they could find in this godforsaken cold." Egil beat his hands against his arms. "Even your thermal mittens don't keep my hands warm enough. How do you expect your men to fire their weapons in mittens?"

"They have liner mittens warm enough for a few minutes in the cold. The outside mitten hangs by a clip while the man is firing. There may be frostbite, but no frozen fingers. I hope. Guardians! Why do I have to make such decisions!"

"Because you're the Lharr," Egil answered simply. "It's too late to change that."

"It was too late the day I was born." Karne's tone was bitter and hopeless.

Egil put a hand on Karne's shoulder. "Let's go back to the shelter and get warm, brother."

Karne paced slowly back toward the shelter, head down, face thoughtful. He stopped several meters from the shelter door. "Wynter won't know right away what's happening out there, and we have no way to tell him. That means we have one or two days more to watch the enemy and do nothing. And that could be an advantage. It could also be a disaster. If we have a bad storm..."

Egil squeezed Karne's shoulder. "You're thinking well. Believe in yourself."

Karne looked up. "Believe in myself? No one else does." The words came out rough and hard-edged.

Egil looked thoughtful. "All the more reason for you to, because you're right and eventually everyone on Starker IV will know it." He shoved his hands into his armpits to warm them and looked out across the plain.

Karne stared at his friend's broad back. There was truth in him. Karne Halarek could not go back to being like the Gharr had always been. He would try new ways when they were better than traditional ways and when he knew the new ways, even on his tradition-tied world, could work if they were given the chance. Karne's determination firmed. It would be better to be dead than to be one with the cruel, arbitrary rulers who had always controlled the Nine Families.

The night was calm and next morning the observer reported the enemy was making feints at the escape entrances. The observer also reported a few motionless bodies beside several of the domes.

"Some soldiers got up in the night and your Specials got them," Willem commented, with some satisfaction.

"So Wynter now knows," Karne said, more to himself than to anyone else. He turned to the observer just leaving the shelter for duty. "Keep your eyes open for a rush from the main stairwell. That's our signal to start back down." He turned to the rest of the men. "Richard's friends are going to think they can beat that rush back and Wynter will let them do it. We're to be at the perimeter of Harlan's camp just after dark the same night. We have to drive our enemies back to their fliers that night and early morning, with help from our allies, God willing. Wynter planned to wait until House von Schuss, at least, arrived, but no one expected the siege to be set early. Wynter can judge what's happening down there better than we can. If his Specials say 'go,' we'll all go."

A young soldier touched Karne's arm. The boy licked his lips. "I've—I've never killed anyone before, lord."

Karne smiled at him crookedly, reassuringly. "Neither have I, soldier, but Richard Harlan has promised to destroy my House to the last stone and has brought his friends to help him do it. We're here to stop them." Karne put a hand on the youngster's shoulder. "How old are you?"

"Sixt—fifteen winters, lord." He rushed on, afraid now he had told the truth. "We needed the money, milord. My mother's a weaver and there are five of us..."

Karne looked at the boy. Was I ever that young? he wondered. Two years' difference in our ages and I feel like it's twenty. "I'm assigning you to guard the shelter when we go down to the manor. We may need to fall back here and I want the supplies protected. Understand?"

"Y-yes, milord."

Karne watched relief flood the young soldier's face and envied him. There's no way I can avoid the fighting, he reminded himself. I have to be out in front and I don't want to die, either.

Karne went to a rock beside the shelter door and sat down. He looked toward the manor. A stiff wind blew from the mountains. Karne heard the boy inside proudly asking Willem for a double ration of beamer bolts to protect the shelter.

Does he know what those to do a man? Karne twitched his shoulders, remembering. I don't know whether I can ever use one again. He brought his mind back to the plain below him. Where, oh, where is House von Schuss? You'd think they'd come a day early to set up.

The skies stayed clear all day and the temperature dropped. No friendly fliers appeared. Karne sat on the observation rock and stared out over the plains.

"Why don't they come?"

The soldier lying beside him on the rock put down the distance glass and looked up. "Storms usually come from the west, lord. Probably von Schuss Holding's in one now. Temperature's been dropping."

Karne curled the icy tips of his fingers against his palms to warm them. "No one expected Harlan to attack before the legal time. Though after the last few months' experience, we should have," he added bitterly.

Karne slid off the boulder and returned to the shelter. Troopers sprawled on the floor and leaned against the walls. Someone had carved several pairs of dice from wood scraps left inside the shelter and two groups of men with dice crouched in circles, playing. Egil, a spectator at the edge of one of these circles, looked up questioningly.

"No sign of them," Karne answered. "I only hope the Gild satellites have been taking pix of this."

"How much longer?"

"I can't believe anything less than impossible flying weather would've kept Emil from coming today. Wynter won't make his charge until he knows von Schuss is in the air. At least that was the plan before the com lines were cut. Who knows what he'll do now."

That night the wind rose. It sighed and whistled around the eaves and corners of the shelter. With morning came snow, hard ice pellets that clicked against the shelter's log walls and rattled on the crust of ice covering the snow already on the ground. When the storm finally howled itself out three days later, an observer went to the rock again. He was back in less than an hour. He saluted Karne and reported, "There's such a layer of ice on the rock I can't climb it, lord. I did climb the ridge behind us until I could see over the trees, but that's all I could see. There's an ice fog below."

Karne's lips tightened into a thin, straight line, but he said nothing for a time. Finally he allowed himself a small sigh. "May as well sit down, soldier, we aren't going anywhere until House von Schuss does."

They waited through fog, rain, sleet, high winds, and more rain, rain often accompanied by midday thaws that glazed and reglazed the fallen snow. On the fifth day of waiting, Karne ordered everyone onto half-rations. To the first man who grumbled Willem snarled, "You going to walk through Odonnel's Centuries to get more?"

"We get two weeks' rations out of one week's supply," Karne explained. "We'll need it if this sort of weather holds up."

Inside himself, Karne no longer felt confident even *two* weeks would see them back inside the manor. His plan for a surprise attack now seemed hasty and naive, his goal of driving his enemies

back to their fliers, hopeless. He watched the food
and fuel stores shrink and resolved that if no help
arrived by 25 Kerensten, he would try sneaking his
men through the Harlan lines and somehow get
them inside the manor barricades.

23 Kerensten dawned clear and cold. The sun
appeared for the first time in twelve days and
many of the troopers went outside to slither on the
ice and enjoy the sunlight. An observer lay on the
rock again. The bluepines' pointed tops drooped
with the weight of ice and snow on them, and several times Karne heard trees crashing down in the
forest, broken by the weight they carried. He
checked over the food again—six or seven days'
full rations left—and had the men check their
packs to be sure all the emergency supplies and
the ammunition were inside. The checking and
double-checking finished in late afternoon. It was
routine by now, this checking of packs every two
days. There had even been some mention, by an
anonymous voice from the back of the shelter,
about old women and their constant worrying. The
remark had been worth a chuckle.

Karne stepped outside the shelter to watch Egil
demonstrating the first moves of elementary Drinn
wrestling. Moves that looked graceful on Drinn mats
looked awkward demonstrated in a survival suit on
packed snow. Others of the men crouched in the snow
whittling or eating, or just enjoying sunshine. Karne
noticed as he walked toward the demonstration that
the snow no longer crunched under his feet. It com-
pressed with a faint squishing sound. And melt was
beginning to drip from the shelter roof.

"There they go!" the observer shouted.

Heads flew up from whatever had been occupying them.

"Quiet!" Willem ordered. "The echo!"

"Sorry, Lord Karne." The observer did not look very sorry; he looked jubilant now that the waiting was over. "Wynter's men rushed a troop on patrol. They're being beaten back now, my lord, just like you said."

Movement outside the shelter had stopped at the observer's shout. Now it began again. Men ran to the shelter for their packs. Others picked up whittling sticks, food wrappers, and other evidence of human passing. Karne stuck his head in the shelter door. "Up, everyone. We're on the road."

The men inside cheered. They flung on their packs and lined up in rows on the snow in front of the shelter. Willem counted to be sure no one had wandered off into the woods briefly, then twenty-five men, their troopleader, Karne, and Egil were slipping from tree to tree down the soggy slope. By the time they reached the edge of the plain, the sun had gone down. Fluffy snowflakes powdered the men's hair and eyebrows and laid a slippery layer over snow turning again to ice. Willem directed soldiers to set up the thermoes behind trees where their small glow would not be seen. The troop settled down around the warmth to wait for full dark.

"Flip your collars blue side out once the fighting starts," Karne ordered. "It will keep your friends down there from killing you. We have surprise on our side—no one on Starker IV has ever done this before—we have excellent manor defenses, and we

have an experienced ground commander in Centen
Wynter. We'll break into Wynter's zone tonight and
from then even I follow his orders. Richard Harlan
is brash and clever, but he has no more experience
leading an army than I have. We will drive Harlan
off. We have to."

Chapter Thirteen

———◆———

WHEN ALL THE lights but the watch-lamps went out
in the Harlan camp, Karne and his men moved out
onto the plain, crouching, creeping, stopping to look
for signs they had been seen. The rest of the men
followed. They heard nothing from the Harlan
watch, not on their side of the enemy camp, not from
Kyle's side. A dark shape crossed the half-moon, its
engine throbbing. Karne looked up with hope.

"Von Schuss transport!" Yan Willem whispered,
and the news spread quickly down the line of
creeping men.

"Landing lights dropping south of Kyle's position, about a kilometer out on the plain," one of
the enlisted men added, his voice speeding up with
excitement.

"We're going to get them. We're not alone anymore. Let's go!" Karne stood and ran toward the
nearest barracks-dome.

He and his men surrounded the dome and

beamed it, melting it and most of its sleeping occupants. They moved quickly, beamed a second
dome, and were heading for a third before Harlan's watch raised the alarm. The third dome was
rousing when they hit it and the troop lost its first
man. Across the encampment another dome's
glowing debris showed where Kyle's men had entered the Harlan camp.

"That's most of four Centuries, men!" Dennen
cried. "Halarek lives!"

The troop joined the cry, voices high with excitement. "Halarek lives! Harlarek lives!"

Beacons flashed on and began sweeping the
area. Harlan and Odonnel troopers poured out of
their barracks, still pressing closed their survival
suits. Some of the soldiers carried homing-
beamers, which targeted body heat. Karne's men
huddled in the shadow of a dome.

"Fools! Those homers don't know enemies from
friends!" Egil snapped. The yellow track of a
beamer flashed over his head.

"They see us! Melt down the dome," Karne
shouted. "We'll get away in its heat-shadow."

The noise—shouting, firing, burning—was too
loud for four of the men to hear Karne's shout; they
continued to crouch against the dome. Egil dropped
to the snow and snaked along the dome wall to
them. "We're burning this," he told them. "When it
goes up, Lord Karne says head for the main stairwell. Wynter's men should be coming now."

The men scrambled to their feet and ran. One
stopped in his tracks and fell. A companion bent,
touched his throat pulse, sprang up, and ran after

the others. "Stunner, milord," he panted when he joined the group. "Peters is dead."

"Stick together," Karne ordered. "We'll all live longer that way."

A beamer bolt zipped into the group. One man spat out an oath.

"Bad hurt?" Karne demanded.

"No, lord, just my cheek."

"If any of you are using stunners, be sure they're set to kill," Karne ordered the others, and checked his own.

"Aye, lord," the men replied.

They burned the dome and escaped toward the main stair. But Harlan's forces were awake now and far outnumbered the two Halarek troops. Karne's men were pushed back to the edge of the circle of barracks by Odonnel troopers, led by the Lharr Timkin Odonnel himself, the checkered circled pennant snapping over Odonnel's head. The noise of battle suddenly rose near the center of the circle, but snow had begun falling again and it and the darkness concealed from Karne what was happening.

"That noise must be Wynter's men," a prefet of Blues shouted. His gun swept sideways and beamed an Odonnel troopleader, whose fall confused the men following him.

"They'll have to fight—their way over here—before—they can do us—any good," Dennen Willem panted, finishing off an Odonnel troopleader. He pulled his knife from his opponent and wiped it quickly against his white pants.

"Watch out!" Karne cried.

Willem dropped to the snow. A heat-bolt zipped

past him at waist level. Two other Halarek soldiers did not dodge in time.

"Fire now!" Dennen's voice rang out over the screams of the dying men.

The front rank of Halarek soldiers fired their beamers at once. Most of two rows of Odonnel men fell, but still the enemy came on.

"There's Halarek, by the big pale one," Timkin Odonnel shouted, pointing. "I want him alive."

Karne braced himself and steadied his stunner with his free hand, then fired. Odonnel looked surprised, then crumpled out of sight among the feet of his men. His men stopped, the pennant dipped, then collapsed as the standard-bearer jammed its staff into the snow beside the dead Lharr. The Odonnel troops milled around until someone shouted "forward" and they began moving against Halarek again, a few at first, solidifying into a wedge that shoved hard against the Halarek line. Karne's men fell back. Soldiers at the rear of the Odonnel force began falling to Wynter's men, who were lying in the snow behind Odonnel, firing long-range stunners with deadly accuracy. A man among Willem's troop screamed and fell.

"Push them back! Push them back onto Wynter's guns!" Karne shouted. He pushed forward into the Odonnel line, plunged his knife into the first man he met, and used the man's body as a shield while he sprayed the man's neighbors with his stunner. Don't think about the men on the ground, he ordered himself. Don't think about their families. It's your Family or theirs.

He plowed farther into the Odonnel ranks with Egil at his side. Now the two sides fought too close for anything but knives and narrow-beam stunning. Karne heard thuds and cries of pain behind him, but the men with him continued to press close.

They follow me! he exulted. Against these odds, they follow me! Elation swept him and he gave a great shout. He felt power sweeping through him and roaring out through his voice. Odonnel's men felt it, too. They hesitated, backed away from him, and Willem's men smashed into the space. Karne fought in a circle of Halarek soldiers now. Egil lunged repeatedly into the enemy, breaking opponents with a wrestling hold long-barred from match-play on Balder.

"Faster than a knife," said Egil, panting. He ducked deeper into the cluster of Halarek men to take a moment's rest, then lunged back into the battle. Karne's men shoved the enemy back onto Wynter's guns until the Harlanites broke and ran. The two Halarek forces joined and fanned out, moving back toward the Harlan domes.

"Von Schuss troopers comin' in from the far side, lord," one of Wynter's men said. "Saw them as we came over the barricade."

There was no time for thought about von Schuss; a Century in Harlan green charged through a curtain of falling snow, smashing into Halarek's right flank, scattering Halarek soldiers in all directions.

"Keep together!" Karne cried to his men.

But only sixteen answered the call. They edged toward the protection of a dome wall. More Harlan troops appeared, cutting between Karne's men and Wynter's. For a time, blowing snow concealed the casualties of friend and enemy alike, then the

wind died for a moment and Karne saw that more
than half the Harlan Century survived. In seconds,
the wind picked up again, hurling stinging, blind-
ing pellets of snow at everyone and erasing sight of
Harlan's men and Wynter's and the main entrance
shelters. They could not move without Egil's sense
of direction. With it Karne knew they could fight
toward the entrance shelter, a fight few would survive, or they could use Egil to retreat to the foothills and live to fight again.

He turned to the snow-whipped troop, his eyes
searching out his large friend. "Egil, I need you.
Lead us back to the trees." Karne looked at the
other men, eyes narrowed against the sharp, icy
pellets. Surely they would not consider retreat
cowardice under such conditions. Would they?

"Just sixteen of us got no chance against what's
left of that Century," a man at the back of the group
said, hesitantly, and looked at the others as if to
judge whether they thought his remark cowardly.

Several others nodded agreement. Karne shut
his eyes for a second in relief, then motioned Egil
to lead.

The foothills were an occasional dark mound
visible only for a second or two through whirling
snow. Behind the troop, Harlan beacons fitfully
swept the plain, but the light was smudged to use-
lessness by the blowing snow. The troop lost four
men to chance encounters with the enemy before
they reached the safety of the hills. They crouched
against tree trunks, panting, and shaking with relief. They were still alive.

"What's the visibility now, Egil?" Karne demanded.

Egil squinted into the snow. He shut his eyes and brushed ice crystals from his lashes, then looked again. "Five meters, maybe."

Karne nodded his thanks and turned to his men. "Who's hurt here?"

The lone prefet set up a light. The trees caught much of the snow and broke up the wind, so visibility was much better than on the open plain. Dennen Willem had a broken nose and finger. Four soldiers had injuries serious enough to make traveling difficult for them and one trooper had been so badly burned he would have to be carried. Karne threw a glance around the survivors. "Set up the litter from your medpak, Yan. On the double. We're—"

"You're hurt, too, lord," the surviving prefet said.

"I am?"

"There's a cut on your shoulder and a bad slice on your right arm, lord."

Karne looked down. His right sleeve was red with frozen blood from a cut on his upper arm. "He must have had a very sharp knife, because I didn't feel a thing," said Karne, wonderingly. He touched the place and winced. "The cold has its blessings. I haven't bled to death." He stamped his feet to warm them a little. "We're going back to the shelter while the snow's still falling."

"How—how'll we find it, lord?" The youngest soldier's voice trembled just the littlest bit. "The snow's coming down harder by the minute."

"Egil got us here. Egil will get us there." Karne glanced at the litter to be sure it was ready. "Lead, Egil."

They had fought from darkness to just before dawn. Morning was a faint gray light when the men began the climb back to the shelter. The slope was steep and the soldiers had to struggle through deep snow that, because it began to thaw as the day warmed, would not support a part of their weight as it had in the cold of the previous night. Melt water seeped through the smallest holes in boots and seams, wetting the men to the skin. The litter's normal speed, which was slow by ordinary standards, was too fast for those conditions. Finally Karne had to set its controls to "hover only," attach a line between the litter and his belt, and push the litter. But even that cut in speed was not enough for the wounded. Before the men reached the shelter, two able-bodied troopers were each carrying one of the worst of the four wounded ones. They reached the shelter at sunset, twice the time it had taken to go down. The group stumbled up to the closed door, tired, hungry, and soaked through.

There was movement inside. "Who's there? I have two beamers on you, whoever you are." The boy guard's voice was both shaky and determined.

"It's Karne Halarek and what's left of our men. Open the door."

"Prove yourself. Tell me, how old am I?" The boy's voice was stronger, more sure.

"Fifteen winters." Karne was bone-tired, shaky, trembling with cold. His words crackled with impatience.

"What's my mother's trade?"

The boy's only doing his job, the way he's supposed to, Karne told himself. "She's a weaver," he answered, with a little more patience.

The boy swung the door open, throwing a rec-

tangular box of light onto the snow. "Welcome
back, lord."

The men piled gratefully into the warm, wind-
less interior of the shelter. A quick questioning
showed Egil had the most medical knowledge of
the group, so Karne handed him the medpak and
let him set the bones and tend the burns.

"Your arm first, Karne."

Karne shoved Egil's hand away irritably. "Take
care of the burned one first. My cut hasn't thawed
yet."

When tended, the men dropped into nightbags
and slept like the dead.

Karne awakened late, according to his chrono.
He sat up, focusing his eyes with difficulty. The
boy was sleeping, sitting up, against the door.
Karne's nightbag rustled as he got to his knees.
The boy sat bolt upright and both beamers targeted Karne. Karne froze, poised on his knees with
his right hand against the shelter wall. The tensed
muscles caused the wound to throb. Hot, sticky
blood began trickling down his arm.

"Oh! My lord, I'm sorry!" The boy neutralized
the beamers and put them on the floor by his side.
"I—I wasn't really awake, lord."

Karne used his left arm to push himself the rest
of the way to his feet. He looked down at his bleeding arm and then at the frightened boy.

"I—I—" The boy stuttered into silence, obviously
terrified.

"What's the matter?" Karne demanded. "It's not
your fault I'm bleeding."

"I—I was asleep on duty, lord. The old Lharr,
your sire, milord, he beamed my father for falling

asleep on duty in the manor house, lord. He died, my father. I thought that with the fighting going on ..." The boy's voice died away.

Karne sighed. "I'm not my sire. And I certainly don't shoot boys, especially boys who have done such a good job protecting our supplies."

The boy sprang up. "Oh, thank you, milord!" He kissed Karne's dangling hand.

Karne felt suddenly weak. He sat down on the dirt floor abruptly. "Get Olafson up," he ordered, his voice thin. "I think I need him." Karne bent his head almost to his knees and held the faintness and nausea at bay.

"Karne?" Egil touched Karne's shoulder lightly.

"I'm bleeding, Egil, I—" Karne collapsed helplessly sideways, like an old cloth doll.

"Too little sleep and too much blood gone," Karne heard Egil say curtly to someone, then the details of what was happening around him got sort of fuzzy. A sharp smell pinched his nose. He opened his eyes and looked up. Egil sat crosslegged beside him, winding up a roll of bandaging. Yan Willem stood behind Egil, looking worried. The three unhurt troopers, in various stages of sitting up, watched from their nightbags.

"Give me a stim-tab." Karne struggled to sit up, discovering his wounded arm was bound firmly against his ribs. He managed to roll up onto his good elbow. "We've got to connect with the von Schuss—"

Egil pushed Karne back down onto a nightbag that had somehow gotten under him and held out a drinking tube. "You're not going anywhere until you can get there without drugs. Here, drink this.

It'll help get you back on your feet, or so the med book says."

Karne looked doubtfully at the tube, then sipped. "Ugh! What is this?"

"Salt and soda in water. People in shock need it. Drink up."

"This?"

"Drink it all or I'll pour it down you!"

Karne put the tube back to his lips and drank. The liquid tasted salty, metallic, and warm. He closed his eyes and let himself drift. When he opened his eyes again, only the other wounded and Yan Willem were in the shelter. "How goes it, Yan?"

"We can't see anything out on the plain. We know von Schuss transports landed but . . ."

Karne pushed himself into a sitting position, but it made him feel so woozy he lay back down.

Willem's forehead creased with anxiety. "You haven't eaten since yesternight. Do you want midday, milord?"

"What is there?"

"Fish soup and fruit pudding. Full ration, 'Doctor' Olafson's orders, lord."

"I'll try some."

Karne felt better for the food and walked around inside the shelter a little. Egil, Dennen Willem, three troopers, and the boy blew in the door, white with snow and sober-faced.

Dennen came directly to Karne. "We walked halfway down, milord, to see what we could. Harlan and Odonnel have let their dead lie. Most of their men and several transports are gone, but there's still a Century or two down there, waiting. The sky will have to clear before we can be sure how many."

"It's going to be treacherous outside if the weather turns colder," Egil added. "What's coming down now's thaw-snow. If the surface freezes, nothing's going to move out there, and the sky's clearing over the mountains, which means cold weather's coming."

Karne's mouth tightened at the news. No one in the shelter was strong enough and quick enough to get back to the plain before the snow glazed over, and if someone were strong enough, there was nothing helpful to do, not against most of two Centuries. They were trapped.

The rest of the afternoon and evening dragged. Although the sky over the foothills cleared by sunset, a Thawtime ice-fog settled over the plain, wiping out all detail. Ignorance created tension and tempers flared often. Long after the others fell asleep, Karne lay awake, restless and tense. He had lost so many men, and to no apparent purpose. Guilt and anxiety gnawed at him. What should he do next? What could he do next? What about the wounded? The same questions went round and round in different form, tormenting, unanswerable questions.

The fog cleared the next day. Karne spent hours outside the shelter, questioning the sentinel on the watch-rock. Several troops and half-troops of men in Harlan uniforms seemed to be patrolling the edges of the plain, though for what purpose, the sentinel could not tell. Von Schuss aircraft had clustered on the opposite side the manor; the von Schuss camp showed little movement. Impatient with questioning when he needed to see, Karne at last climbed the slope above the shelter until he could see the plain below. The scene was as the sentinel had reported it. What did you expect, Karne asked himself scornfully, something completely different? At least there's not been enough cold to glaze the snow. I should be grateful for small blessings.

He stood for a long time on the side of the hill, looking without seeing, wondering what he could have done differently, what he could have done to drive Harlan and his ally off. Accusations and doubts chased themselves around inside Karne's head.

I should have waited for the von Schuss transports. I should've waited. I sent too few men, and now we're fewer still. With us, Kyle, and Wynter mainly on the northeast, the Blues at the other, two exits had to defend their backs against a Century apiece. Most of the Harlanites are gone, but Richard left searchers and we'll have to break through the patrols down there if we try to get the wounded back into the manor. Will Wynter take charge and do something? Will the Baron? Can I get a messenger to either of them, as thick as the Harlan patrols are? Can I get around the Harlan patrols and if I try it, what do I do with the wounded? The litter case isn't going to live much longer without the clinic.

Karne did not see the changes in the scene on the plain for a long time, though he was looking at them. Then a bright flash to the east caught his eye. It was sunlight on the wings of a Harlan fighter which swooped suddenly over the edge of the foothills. A heat-bolt shot out of one of the wing guns and the purple tracer showed the bolt's path into a snowdrift on the eastern edge of the manor grounds. The fighter zigzagged close to the edge of the foothills and shot again. Karne stood taller to see what the craft's target might be. He saw a line of men in

Harlan green following the fighter on the ground. The men cast back and forth like hounds.

They're hunting someone. Kyle's men. They'll be easy prey for such a hunt and so will mine. The thought was a bitter one.

A brown fighter zoomed down on the silver one, purple tracers spitting from it. Sunlight caught for a moment on the gold von Schuss medallion on its side as it swooped in pursuit of the Harlan craft. Karne's stomach tightened in anticipation, but the bolt missed the Harlan fighter. There was help, but he could not attract the von Schuss pilot's attention without attracting the Harlan pilot, and Harlan had men on the ground already, searching, while von Schuss's men were across the plain, on the far side of the manor. More soldiers in Harlan green appeared, nearer, sweeping the edge of the foothills. Karne stood very still, watching the hunt and softly cursing Harlan and clans and feuds and his own vulnerability, with only eight men still in fighting condition.

He walked carefully down to the shelter, for the snow's surface was beginning to ice over. He formed a tentative plan to save his remaining men as he went. He did not notice snow was falling again until he reached the shelter. He entered the building and stopped just inside the door. "Harlan had fighters up, hunting," he said bluntly, "and soldiers are on the ground to flush out the game. Us, and Kyle."

He had all the men's complete attention. "I can see no way for us to get into the manor and there's no way for the manor to get through to any other Holding or to Council. That's part of what those Harlan soldiers are still here for, to keep the com dishes from being repaired. This shelter will be found, eventually." Karne took a deep, unsteady breath. "I propose that Egil and I and the three fit troopers circle around Harlan to the Council patrol hut in Zinn and contact Council from there. Harlan wants me. I don't think he'll kill the wounded, or two Justin men." Karne inclined his head a little toward Yan and Dennen.

"We can turn the thermoes off at night to hinder heat-seekers. We could hold out here, lord, until von Schuss drives Harlan off." The boy soldier was eager, alert.

"Eight of us who can still fight, against even a squad?" Karne shook his head. "If we're lucky, this shelter won't be found for three or four days. If we're not ..." Karne looked past his men to the farthest corner of the shelter. "Egil, the three troopers, and I will cross the first ridge of the hills here and circle east. We can follow the Ednov River upstream, reach the patrol hut through the low pass, and have a direct connection to Council in two or three days. Harlan and Odonnel have broken the law of siege, again. That should get us Council help without argument. We'll leave the boy and the Willems here to protect the wounded."

Yan Willem shook his head. Karne looked at him intently. "Is there something wrong with that plan?"

Willem shook his head again. "No, lord. It isn't that. I just don't want to stay here if there's fighting to be done."

Karne looked grim. "You're the ones most likely to meet Harlan. I'd stay and send someone with a message to Council if I thought Council would take the word of anyone else but me." He looked at the others who were to stay and went on in a confident tone, a confidence he did not feel. "It's snowing again. We'll take empty food packages and some wastepaper with us and sweep away our tracks behind us. Halfway down the hill we'll mark tent-squares, melt a few cooking circles inside the 'tent' areas with thermoes, leave the trash, and make a wide, muddled trail away from that camp and this one. If we make the campsite look real enough, searchers will never think of looking somewhere else." Karne hesitated a moment. "We could even leave one of the pack tents up, as if we'd left in a hurry. That should protect you up here, long enough for us to reach the patrol hut, at least."

Egil looked thoughtful. Karne watched him with well-concealed anxiety. Egil, despite his joking comments about his marks, had been one of the best tactical planners at the Academy. Egil finally nodded, slowly. "I don't see any other way with a hope of survivors, Karne. A brave attempt to fight through to the manor would end up with everyone here dead, and a dead Lharr is of no use to your House."

Chapter Fourteen

———◆———

THE FIVE MEN who were going to the Council post spent the late afternoon and part of the night preparing. Karne carefully divided the food and fuel. "There's fourteen days' full rations for each of us. We'll take six days' food and twelve days' fuel rations." Karne sat back on his heels and looked at the piles to stay and to go. "That leaves twenty-two days' food rations and sixteen days' fuel here, plenty of margin for delays, bad weather, more attacks by Harlan and Odonnel." He glanced significantly at the Willems and then at the beamed trooper. The Willems looked grim and nodded. The trooper had no chance at all if rescue did not come within two or three days. Karne talked directly to the wounded. "Someone will find you long before the supplies run out. God willing, it will be Halarek or von Schuss that does the finding."

Each man going with Karne packed his own food, fuel, and tent. Egil also packed the extra tents and the sacks of trash for the fake campsite. Then all of them lay down for a few hours' sleep. Karne lay down like the others, but he could not sleep. He knew how to make his muscles relax, but he had never found a successful technique for making his mind relax as well. His mind struggled with the choices he'd made. The trail to the edge of Zinn was a high risk, but no one in his troop was likely to survive a rush for the Ontar entrance shelters. In Thawtime, there might be Runners from the Desert in the pass, before the Council patrols drove them back to finish their sentences. Runners were always dangerous—Zinn itself was always dangerous. That's why Starker sent its convicts there. Even if Karne and his men were the only people on the ground in the pass, they could be seen from fliers and attacked from above. With beamers. Karne shuddered, remembering.

He rose at dawn, physically rested and mentally on edge. Each time he had made what he thought

was the best decision for his House, the decision
had somehow turned against him. He had to suc-
ceed this time. He would get no more chances. If
Harlan captured him, he was dead.

He stepped outside the shelter. Ice-fog hung
again over the plain and clung in crystals to trees
and bushes and rocks. On any other morning,
Karne would have enjoyed the beauty of the sparkling twigs and pine needles. This morning, the
frozen fog only meant that by midday any brush
marks he and his men accidentally left in the snow
would be buried by the crystals falling from the
trees. He threw off his reluctance to begin the trek
and reentered the shelter. "Roll out of bed, men,"
he ordered. "It's time to be on the trail."

Preparation required only a few minutes, then
the men were at the door, munching on trail bread
and gulping the last of a mug of klag. Yan Willem
saluted the men who were leaving.

"Olafson, Lord Karne, Gissen, Treece, Fellan.
The Lord be with you."

"And with your spirit," they answered.

"Pray for us," Karne added as he went out the
door, repeating silently to himself, we're not going
to die, none of us are going to die. He said the words
over and over to himself like a litany—we're going
to cross the ridge and work east to the lower Zinn
pass, we're not going to die, we're not going to die.

Karne stepped carefully outside into a bitter
cold morning. "Watch your step!" he snapped. But
not ten paces from the shelter, Gissen slipped and
fell. Treece started toward him to help but had to
windmill for balance instead. Egil grabbed a tree
trunk just in time to keep from falling.

"We're not going to be able to walk at all!" Treece snarled.

Egil loosened his grip on the tree and turned to Karne. "I have an advantage here, brother. My people go outside in winter. We can be all the way down the hill in just an hour if we slide down."

"Slide?" The three troopers looked at the big man with no understanding at all of sliding on purpose.

"Slide," Karne repeated with satisfaction, remembering the children of Balder.

"That means to sit on a board or piece of stiff something and ride on the ice, like a boat over water." Egil paused. "You don't use boats, either. I'll have to show you, then." Egil walked gingerly back to the shelter and went inside. In a little while he returned and handed each man a plasti-board rectangle. "The backing boards for the others' packs," Egil explained. "Watch."

Egil sat on the rectangle, pulled his feet up onto it, and pulled the front edge up into a curve. He hitched along on the snow until the plasti-board began to slide. Egil zipped past the Gharr, down the hill, spun into a turn, and fell on his side. The Gharr gasped.

Egil stood up, laughing and brushing off snow. "I haven't done that since I was a boy. Before you try it, cut handholds back from the front edge. This is going to be a longer slide than I've ever had before. You'll need the holes." Egil laughed again, flung his arms wide, and stuck out his tongue to catch snowflakes. Then he picked up his sled and came back up the hill. Coming up, he could jab his toe through to the soft snow under the crust and walk with confidence.

"There are a few things you need to know about

steering," he began while he was still a distance away. "You can lean the direction you want to turn or pull up the opposite front edge and lean, or fall over and stop, which is the best idea if you're about to meet a tree. You can't get hurt if you're careful." Egil stopped beside Karne, not even panting from the climb. "We can reach the camping site long before dark this way. Lord Karne, may I set the order of going?"

Karne nodded.

Egil's mouth twisted as he thought. "The first man breaks trail and the last man gets the fastest ride. I'll go first, because I'm heavier and know more about sliding. Lord Karne, you follow because that's the safest position for you, having only one arm." He looked at the others. "Men, we'll make only left turns, since that's the only direction Lord Karne can turn without hurt. You three troopers pick your own order. If one of you races horses or fliers, though, that one should be last."

Fellan moved up the slope, behind the others.

Egil nodded approval at him. "All of you, keep to the one track if you can. The fog falling will probably erase it by midday, but if it doesn't, one track will keep Harlan guessing. He doesn't know about sliding either." Egil sat on his sled. "Sit, dig your heels through the crust, and cut your holes where they're comfortable." He watched until the holes had been cut. Then, "Let's go!"

Egil shoved off with one hand, Karne and the other men followed. Speed caught Karne's breath. Snow crystals blurred into a glistening white sheet as he zipped past. His stomach felt gone, as if he had left it on the shelter doorstep. Egil's track bent around a pile of boulders and Karne skimmed after him without trouble, but his heart pounded heavily and he had to swallow a large lump in his throat. The path led straight between rows of pines and Karne felt the first glow of exhilaration. "Guardians! What the Gharr have been missing!"

Joy possessed him. He was so filled with it he saw the bend in the track too late and threw himself sideways just in time to miss a massive bell-wood tree. He heard a squawk behind him, a crunch and thump, then another thump. Sitting up again once the ice crust had been broken was difficult with just one arm, and when Karne finally succeeded, the three troopers were again sitting on their sleds, heels dug in, brushing snow from their faces, hoods, shoulders, and legs.

"Are you all right, milord?" Fellan asked.

"Aye." Karne laughed ruefully. "I apologize for not paying attention."

The troopers shrugged and lined their sleds in the track on the downhill side of the stirred snow.

Egil had a good eye and had selected an almost straight course cutting slightly across the slope. At one place he had made a left-side fall-stop, then corrected the track toward the right. Karne saw the blurred mark where Egil had fallen sideways far enough ahead of time to make the same fall-stop himself. Near the bottom of the hill, Karne's sled zipped past Egil's empty one. Karne stuck out his footbrakes. Egil had stopped in the open center of a grove of bluepines and was bending over the unrolled tent, fitting the gas cylinder to the setup connection. Karne left his sled and sat on a snow-covered rock, resting his left forearm on his thighs.

The entire arm arched and trembled from the strain of steering. Gissen, then Treece, then Fellan slid to a stop in the clearing. Without needing orders, they set up a thermo and a two-pot and started cooking midday. The tent went *whump* and erected itself. Egil stepped back and examined it.

"It's a four-man, but if we trample the snow a lot, searchers will never figure out how many were here."

Karne heard clicks and slithering noises behind him and turned quickly. Treece had loosened his pack clips and was sliding the pack off. "Leave it on, Treece," Karne ordered. "Loosen it if you like, but leave it on. Visibility's still good enough for fliers. We might be spotted and have to dive for cover."

Treece winced as he slid the straps back over his shoulders. He trudged back to the thermo and stripped off his mittens, letting them dangle from their safety clips while he warmed his fingertips. "Keeping a tight hold so long sure numbs the fingers," he said to no one in particular.

Karne forced his shoulders back, then forward to get rid of a crick in his neck. He stood up slowly and tried to brush the snow off his rear. His tired left arm obeyed him poorly. All the muscles creaked and they hurt when tightened. The troopers crouched around the thermo and served themselves stew and hot klag.

Gissen wrinkled his nose. "This stew has garlic in it."

"It's food," Fellan snapped. He scooped a spoonful up, blew on it, ate it.

A gust of wind rushed under the pine branches and blew snow against the two-pot. The pot hissed and sizzled. No one spoke until the food and drink were gone and the utensils wiped out with snow and put away.

Treece licked his lips. "That was good. I wish there were more."

"Later, when we're out of Harlan's reach," Karne told him.

Karne leaned back against his packframe and closed his eyes. He felt weaker than he would ever tell anyone, and very tired. The trek to the patrol hut would take two days and the foothills beyond this one were not hard to cross, yet, right now, the trip seemed more than he had the strength to do. Snowflakes made tiny, cold prints on his face, more and more of them, until Karne had to wipe them away. He sat up. Snow was falling hard again, the wet, heavy snow of thawtime. Visibility for fliers would be about zero. Karne looked around their camp. Egil had left wastepaper where wastepaper would be left and had dropped the food wrappers and containers outside the tent door and around the thermo. He had also stacked the plasti-boards in the snow beside the tent. It was time to muddle their trail and move on, so they could set up a real camp for the night before the weather turned much worse.

Karne looked at his companions. They, also, were leaning back against their packframes, napping. For Egil, the standard Gharr-size frame was far too small, so when he leaned against it, his head flopped back onto the top of the pack. The position had not stopped him from sleeping. He snored quietly. Karne started to rise. He heard the buzz of an engine.

"DIVE FOR COVER!" Karne shouted.

His companions jerked awake and sprang for the low-hanging pine branches. The flier, invisible in falling snow, came over. A purple tracer lanced into the center of the clearing, striking the thermo. Flames flew outward.

"Heat-seeker! Up the hill!" Karne cried to his men. "Split up! Meet over the top of the ridge." He did not wait to see if everyone obeyed, but burst from his hiding place among the pines and scrambled up the hill, using his left arm as a sort of third leg. He saw one trooper climbing near him, but falling snow hid the other men. He knew the others were coming because he heard snow-muffled scuffing and crunching noises and once in a while an "oof" when someone slipped or fell. He paused for a fraction of a second at the crest of the ridge to look back. Snow hid the flames of the thermo, but not the ominous orange glow. He was not the only one watching.

"Heimdal! The whole grove's burning," Egil shouted from Karne's right.

"Fire must've overpowered the piddling little body heat we put out. We're safe!" Treece shouted, jubilant.

"Don't be a fool!" Fellan snarled from somewhere to Treece's left.

"Gissen?" Karne called into the snow silence that followed Fellan's retort.

"Here, lord."

By calling, answering, listening; calling, answering, listening; they found each other. Treece, who had been a little slower leaving the pine grove, had a singed hood and jacket.

"Whew," he said, wiping away snow-water that

was dripping off his icy eyebrows. "The flier can't find us with all that heat around. Do we stop here?"

A blot above the fire's glow moved slowly toward the ridge. Fellan stared at the blot and at the bright, white light on its bottom. "They can't find us with a searchlight."

"Right, Fellan, but up here on the ridge our body heat will be like a beacon to them. They'll need the light to find us afterward." Karne raised his voice to be sure everyone heard. "That could be a von Schuss flier, or one of ours, but I won't bet on it: Our people don't need to hunt us at dark in a snowstorm. Scatter, now, at least two hundred paces from each other. It'll be a cold, cold night, but at least we'll likely live till morning."

The other men moved away. Karne waited until he could no longer hear the *shuff, shuff* of leg-plowed snow before he scrambled up the side of the ridge and a little way down the other side to a jumble of boulders. He curled up in a cranny and leaned against his pack. Several times he heard the hiss of a heat-bolt blindly zapping the crest of the ridge above him, but the flier itself never crossed the ridge-top. "They know we're here," he whispered as his eyelids grew heavier and heavier. "They know we're here."

Dim morning light showed Karne he was in a rocky, deep, and very narrow ravine between two ranges of hills. The ravine was bare of snow wherever its steep, leaning walls protected it from the wind. The men gathered, ate a fast-breaking biscuit, drank snow-water, slid to the bottom of the ravine, and followed the direction Egil said was almost directly east. Snow covered the protected ravine floor only thinly, snow that glistened in weak sunlight. By the time the men stopped for midday, the sun had come fully out and the air was thick with dripping and trickling sounds. They set a thermo on a flat rock and heated an energy-rich mush. While they waited for the mush to boil, the men joked and talked.

Egil took off his boots and held his feet toward the thermo's heat. "My toes get numb walking in snow so long. My fingers are cold, too. I bet ice melts at a lower temperature here than it does on Balder." His aggrieved tone earned him smiles from the Gharr.

"This is Thawtime," Gissen reminded him.

"So you say," Egil retorted morosely.

The first warning of danger was a tracer bouncing off a cluster of boulders above them.

"Heimdal!" Egil grabbed his boots and ducked behind the cluster of flat rocks the thermo sat among.

"Scatter!" Karne ordered. "Get those green packs off and lie down on them, then don't move. Egil, damn it, you're hiding behind the biggest heat source down here!"

Egil whacked the thermo away into a snowdrift and scuttled the opposite direction. The thermo sizzled, turning the snow around it to steam, then it went out. Egil whipped off his pack and sprawled over it. The flier descended. Karne heard clearly the buzz of its engine coming closer and closer until the narrow ravine hummed with the noise. A heat-bolt zapped the rock the thermo had been on. Karne wanted to get up and run from the death the flier carried in its wings. His memory screamed the pain of burning. Run! Run! The flier came nearer. If it's a flitter, they'll come right down the ravine and burn us by hand. Karne's legs twitched with the urge to run. The flier's heat-beam sizzled across nearby rocks. Karne's mouth felt dry and his muscles knotted, aching with the wild need to get away from the burning. Then the flier was directly overhead. Karne's breath came hard, he shut his eyes to close out the flier, knowing if he watched it his terror would be too great for him to control. The engine sounded like a fighter's. It flew down the ravine, then turned and came back, the sound of it coming closer and closer again. Karne took an iron grip on his fear and forced himself to look up. He was a commander and had to know what he and his men were facing. He told himself that again and again as the flier's engines thrummed closer. It *was* a fighter and too wide to come lower. Karne's entire body trembled from the effort of will needed to stay motionless so near the deadly beam. The craft passed. Karne heard a sizzle as the fighter rounded a bend in the ravine, then the sound of its engines faded.

"Can we get up now?" Gissen's voice was plaintive. "I'm getting cold."

"You're cold—"

"Shut up, Olafson," Fellan snapped, "and get down! We're not safe yet."

Irregularities in the ravine hid the speakers from Karne's sight. In the quiet following Fellan's order, the ravine itself seemed quieter than before the attack. Water ran gurgling over rocks, dripped from the twisted trees that clung to the steep south wall, trickled through places hidden under snow. In such quiet, the returning buzz of the fighter seemed more ominous, more dangerous than it had before. Karne felt himself shaking and cursed himself for a coward. The flier passed over his hiding place, fired several bolts beyond it, and disappeared far down the ravine. Karne heard a rushing sound as thaw-softened snow somewhere, disturbed by the flier's vibration or loosened by the heat of a bolt, slid down the ravine side. Karne lay without moving a long time after the last throb of the flier's engines had died in the distance. He hoped his men interpreted the wait as prudence; he knew it was caused by bone-melting terror as well.

"Let's try it," he called out at last, keeping his voice steady by an act of will. "Get up, but be prepared to duck again."

"Must've been a fighter," Gissen said. "Too wide to come down."

So, someone else had been afraid to look. That made Karne feel a little better. "It was a fighter," he said. He looked down the ravine to where he had last seen Egil. "Egil? Egil?" His voice sharpened with concern. "Are you all right?"

Egil crawled out from under an overhang. "That was too close." He took off one mitten and stuck his fingers into his mouth to warm them.

"Pilots couldn't aim," Gissen added smugly.

"Don't talk till you know what you're saying," Fellan snapped, coming around a bend in the ravine wall to join the rest of the men. He held up a slightly burned pack. "Treece—isn't, anymore. Said something about this being too uncomfortable to lie on. He threw it to one side when he lay down."

Gissen looked at the pack wide-eyed. "Did he run away?"

"Don't be more a fool than you have to be, Gissen." Fellan dropped the pack to the snow. "All that's left of Treece are the soles of his boots and his pack. Guardians, Gissen! A fighter's bolt will burn a flitter out of the sky!"

Gissen swallowed noisily and began to look greenish around the mouth and nose. "Are we—are we going to bury him, Lord Karne?"

"There's nothing left to bury, according to Fellan," Karne replied, feeling a little sick himself. "We'll take what we can use from his pack and get out of this ravine." Karne turned to Egil. "You warmed up enough?"

Egil shook his head.

Karne's mind raced. There had to be something to keep Egil from freezing. "Carry the thermo for awhile," he said abruptly, hiding his worry with the curt tone, "it can't be completely cooled off yet. We're changing routes, men, going over this ridge and the next one instead of staying on this side of the mountains. We're too easily seen on this side. Harlan knows we're here now. We'd be ducking bolts until none of us were left. We can reach the patrol hut by crossing Spider Mountain and walking along the edge of Zinn."

"Go into the mountains in Thawtime, lord? And Zinn? What about the Watchers and the Runners?"

Fellan's voice was calm and respectful, but Karne knew the man's doubts had to be pressing for him to even think of questioning his lord. The man was a good soldier and deserved a respectful answer. Karne shut a mental door on what he knew was "correct" behavior for a lord facing such questioning and answered honestly. "I'd rather take my chances with all of those than try to stay alive for three days as a beamer target. Those who don't want to try the edge of Zinn can stay on this side and try to get back."

Gissen broke in. "But we'll die over there, lord."

"I've been burned, Gissen. I'd rather die of cold or hunger or a Runner's lance. But we won't. There are four of us, and I've been on Spider Mountain before, hunting with my sire."

"What if a flier comes before we—"

"Stop your whining, Gissen! Matters are bad enough as is. I won't put up with whining."

Gissen's mouth shut with an audible snap. Karne pulled on his pack, with Egil's help, and started down the ravine at a fast pace, not looking back to see who, if anyone, followed. He reached a place where the ravine met a gentle hill, a place where a man with one hand to use could climb out.

As he came closer and closer to the crest of the hill, Karne crouched lower and lower. The men behind him followed his example. By the time Karne reached the crest, he was crawling. He stopped and looked back. All his men had followed him toward Zinn. Beyond them, Karne could see over two ranges of hills to the plain, where strings of men were struggling up the hill to where the fire had been. Sunlight flashed from the barrels of long-range stunners. "Look." He pointed.

The others looked. Their mouths tightened. They all turned and slid down the barren slope on the far side of the ridge to the foot of the next hill, then climbed to the top of that. Bare trees spread empty branches above soggy snow. Above the bare trees, pines drooped under cloaks and hoods of ice. Karne stopped among the pines for a breather, his forehead gleaming with sweat. "Warm now, Egil?"

Egil grinned. "Aye, lord. Is it time to eat?'

"Aye, but only a fast-breaking biscuit, a piece of choc, maybe some dried plums. Suck snow if you're thirsty, because we're not lighting the thermoes again until we reach the mountain, where we'll be out of sight."

"How long, lord?" Again, Fellan was questioning. Again Fellan's voice was respectful.

Karne wondered if he had made a mistake with Fellan. Would it make him less willing to follow orders if he could ask questions? In Federation forces it would not, but the men of Federation worlds had long been used to independent thought. Did Fellan see Karne's willingness to listen as weakness? But it was already too late to go back to a traditional way of dealing with questions. Karne met Fellan's eyes. There was no contempt in them. "With luck, we'll be on the side of Spider Mountain tonight."

Fellan nodded, reasssured, slid off his pack, and began digging out the food Karne had listed.

The men ate standing, then scrambled down the sharper slope on the other side of the pine-topped hill and slid out onto the black ice of a wide river. Karne stopped, balancing himself against the slipperiness, and cursing the overconfidence that had sent him out into the foothills without direks. He had thought them unnecessary; after all, they would never be out of sight of the plain and Ontar manor. It was too late for regrets. They did have Egil with them.

He turned to his friend. "Spider Mountain is north, northeast of this river, Egil. Which way do we go?"

Egil pointed, then started walking and the men

followed. They climbed through old, broken pines and tall underbrush to the top of the next ridge, a narrow, rocky spine scoured bare by wind. A fierce wind funneled down a gorge that might have been the river's old bed.

Egil stopped with a gasp. "We're too wet for this wind, Karne. My clothes are soggy with snowmelt and so're everyone else's." The wind whirled around Egil, making his teeth chatter so much he quit talking.

Karne took Egil's arm and led him off the wind-swept rocks. "My sire took his sons hunting Dur cats in Zinn once. We came down this gorge. There's a flat place not far from here. We'll set up tents there and dry out, Egil. No matter how cold we are, we can't set up a heat-beacon like a tent camp on a hilltop."

"It'd be suicide," muttered Gissen.

Karne plunged down to a game trail that cut into the side of the rocky ridge and curved its way gently toward the gorge floor. Across the gorge from the trail, tons of sliding rock from a rotting cliff lay in a jumble of boulders and debris that half filled the space between the ridge and the cliff. "Careful, it's a bad drop," Karne warned, keeping close to the ridge side of the game trail himself.

The trail eventually flattened out between the ridge wall and the snow-covered side of a mountain. A narrow neck of rock that had probably once been under a waterfall connected the mountain and the ridge the men had left. Karne looked at Egil. He had both hands inside the opened front of his survival suit.

Karne stopped. "Set up a thermo, Fellan. Gissen,

we're putting up two tents." Karne took off his sling and struggled to get out of his pack.

"Karne, I can do that for you." Egil pulled his hands out of his suit.

"There's heat," Karne snapped, pointing to the thermo. "Get your hands warm."

Karne watched, carefully keeping the worry from his face, until Egil hunched over the thermo and held out his hands to the heat. Karne put the sling back on and attempted to connect the gas cylinder to the first tent with one hand. Fellan took the cylinder away without a word, inflated the tent, and set up another thermo inside. "Better get in there, Olafson," he said.

"He's right, Egil," Karne added. "Go in and get out of your wet clothes. We'll all come in to eat in a few minutes."

Egil hesitated only a moment before limping into the tent.

Chapter Fifteen

———◆———

THE MEN SET out again after sunrise. Frost had whitened the tops of the rocks they had cleared to sit on the night before, but the snow was still soggy, with no ice crust to make walking treacherous. Karne pointed to a narrow ledge, several hundred meters above the gorge floor, that switched back and forth across the side of the mountain. "That's where we're going. Wom trail."

"I haven't got a wom's tiny hooves," said Gissen, pointing to his boots.

They all looked at Egil, who had much bigger feet. He seemed pale.

"Egil?" Karne's voice sharpened with concern in spite of himself.

Egil grinned weakly. "I'll manage, Karne."

They climbed to the wom trail through a jumble of rocks and small boulders. A strong wind still swept down the gorge, reaching them even so high above the gorge floor.

"Keep moving," Karne ordered as the men began to slow. "We won't be out of this wind until we're past the end of the ridge we were on last night."

Egil began to move forward in the direction Karne said, limping. Karne watched him only a moment before stepping up his pace and catching up to his friend. "I'll lead, Egil. I've been over this trail before." Karne hoped the face-saving explanation was convincing. He was not tall enough to make much of a windbreak for Egil, but anything had to be a help.

The trail wove back and forth, slowly climbing above the sheer face of the former waterfall. The air was colder at this altitude, the snow dry and hard. The trail crossed the foot of a cliff on which the melt-water of the day before had frozen into a thin, gleaming sheet. The men had to walk with one mitten on the cliff wall for balance. Then, with one more step, they rounded the end of the cliff and were out of the biting wind. Egil sighed tiredly and leaned against a large boulder. Karne surveyed the way ahead. On this side of the mountain, the sun had remelted the top layer of ice, making the trail much slipperier. Here, above Zinn, Thawtime showed more than on the plains. The barren slope above and below the men showed patches of brown rock, a stretch of ice-glazed gravel here and there, a dried clump of grass, the skeleton of a bush. Trees had lived on the slope once, before some ancient fire, but now their yellow wood stood open to the weather, their trunks reached upward, giant poles striped and streaked with wind-polished charcoal. Below the trees, at the mountain's foot, lay the still-white expanse of the Desert of Zinn. To the north, on one of the mountains ringing Zinn, Karne saw fire flare toward the pale blue sky. Gissen, too, saw.

"Watchers!" Gissen could not hide the tremble in his voice.

"Either we've been spotted or Harlan has people out here. No one sends convicts to the Desert this early."

The excitement in the others' voices roused Egil from his numb silence. "Watchers? What are Watchers?"

The troopers looked to Karne to explain. "It's hard to say, Egil." Karne thought a moment, trying to remember what, if anything, he had told Egil about the Gharr and Starker IV. "The Watchers were here before the first of the Gharr, missionaries of The Way, settled this world. "They—watch. That's all we know of them. The Runners, who are convicts sentenced here by the Families, see the signal fires and hunt down what was seen. Runners rob humans they catch of everything that's usable here, but they don't kill unless they're starving. And they leave their victims with enough food and water to get out of the Desert. Part of every catch the Runners take to one of the places-of-leaving, as payment for the signal fires. But the Watchers are never seen, according to the men who survive their sentence and come back to the Holdings."

"I don't want to find out what they look like," Fellan said, shivering.

"Me, neither. Let's go!" Gissen looked about vainly for the trail.

Karne looked at Gissen, his face grim. That trooper should have been left in the shelter. "No trail here, Gissen," he told the man sharply. "The guard-post stands in that pass." Karne pointed across a long, shallow bay, where Zinn invaded the foothills, to a notch beyond to the southwest. "The Council sets patrols on this side of the Desert from Thaw-time till Frosttime to keep the convicts here," he added for Egil's benefit. "We need your sense of direction here, too, Egil, because we won't be able to see the pass from the Desert floor. Do whatever it is you do to keep your bearings and let's get started."

Egil looked steadily at the place Karne had pointed to. When he nodded, the men set off down the mountain, zigzagging across the gravel slope, slipping, sliding, sometimes falling down. They ate midday halfway down. By sunset they were nearly a fourth of the way across the bay of desert. They set up camp in the shadow of the sentinel rocks, upright black stones several times the height of a man, that followed the line of foothills. Karne kept a close eye on Egil, worrying, yet unwilling to shame his friend in front of the troopers when there was nothing

Karne could do to ease the misery the cold was for him.

The next morning, snow was falling again and the men set off into a snowy haze. Egil, because of his directional sense, led still, complaining continually of the renewed cold, and that was so unlike him that Karne took him aside at midday while the two troopers were preparing the meal.

"What's the matter? You're as hard to live with as a hungry Zinn bear."

"Nothing's the matter, Karne. Nothing that anyone can do anything about. I'll be all right when we get to the guardpost. I just can't be comfortable in Gharr clothes in the cold. Too warm-blooded, I guess." Egil stripped off a mitten, opened his top coat fastener, and slipped the hand in against his chest.

"Egil, show me that hand." Karne knew his voice betrayed his anxiety, but he could no longer help it. Egil was in real trouble with the cold.

Egil shook his head deprecatingly. "It'll be all right, Karne. It's just cold."

Karne thrust out his own hand. "Let me see it, Egil."

Egil reluctantly pulled out his hand. It was red and very cold. That was not good and they had an entire day left to travel. There had to be something Karne could do to keep those hands warmer, because carrying the thermo worked only until the thermo cooled. "How does it feel?" he demanded.

"A little numb."

"A lot numb, I'd guess." When Egil nodded sheepishly, Karne's voice sharpened. "And the other? Is it the same?"

Egil nodded again.

"Here." Karne held Egil's hand between his until it warmed, then he warmed the other the same way. He dared not rub the skin, fearing it had already been damaged. "Go sit by the thermo and keep them warm."

Karne looked anxiously across the bay to where it bent back into the Desert. Somewhere along that bend was the trail to the guardpost. If Egil could get to the post without more damage to his hands, the com connection with Council would bring medical help as soon as it could be flown in. Karne swallowed hard and looked at his friend, hunched over the small warmth of the thermo.

"His hands," Karne whispered to himself. "Guardians! I have to get him to the guardpost in time to save his hands!" Karne brushed away a large snowflake tickling his nose. Getting Egil there without more damage would not be easy. If the Watchers' fires this morning were the first, Runners were on their way. If those fires were not the first . . . Karne would not let himself think of that. Either way, they would not have time to stop and light the thermoes for the sake of Egil's hands. He went back to the thermo and stood looking down on the heads of the men who crouched around the two-pot. They were probably as tired as he was, and stiff as well from plowing through snow and keeping balanced on ice.

At least there's no wind here, Karne thought, and crouched beside the thermo until he, too, was somewhat warm.

The men ate nightmeal and moved into the tents. Karne sat long on his nightbag, thinking. Speed back to Ontar was very important. However, Karne had heard that exhausted people suffer more from cold than rested ones. He glanced at Egil, stretched out in his bag. His hands, which probably hurt, lay near his face. Karne dialed the tent thermo up two decades and lay down on top of his bag. They were only one day away from the post. There was an unused thermo in Fellan's pack. They could afford to spend the extra fuel to save Egil's hands.

Strange, faraway howls floated on the still night air. Karne shivered in spite of himself. The Runners were out, and they were hunting.

Egil's hands looked normal the next morning, but Karne was not sure that meant they would continue to be all right and the spare mittens among the men were all too small for Egil. Karne pushed everyone to hurry, hurry, hurry through the sunny morning, yet stopped several times, against his better judgment, to fire up the spare thermo until it was just on the cool side of too hot to hold, then hand it to Egil. Too soon clouds covered the sun and a fine, light snow, the sign of colder weather, began falling. By the time the men reached the sentinel rocks at the other end of the bay, the snow had become a fog. Runners' howls came through it eerily, making the hair rise on the men's necks.

"They're closer," Gissen whined. "We're going to be caught!"

"They haven't got a guide who could find the way blind to the guard hut," Karne snapped. "We have."

The falling snow became a wall of white that hid anything more than an arm's length away. Egil stumbled from tiredness and, Karne suspected, numbed feet. Karne ordered each man to hold to the belt of the man ahead so no one got lost. The Runners howled closer.

They were climbing a hill. Egil stumbled and fell. Karne helped him up and whispered, "Not much farther. It's not much farther, Egil. Keep on till we're inside."

"What? Inside? Where?" Egil's bewildered voice frightened Karne.

"The Runners are on our trail, help us get away, Egil," he urged, ashamed of using a threat to force the exhausted, freezing man to move on.

Egil responded. He straightened and walked a little faster, but his breath rasped in and out. That was the only sound in the eerie, snow-thick silence, Egil's harsh, painful breathing.

"Where are we, Karne?" Again, Egil sounded like a lost child.

No, don't let him be lost. Guardians, keep him on his track! Karne prayed silently. Aloud he said, "We're going to a warm house, Egil. You know where it is, remember?"

The walking and stumbling and the pull of arms on belt before and belt behind seemed to go on forever. It was a nightmare without sight or sound, only muscles telling the men they were moving. Snow collected in Karne's eyebrows. It melted where his outstretched wrists were exposed, turning his cuffs into icy knives. Egil walked into something. Karne let go of Egil's belt to feel what that something was.

"It's a wall! It's the guardpost!" Karne reached for Egil's belt. It was gone. "Egil! Egil!"

Only the shush of snow falling against the wall answered him. He turned to the men who had crowded close to him. "Fellan, Gissen, follow the wall by hand till you find the door. Press against the tube under the bottom edge, then get some lights on out here. Fellan, come out immediately with a torch and help me find him."

Karne heard the two men's mittens sliding along the stone wall, something made a small rumble, then Karne heard a click. Light fell from a window onto the snow behind him. "A rope, Fellan," he shouted, feeling his way toward the door, walking sideways because the wall was on his right. He waited by the door with the faint sound of snow falling for his only company. The urgency of finding Egil tore at him. "Egil!" he shouted into the muffling snow. What was taking Fellan so long? "Fellan!" Karne dared not take his hand from the building until he had a rope to follow back again. "Egil!"

Time dragged on in awful silence. Then four brilliant lights came on, illuminating the area around the hut for a hundred meters, drastically shorter than the lights' normal range. Fellan jumped from the raised doorway into the snow, slid the door shut, and tied a rope around Karne without waiting for orders. "I had trouble finding the rope, lord. And I found the lights instead of a torch," he said, matter-of-factly, then added, "He was too done to go far."

Knowing one end of the rope was tied fast inside the hut, Karne and Fellan moved to the other end and trudged slowly, about two meters apart on the rope, in a circle from the hut wall outward. Karne saw a faint depression in the snow that might mark Egil's path. He pointed, Fellan nodded.

"Egil!"

There was no answer. The two men moved forward again, both feeling with their feet as well as looking for Egil. The snow fell silently, smothering shapes and sounds.

"Egil!" Despair swept Karne. The person who meant more to him than anyone else did was gone. Karne plowed forward, feeling the resistance of the snow against his shins as a heavy weight. Then, off to the left, he saw an oddly shaped mound of snow. Surely nothing that lived out here grew like that. Karne plowed forward and dug swiftly with his good hand.

"His pack!"

Fellan slid along the rope and was with Karne in seconds, digging frantically at the mound. First the broad shoulders, then the shaggy blond head, then his face. Karne touched Egil's throat. "He lives."

As if they had worked as a team all their lives, Karne and Fellan hauled Egil's body out of the snow and dragged it back to the post. Within moments after they had hoisted him through the door, they had stripped Egil and wrapped him in warmed blankets. His hands and feet they set in basins of tepid water.

Fellan sank back on his haunches when the work was done and stared at the off-worlder's face. "Will he live, Lord Karne?"

"God alone knows." Karne sank to the floor beside his friend, blank with exhaustion, knowing he should try to reach Council and too weary to move.

When Karne awoke, it was a gray snowy morning and Egil was watching him. The blue eyes were puzzled. "How did I get here?'"

Karne rolled onto his side, aching from the night on the hard floor. "You led us here, then wandered off and fell or lay down in the snow. You could've died, Egil!"

Egil struggled to sit up and could not. He sagged back onto his blankets and his voice had the sharp edge of panic. "I—Karne, I can't feel my hands!"

Karne lifted one of them from the blanket. It was not stark white, as it had been the night before, but it was still glossy, unnaturally pale, and heavy as lead. Its mate was just like it. Karne looked at those hands and thought of the ancient heroes painted across his bedroom wall. Without hands—he looked at his friend and saw the same thought in Egil's eyes. "Egil..." But there was nothing comforting to say.

Karne sprang up and over to the com-console. It came on at a touch. "Council, this is Guardpost 105, the Lharr of Halarek speaking. Medical emergency. Repeating, Post 105 is reporting a medical emergency. Do you hear me?"

No one answered. Karne tried again and again, every hour. No one ever answered. Karne hurled the patrol logbook across the room. "I know it's hooked up. It's always hooked up!"

Egil turned his face away. "There's nothing they can do anyway, Karne. If I can't feel them, it's too late."

"If I'd set up the tents last night—"

"It's not your fault, Karne! I walked off on my own. Maybe I should've gone farther."

Karne heard the bitterness and there was nothing adequate he could say in reply. A long, uncomfortable silence followed, broken only by Gissen's gentle snoring. Karne paced across the hut and back, stopping beside the front window. "If I can't com help,

Egil, I'll walk to Ontar for it. It's only a day and a half or so."

"Don't be a fool!" Egil snarled. "If you do that, this whole trek will have been for nothing. I will've lost my hands for nothing. Council has to staff this post. If the com doesn't work, stay until the patrol arrives. Heimdal, Karne, your House is at stake!" Egil rolled with difficulty to his side and one hand dropped to the floor with a sound like a rock.

Egil's anger shook Karne back into remembrance of priorities. Egil was very important to Karne, but several thousand lives would end if Richard Harlan managed to carry out his threat to destroy Halarek to the last stone and distant cousin. *Guardians! No wonder the lords of the Gharr feel nothing but anger, pride, and a sort of mild affection. They can't afford to know more about their feelings with Gharr rules the way they are! They'd go mad or tear themselves apart otherwise. As I'm tearing apart.* Karne looked down at Egil's rigid back and turned his face to the window to hide his tears from the awakening troopers.

Snow was falling more heavily than the night before, if that were possible. Karne could not see beyond the windowsill. *Guardians, where are you? My friend, my brother, may die!* He spun away from the window and paced the square hut floor. For hours the storm whirled and howled outside and Karne prowled from one side of the room to the other inside, trying to reach Council on each swing past the com unit, struggling to make his feelings accept Egil's decision, worrying that Harlan had somehow cut off even Council transmissions. House Halarek was in deadly danger, Egil would likely die, and the patrol hut's only link with Council would not work!

Karne slept fitfully that night and got up before dawn. Egil was moaning with pain. Karne knew how bad the pain must be for a man of Balder to admit it: pain was to be laughed off, dismissed as of no importance. He dug painkillers from one of the medpacks and ordered Gissen to dose Egil on the prescribed schedule. The night's sleep, scant though it was, had helped Karne regain his strict self-control. Egil had made his own decision about his life. That was his right. Now Karne had to decide how best to protect his House if he could not reach Council headquarters. After hours of struggle and internal argument, Karne could find no better answer than to return with Fellan to Halarek Holding and try to reach von Shuss's men. Karne's personal danger would be no less than before, but Gissen and Egil, if he lived, would be still alive and out of Harlan's reach to be witness to what had happened to Halarek. That was cold comfort, but it was all the comfort there was. Council must know about the illegal siege. Perhaps some remnant of his House would be saved.

The snow stopped falling in late afternoon, but the wind rose as the snow lessened. Sometimes the men could see the Desert from the front window and sometimes they could see only plumes of snow. Karne and Fellan prepared for the trek back to Ontar by packing all the food and other supplies they were likely to need. The patrol hut's supplies would feed Egil and Gissen. Gissen stood by the window, watching. Suddenly he called, "Hey, what's that?"

Karne and Fellan rushed to the window. Two

gaunt figures stood at the edge of the trees almost one hundred meters away.

"Runners?" Gissen asked.

Fellan and Karne nodded.

"Why are they here?" Gissen's voice had begun to tremble with apprehension.

"Because we know how to open the guard hut, which is warm and dry and full of food." Karne looked again at the figures and wondered how many more lurked in the cover of the trees. "The convicts who survive their first trip across the Desert live in caves deep under the mountains on the other side. They heat and cook with wood and eat whatever they can catch. There are no fat Runners."

The Runners watched the guardpost for a very long time, then disappeared. Karne finished packing. Fellan kept watch at the window. He turned and watched Karne press down the last pack closure. "Is this building armed, lord?" The question held none of the fear Gissen would have put into it.

Karne looked up. "It should have perimeter stunners, medium-range, with automatic track and fire. Probably a long-range beamer, fired from the roof. Why?"

Fellan turned back to the window. "There are ten or more Runners out there now, Lord Karne."

Karne went to the window. The Runners stood along the edges of the trees, thin as shadows in the gathering dusk and much closer than they had been before. That they came so close to an occupied Zinn patrol hut showed their desperation. Karne bit his lip. Runners made leaving the hut far more dangerous. Yet Halarek needed help. Egil needed help. Karne's hands clenched and unclenched. The Runners would attack eventually; they only needed to work up their courage, though Karne, with no knowledge of Runners' ways, had no idea what sort of weapons they might use.

A harsh gasp broke into Karne's thoughts. He spun. Egil was sitting, using one of his dead hands as a prop. He was breathing hard against the pain. "Take these two and go, Karne. I'll cover you with the beamer."

"I won't trade my life for yours."

"How else are you and Fellan going to get past the Runners, smart boy?"

Egil's words stung. Karne could not pass the Runners with just Fellan's help, nor with Fellan and Gissen together. "I won't trade my life for yours," he insisted stubbornly. "The only way I could make myself leave was by convincing myself you'd still be here when the patrol arrives, to tell what happened to Halarek."

"You're my brother, Karne. I love you. I want you to live." The two troopers looked away, embarrassed. Egil went on. "You can live. I know it. You have the skill and wit to make it to the von Schuss camp." Egil took a deep breath and continued. "Everything I'm good at requires hands, Karne, and my hands are gone. But even if my hands worked, I'd still offer you this chance. Don't you know that?"

"No," Karne whispered, "I didn't know that. Even members of my own clan wouldn't offer me that."

"Karne, your whole House dies if you do. But you'll make it to von Schuss. You can make big changes in your world, important changes." Egil paused to clear his throat. "Take your life as my gift and tell your children about the friend who saved you by pressing beamer buttons with his nose." Egil's voice held the amusement and joy a Balderman would feel at such a way of dying, a way worthy of saga.

Karne looked into Egil's eyes for a long time, then nodded. "Gissen stays with you."

Egil shook his head.

"He stays, Egil. You can't feed yourself. You can't even get to the beamer without help. Believe me, there'll be someone here for you within three days. You can hold off the Runners for that long." Karne hoped with all his heart that was true.

"I don't want to stay, Lord Karne," Gissen whined.

"Gissen, you're a soldier. This is your post. Help will come. Now take Egil up to the beamer."

Gissen's mouth sulked, but he bent his head, accepting the order.

For Karne, the following night dragged by. He was up at first light, slipping into his pack with Fellan's help, waiting by the back door while Gissen helped Egil up and into the tiny lift that went up to the beamer hole. "I'll yell when I'm ready," Egil said as he went.

Moments after the lift stopped, Egil roared down, "Ready!" He sounded almost normal.

Karne and Fellan slipped out the door, through the softening drifts, and into the bluepines covering the sides of the pass. Runner howls frayed the air, answered by sizzling beamer bolts. The two men did not speak or look back or stop moving until they were over the crest of the pass and walking down the gentle valley that widened slowly on its way to meet the plain. Karne heard a flier and held up his hand. Fellan stopped beside him.

"Hear that?"

Fellan nodded.

"Let's duck out of sight until we see whose flier it is." The men stepped under the branches of some pines and waited until the flier came into sight.

The flier was a small Zinn-patrol transport in Council red. Karne hesitated. Gormsby would be the chairman at the Thawtime meeting, and Gormsby was a Harlan ally. But Council was Halarek's only hope. He had to take the chance he could convince Council to protect his House. Karne stepped out of hiding, more boldly than he felt, and jumped and waved to attract the transport. It passed over, then banked and returned just above the top of the trees.

"Looking for a proper landing place," Fellan muttered.

The transport landed down the valley and a squad of patrolmen jumped out onto the snow. Half were wearing Druma's electric blue and half deVree's light orange. The squadleader wore Council red. They fanned out and moved toward Karne and Fellan, stunners drawn. Karne tensed. There was nothing else he could do. He had committed them to Council hands.

The squadleader stopped a pace from Karne, his stunner pointing at Karne's head. "Karne Halarek, you're under Council arrest."

Chapter Sixteen

———◆———

A THOUSAND FEELINGS raced through Karne's mind in the seconds following the squadleader's announcement—despair, hopelessness, anger, grief, helplessness. He was trapped. His House was done. Gormsby's alliance was more important to him than the fairness of Council. He and Fellan had made good time over the pass and it was all for nothing. Yet, perhaps, he could salvage something for Egil from this disaster. He willed his voice to show nothing of his anguish and despair.

"An off-worlder, a neutral in our wars, lies at Post 105 in severe need of medical help. For the sake of Starker's reputation with other worlds, send him aid."

"My lord," the squadleader replied respectfully, "you broadcast that need. Chairman deVree ordered the team out as soon as you started broadcasting, but the pad was socked in until early this morning. Are they too late?"

Karne shook his head. "Council heard me? No one answered. Why?"

The squadleader shook his head, puzzled. "Every call was answered, lord. The com-techs didn't understand how you could be in such distress and not respond. The receiver has to be out. Had a lot of trouble with receivers these past two winters." The squadleader then motioned toward the transport. "Get in, lord. We're ordered to take you to Council ground before we start dropping off patrols."

"But my friend—"

The squadleader waved toward the transport impatiently. "We'll contact the med team from the air. We must deliver you and get to our posts. The Runners are bold this year. Several have been seen out of the Desert on Holdings already this year. Please enter the transport, lord."

Karne stood fast. "Why arrest me? It's Harlan who's broken the law."

The squadleader shrugged. "I don't know, lord. I just follow orders. My centen didn't explain them. I do know the siege of Ontar manor will be lifted the moment you're in Council custody; in other words, the moment you're in the transport and I com the chairman." The squadleader turned Karne's body, ever so politely, to face the ramp and gently removed his stunner and knife. "Better get aboard, lord. Word is that food's getting scarce in the manor and medicals low. You lift the siege by coming peaceably to Council ground."

Karne's shoulders sagged. He began walking up the ramp, although his feet felt as if they wore lead boots. He heard the squadleader grumbling to another solider. "DeVree could've ordered a centen and a smaller ship to pick Halarek up. A centen's more proper. Besides, if these two can travel through the pass, so can Runners."

Karne knew that though a centen would be proper, Council usually sent either the liege lord of the head-of-House or a highborn vassal. But then I'm not really the head of my House, Karne thought bitterly, and won't be for forty more days. And I have no liege.

He ducked through the transport's door. The deVree and Druma soldiers serving as border patrol for this sector this season sat on rows of benches in the body of the transport. The squadleader respectfully showed Karne and Fellan to a bench near the front of the transport. Karne looked up at the smooth, gray plasti ceiling. Looks like my future, he thought, what there is left of it.

The squadleader slid into the seat beside the pilot, spoke to him quietly and hurriedly, then turned to Karne. "We should receive a reply from the med team in a moment, lord." He paused, as if considering something. He met Karne's eyes directly. "The Gild report is done. Council is meeting early, tomorrow, to decide what to do with it."

A spatter of static came over the com, then a coded sequence of numbers and letters. The pilot asked to have the series repeated, then turned to Karne.

"The med team is in the air and expects to be at Post 105 within a few minutes of the time you land at Council, my lord."

Karne's voice obeyed him unwillingly, and cracked a little on the words. "Thank you."

Karne later remembered nothing of that flight beyond the smooth, gray ceiling and the hardness of the bench. At the Council building, the transport's pilot led Karne and Fellan through an entrance Karne had not known of and down a flight of stairs to a hall lined with doors. The pilot unlocked a door a few paces from the stair and motioned Karne in.

"Make yourself comfortable, milord. Chairman Gormsby and other members of the Houses-in-Council are on the way from their Holdings. They plan to talk with you before Council meets. Your man here will stay with Council's enlisteds. He'll be well taken care of." The man gave Karne a look he interpreted as sympathy and went out, shutting and locking the door.

Karne was alone. He felt a sudden, powerful, and unreasonable surge of panic. He had no one, and he was at the mercy of the chairman.

The room had been tastefully decorated with soft-napped wall hangings, a fur rug, a wide bed, and a stuffed bag-chair, wall lights, and a large hide chest for the occupant's belongings. "Luxurious, for a prison," Karne muttered, the wall hangings muting his voice even further. He tried the door to be sure. Locked. "But it is a prison."

He slumped onto the bed and gave himself up to despair. He ran over and over his actions since his return home and each, still, looked like the best answer to its situation. But he had not been attuned to Gharr ways of thinking and behaving and that had been his downfall. His thoughts raced round and round, like rats in a trap, increasing his grief and despair. Everyone, everyone falls with me, he cried silently.

When he at last found his way back out of the mental fog, two trays of food lay on the floor inside a wide slot in the bottom of the door—nightmeal and fast-breaking. With the fast-breaking tray was a note: "Karne, you didn't answer and the guard wouldn't let me in. Buck up. The siege is lifted and the Larga Alysha is here with me at Council. Emil."

Karne crumpled the note into a ball and threw it at the wall. Months of work and rigid self-control and careful thought and he was a prisoner, not even allowed to see family or allies. Karne stalked to the door and pounded on it imperiously. "I know there's a guard out there. Open this door!"

No one responded and that only increased Karne's helpless anger. He sat on the edge of the bed in fury and started counting hairs in the fur rug just to keep the rage in. He did not know how long he had been at this pointless task before he heard the door open. He did not turn around.

"Karne?"

Karne looked up. "Lady Mother," he answered listlessly.

The Larga stood in the doorway, a Council centen and perhaps a squad of Council soldiers behind her. Karne stood slowly. He could not greet her with joy that she, at least, was free. He could not even feel joy, not when his ignorance of Gharr politics and his misjudgments of Gharr ways were bringing down his entire House. The Larga swept across the room and gripped his upper arms with surprisingly strong fingers. She looked up at him with deep lines between her brows.

"What's wrong? You look—drained, beaten. We have our chance to lay what's happened before the World Council."

Karne looked down at her in disbelief. "Don't you know? I'm not here by invitation or choice. I've been arrested, Lady Mother."

The Larga whirled, every line of her taut with outrage. "You!" she stormed, stabbing her finger toward the portly Council centen. "Didn't you make clear to his lordship this was *protective* arrest? Didn't you tell him I requested it of Chairman deVree before he left office? Didn't you tell him it was to protect his life?"

The centen cringed and backed a step away from the tiny, furious woman. "I—I haven't seen his lordship till just now, milady. Chairman Gormsby said nothing to me about his lordship, my lady. I was only under orders to have him arrested by the nearest Zinn patrol. I didn't know—I had no idea—"

"Some commander! You let the Lharr Halarek be brought in on a common transport, filled with soldiers of the line. No officers, no member of any Family, not even a centen among his guard! You neglected everything due his rank and blood!"

The centen blanched and backed up another stop. The Larga whirled from him to face Karne again. She laid a light hand on his arm. "Has no one visited you? None of our vassals? No one?"

She needed no answer but the look on Karne's face. She dropped her hand and shook her head. "I can't understand it. Common courtesy between vassal and lord . . ." Her voice died away, unbelieving.

"Excuse me, my lady." The centen's voice was ingratiating. "Chairman Gormsby ordered no visitors. You yourself, lady, were allowed to visit only by intervention of Justin, von Schuss, and Davin Reed of Loch, a leader of the Freemen, lady."

The Larga flushed with her anger, but she did not speak it. She lifted her chrono, examined the time, then let it drop again. It slid with a quiet *clinkle* of gold links to the end of its chain. "Gormsby is settling a score with Trev by these petty cruelties," she said under her breath, "I know it. I just know it!" She glanced at Karne to be sure he had heard her, then settled a formal smile on her face. "We'll have to see about that in Council, won't we, Centen. Karne, the session will start soon. The men here will see you arrive at the chamber alive."

Karne allowed himself to be shown out and led

down two more levels to the tiled hallway that surrounded the Council chamber. He had little hope of being free again, let alone of saving his House. Too many powerful Houses stood against him now— Gormsby, Harlan, Odonnel, Kingsland—all the most powerful of the Families except Justin. House Druma had no backbone and could not be counted on for support. Druma would not oppose, but it would not support, either. As for his other vassals, there was the matter of his treatment of Nerut, Melevan, and Roul. Karne shook off the thought. It was past time for worrying about what his vassals would do.

A pair of Harlan soldiers pushed away from the wall when they saw Karne, who stiffened and reached for his appropriated stunner. The Harlan men turned abruptly and walked away when they saw the soldiers in Council uniform immediately behind Karne. Thank you for the guard, Lady Mother, Karne thought, sure that without them, he would now be dead.

Only a few other people stood outside the chamber and most of these belonged to House Odonnel and House Kingsland. Just inside the door of the chamber, a cluster of minor-House lords and Freemen blocked entrance.

"Make way. Make way, please," the Council guards ordered.

The group spread apart and the soldiers guided Karne through, encircling him so tightly he had trouble walking. He was led to the section reserved for his House, but instead of being seated behind the prep table, as was his right, the soldiers pushed him toward the door of an open-topped plasti box. Karne stiffened and stopped.

"No. I've been locked up long enough."

The centen coughed in embarrassment, glanced at the Larga for help, which she did not offer, looked toward the chairman's chair, which was empty, then at Karne. He would not meet Karne's eyes. "It's for your own safety. The Freemen insist on it, my lord. You and Lord Richard may kill each other if you wish, but not in the Council chamber."

"Then put Richard in it," Karne snapped.

The centen cleared his throat. "Ah, Lord Richard, ah, he has a powerful friend in the chairman, my lord. You will sit inside the box or you'll be taken back to your room upstairs. It's up to you."

Karne looked around the chamber. The section for the Nine looked full and the upper gallery as well. There were many gaps in the benches of the Freemen and minor Houses, but many of those places belonged to the men at the door. Karne entered the box, burning with indignation and anger, and sat in the chair provided. The centen shut the door, pointed his stunner directly at the box, dialed it to "kill," and fired directly at Karne. The wall of the box flushed lightly pink, but Karne felt nothing. He smiled, thinly, at the centen, who smiled back, waved good-bye, and marched out with all but two of his men. The two remaining behind blocked the door from the box. Karne could hear the rattle of their equipment as well as if he were outside with them.

That was kind of him, Karne admitted to himself, reluctant to give any credit to the man immediately responsible for his capture and imprisonment. He then looked at his chrono. The time of meeting had come but the chairman had not, and several of the benches behind the prep tables of the Nine lacked important occupants. The murmuring in the chamber had a questioning quality about it, as if everyone were asking his neighbor, "What's the matter? Council always starts on time." Karne put himself briefly into the mode-that-gives-distance-from-pain to quiet his inner tension. Calm after that, he watched the shifting colors and alliances in the chamber without feeling them.

Half an hour passed, and the calm Karne had reached after the centen's kindness began to ooze away. He heard an excited stirring behind him and turned around. Karne saw the wave of heads turning, like wind through long grass, as astonished Family members watched Richard Harlan stride down the aisle toward the Halarek prep table. Karne sprang to his feet and was at the door in a moment. The two Council guards moved close together in front of the door, facing Richard, blocking the exit from the box.

The Harlan Duke-designate stopped beside the Larga's chair, went down on one knee, and lifted the Larga's hand to his forehead in the ritual gesture of deep respect. The Larga jerked her hand away. Richard laughed and stood. "Don't be angry, my lady. When today's meeting is over and its issues settled, our Houses will no longer be at war with each other. The feud will be ended. I hope this pleases you and the Lady Kathryn. Please express my admiration to her and tell her I hope to tell her myself in person soon."

The Larga paled at the implication of Richard's

words. Karne's hands clenched and he raged at his inability to break out of his prison and clench those hands around Richard's handsome neck. He saw Nik, across the room, standing flushed and rigid, the Baron's hand restraining him. Richard laughed at the effect of his performance, bowed to the Larga with practiced grace, threw a triumphant look at Karne, cast a speculative look at Nik, and walked across the center space to the Harlan table. The Larga Alysha spun toward Karne, her hands fluttering, her face still pale, her lips caught between her teeth to keep back tears.

"Never," she whispered. "I'll never let him have Kathryn."

"Don't let him see how effective he was, Lady Mother," Karne said very quietly. "We've given the bastard too much satisfaction as it is."

Just then, with a blare of ceremonial trumpets, quite out of place in Council, the Marquis of Gormsby entered with an honor guard of Council soldiers, one of the few customary parts of the brief ceremony of Installation. The soldiers marched with him to the chairman's table, handed him the chairman's gavel, and marched up the Freemen's aisle to posts by the side doors. The new chairman had just been Installed. He rapped for attention.

"Peace be on your Houses."

"And on yours grace, and peace."

"The Council of Starker IV is now in session. I apologize for the late start, but there's been some unexplained delay in getting the Gild report. The Gild insisted it be delivered to Council in person by official Gild representatives, an idea quite out of the customary order of things." Gormsby cleared his throat, took a sip of water from a glass on the table, and continued. "We have several other matters of urgent business to consider this day. The first matter we will take up is that of the Harlan trusteeship. By order of the last Council, the trusteeship was to last until the Gild made its report on the *Aldefara* case, or until the Thawtime Council, at your pleasure, lords and Freemen."

"Hareem Gashen, freecity of Neeran. We Freemen believe the Gild report is vital to a just decision. Therefore we, as a group, vote to continue the Harlan Holding in trust as it is until we hear the Gild."

"Are there 'nays' among the Freemen? Then record each Freeman as voting to continue Kingsland as trustee. Does anyone else wish to speak to this matter?"

The young lord of House Koort stood. "Arlen of Koort. Since the difference in time isn't likely to be more than an hour or two, I vote my House in favor of waiting."

A murmur of approval followed his speech. Karne felt a little relieved. At least his House and House von Schuss were not entirely alone. The Duke of Druma stood for recognition. *My one vassal from the Nine*, Karne thought, *and a man I thought most unlikely to take sides today.* The chairman nodded to Druma.

"Paul III Druma, here. My lords, I fail to see what the Gild has to do with this matter. This is a matter of sovereignty. Starker belongs to no over-government, such as the Federation. The Gild's conclusions should have no bearing on our decisions because the Gild is an intergalactic merchant monopoly and neither a legal nor a political organization, yet if we judge one of our own Families by the conclusions of this merchant group, we have yielded some of our sovereignty to it, sovereignty which we have protected carefully against all outsiders for fifty generations, into the hands of traders and—"

"Sit down! Sit down!" came from the Justin back benches. The Earl of Justin glared at the young men, then turned around to face the center of the chamber again.

"You speak against waiting, my lord?" The chairman waited courteously for a reply.

The Duke of Druma could not answer, he was so angry. He sopped his grayish, wrinkled face with a large handkerchief, nodded, shook his head, and sat down.

"With Druma to speak so, we don't need enemies," the Larga said savagely.

"SHHHHHHH!" said the Larga's neighbors.

The Larga rose with dignity. "Alysha Halarek, regent in Halarek. The trusteeship decision must also include siege laid three days early by Harlan and his trustees."

Her statement brought a gasp of surprise from those who did not know what had happened. The chairman rapped his gavel on his desk.

"Women do not speak here, milady. Richard Harlan was already standing."

"Richard may not speak for Harlan now, but I am the regent for my House," the Larga protested.

"That is unfortunate for your House, milady, because that means your House has no official voice here. I recognize Harlan."

Karne sprang to his feet. "I am Lharr in Halarek! If the Larga may not speak, it is my right!"

Members of Council began murmuring angrily. Gormsby ignored them and Richard Harlan began speaking, long before the murmuring died down enough that Karne could hear him.

"...Houses consider my position, there are a number of matters they should consider. The most important of these is the continuing humiliation of being governed for, as if I were a minor." Richard paused long enough to looked pointedly at Karne. "And it embarrasses my House to be punished for even so long a time as one winter for such a small offense—"

"Small offense!" the lord of House McNeece roared, bounding to his feet. "You laid siege early. You laid siege without notice. The forty-day law is all that keeps the wolves among the Nine from eating up small Houses like mine!"

"I have the floor, Van," Richard cut in smoothly. "You'll get your turn to speak." Richard turned again toward the chairman. "As I was saying, such a sentence humiliated my House and that lessens my credibility with my vassals. To this shameful sentence, the Council had added the disgrace of compelling my trustee to withdraw my forces from the site of a lawful siege."

"The lawfulness of that siege had been questioned, Lord Richard," Gormsby put in.

Richard bowed to indicate he had heard the chairman's remark. "I gave the required public notice." He turned toward the center of the half-circle of Families. "I also wish the Noble Houses to consider, in making their decision, that the charges laid against my House at the last Council by the minor, Karne Halarek, and his regent, caused the paralysis, eventual insanity, and death of the noble Duke Asten of Harlan, my sire. My House has suffered enough, lords and Freemen, at the hands of this foreign-bred, foreign-trained incompetent. Give me the reins, let me rule my House as it was my sire's wish that I do." Again he looked significantly at Karne, who clenched his teeth and did not retort.

I have long lived with knowing my sire did not wish for me to rule, Richard Harlan, Karne told the young Duke silently. You misjudge me if you expect to taunt me with such remarks.

A new voice entered the discussion. "My Lord Chairman. Emil von Schuss, here. Please remind the young Duke-designate that the Nine refrain from insulting other heads of Families, however subtly, on the floor of this chamber."

The phrase, "Duke-designate" stung Harlan. His face reddened and his lips tightened.

"Consider it done, Baron." Gormsby looked at the papers on his desk, not at von Schuss.

The baron remained on his feet, but the chairman continued to refuse to look in his direction. The baron had been insulted, before the entire Council, apparently intentionally, for the request of a head-of-House had always before been honored, to the letter, on the floor of Council. Yet Gormsby had just refused to do so.

"Are we ready to vote?" Gormsby glanced around the chamber.

"My lord Chairman, you have yet to honor my request." Baron von Schuss was holding his temper with considerable difficulty.

"I said to consider the matter done, my lord. If

there are no other objections, we shall begin the vote on the trusteeship of House Harlan."

"My lord Chairman!" shouted a voice from the Freemen's section. "I object to this rushing. The Gild will soon bring us—"

"Frem Reed, you neglected to identify yourself as required. Bailiffs, bring down the ballots."

Angry whispers, over-loud rustling of papers, and much coughing and shifting in seats followed the chairman's order. He looked disconcerted and glanced toward Garren, new Lharr in House Odonnel, who shrugged. Before Gormsby could order the ballots distributed, the chamber boomed with furious pounding on the main doors. Men from the back benches of von Schuss and deVree forced their way through the throng of observers that clogged the circular aisle at the back and shoved the doors unceremoniously open. Everyone who turned to look saw the unusual sight of soldiers in Council red pushing a delegation of Gild First Merchants away from the chamber.

"My lord of Gormsby, what does this mean?" the Earl of Justin roared.

"Aye, tell us!" The angry chorus shook the gallery floor until it rattled.

Baron von Schuss rose, his usually florid face almost purple with anger. Other heads-of-House rose, many of them clamoring for attention. Gormsby's eyes flicked from side to side. He wet his lips with a dart of his tongue. "Why, my lords, why, I—I have no idea what's happening. Bring those men in, Lord Emil."

Von Schuss and deVree escorted the ruffled Gild officers to the center of the chamber. The lords stepped back to their tables. The First Merchants brushed their rumpled uniforms into order with quick, short strokes. The room had become so quiet everyone could hear the rough sound of hands against stiff fabric. A gray-haired Terran at the center of the group faced the semicircle of the Nine.

"Lords of the Nine Families, I, John Gaunt, of Gild Central, say to you that I have nowhere been treated so badly in my entire career, and I have dealt with the barbarians of Joren and the cannibals of Sabo! If the matter before you were not of great urgency, I would take my delegation back to Gildport and recommend that Starker IV be made off-limits to Gildships for an indefinite time!"

Lords and Freemen alike gasped at the idea of such a disaster. Gaunt continued, his voice still shaking with anger. "The Gild has spent months and untold decacredits to investigate the murders and attempted murders aboard the *Aldefara*. We have held, against their wishes and at great expense to the Gild's goodwill on their home worlds, the three sentient beings still living, other than the crew, who were present at the time of the attacks. We held them because we had to have their testimony both during the investigation and during the trial. The trial is now completed. I will come to the verdict in a moment, after I've read the conclusions of the investigation."

Gormsby's obvious alliance with Harlan, his avoidance or obstruction of the normal rules of Council, his clear dislike of Halarek—Karne suddenly did not believe Gormsby would help Egil, because Egil was Halarek's friend. Perhaps Egil was already hostage somewhere, waiting his use as an item of barter. Karne shoved open the door of the plastic box, pushed aside the Council soldiers and several Halarek cousins who leaped up to stop him, and strode to John Gaunt's side. He grasped the man's arm urgently. The Gild was the only agency that could save Egil now.

"Gentlehom, I interrupt you for the sake of a man's life. He needs off-world medical attention at once. He's—"

The Gildsman looked Karne up and down coldly. "And who be you?"

"Karne Halarek, gentlehom. Please, send men for Egil Olafson before you continue your report. Your ship's med-officer may be able to save his life."

"Olafson claims to be Halarek's brother," Garren Odonnel sneered, loudly enough that the Gildsman could not miss what he said.

Thoughts flitted like shadows across the Gildsman's face. "If he's your brother, there's nothing I can do for him. The Families were told months ago that the Gild carries no more passengers from Starker IV anywhere."

Karne stiffened. "My enemies would hurt me through my friend, gentlehom." He kept his voice quiet and reasonable, though he was shaking with rage at Odonnel inside. "That's why I interrupted you to begin with. Egil is a citizen of Balder. His father is freemerchant Odin Olafson, who—"

Gaunt's face lighted with recognition. He turned quickly to one of his companions and spoke to him in a language Karne did not understand. The companion left the chamber running and Gaunt turned to Karne.

"First Merchant Ronoke goes to prepare our

shuttle. Your friend will be taken to our ship the moment your Council turns him over to us."

Karne bowed deeply. "I'll always be grateful to you, gentlehom. Egil Olafson is closer than kin to me."

"How will we know the chairman has given us the right man, young sir?"

Karne felt glad for the first time in weeks. He grinned at Gaunt. "He's the image of his father, gentlehom."

Gaunt grinned back, then sobered and turned to Chairman Gormsby. "You will release this young man to us immediately on pain of Gild embargo."

Gormsby licked his lips and looked at Odonnel and Harlan. Garren Odonnel doodled with his stylus on the tabletop. Harlan looked at the ceiling.

"We of the Gharr always deal honorably with the Gild, First Merchant."

Gaunt looked down his nose at the Marquis, his disbelief plain, and pointedly turned away. Gormsby flushed and licked his lips again. Gaunt spoke, more to the Council than to the chairman. "You will regret for years anything but the immediate release of this young man, Council of Starker IV. He comes from a great merchant family and a powerful ally of the Gild."

Gormsby cleared his throat and fumbled through the papers on his desk, sent for a Council medical officer, conferred, fumbled through his papers again. "A med team was sent to care for him this morning, but—we do not—we do not have the young man, First Merchant."

Karne went rigid. Gaunt turned slowly, his eyes

and face hardening. "Then who does?" he asked ominously.

Gormsby shuffled through the papers as if the answer were somewhere among them. "The—ah —the rescue party found the guard hut ransacked and empty, First Merchant. There was no food, no medical supplies, no clothing or blankets, and no Egil Olafson. The Runners seem to have taken him, First Merchant."

No Egil! Shock and then a wild grief tore at Karne. Egil! All my brothers and now Egil! Karne took deep, gulping breaths to control the wildness. He summoned all the training the Academy had given him, concentrated on it, and put his grief to one side with great difficulty. If he were to come out of this at all, he must think as he had never thought before. He would have to mourn Egil later. No one came back from the hands of Runners. As if from a distance, he heard Gaunt speaking.

"...the evidence the Gild collected over this long period of time, and with help from the laboratories of the Patrol, the Gild and Patrol have reached these conclusions:

"One. That the various shooting, exploding, gassing, and poisoning incidents aboard Balder's Orbital port and aboard the *Aldefara* were, in fact, attempts against the life of Karne Halarek, here present.

"Two. That these murderous acts were committed from a plan and for a reason, not out of insanity.

"Three. That the only personal benefit from said Karne Halarek's death would be to someone on the intended victim's home world. Therefore, no one among passengers or crew had a personal motive.

"Four. None of the passengers could have been involved in the attempts, for various reasons I won't go into here."

Gaunt stepped to the chairman's table and took a drink from the glass of water there. Some of the younger members of Council tittered. Gaunt resumed his place and his sober mien.

"There are more conclusions, gentlehoms.

"Five. That although no one of the crew had a personal motive, someone might have a profit motive for killing or helping to kill Halarek. A check of financial records helped betray this person, Captain Alonso Telek.

"Six. The Gild has proof that Telek acted in the payment of and on behalf of one Asten Harlan, now deceased. As a result of this investigation, Captain Telek has been sentenced to ten years' hard labor in the mines of Arhash and been barred from interplanetary command for life.

"Lastly, I leave with Frem Gashen of the freecity of Neeran photos of Gild drafts from Asten Harlan to Alonso Telek, ostensibly for cargo. Such cargo was never manifested on Gildships and was never received through customs at the ports listed on the drafts. Do with these as you will." Gaunt walked to Frem Gashen's desk and put some papers in his hand. He folded his own papers over with a snap. He looked at the Freemen and minor Houses. "Lords and Freemen of the Gharr, the Gild has acted to the limit of its codes and charters. However, I also leave with Frem Gashen, as information only, not as an interference in Gharr politics, Gild satellite pix of House Harlan flitters in Zinn, pix taken 20 and 21 Narn."

A roar of outrage and anger swept through the chamber like an avalanche. Gaunt and his delegation filed quietly out before the noise had died away. Karne strode to the center of the open space ahead of the chairman's table. He raised his arms for quiet. The uproar continued. "Lords and Freemen! Lords and Freemen!" he cried.

Slowly, starting with House Halarek and spreading to its allies and the minor Houses, the noise abated. Karne did not face the chairman, as custom required, but spoke to the semicircle of Families and minor Houses directly.

"My lords, the Gild has presented evidence. The physical evidence is aboard the *Aldefara* if anyone wants to check it, but the Gild has always been scrupulously honest. Does anyone here doubt the word and the honor of the Gild?"

No one said anything. No one dared. The Gild was Starker IV's only commercial link with the rest of the universe.

Karne waited long enough for his point to sink in, then continued. "I say, accept the Gild's report and the Patrol's conviction of Captain Telek as sufficient evidence to continue the Harlan trusteeship indefinitely. If the Gild report is not enough, there," he pointed to Gashen's desk, "are the photos that support my claim to have been attacked by Harlan assassins in Zinn."

Richard Harlan slammed the Harlan table with his open hand, making a cracking sound that startled everyone. He sprang to his feet. "The attack in Zinn was my sire's act. What do my sire's acts have to do with me? Nothing! Nothing at all! I won't listen to an enemy of my clan plot its destruction!"

Karne pointed a trembling finger at Harlan. "You set this last siege too early."

Richard looked at Karne coldly. "I gave the notice required by law."

Karne laughed, a grim, frozen sound. "That you did. The whole planet heard you. Only my House heard your transports landing three days early."

"You lie!" Richard Harlan was leaning over his prep table now, his face reddening with anger.

"I tell the truth!" Karne spun away from Harlan and fixed each of the lords of the remaining Nine with his eyes. "I have Gild pix to support what I say. Perhaps Council will now believe what I said at the Frosttime meeting: Harlan set illegal siege on my House, then attacked me and my escort in Zinn; Richard of Harlan himself was there. House Harlan thinks itself above our laws. Vote now to continue the trusteeship!"

Gormsby rapped his gavel. "I am in charge here! I say when we vote!"

"The vote! The vote!" cried many voices from the minor Houses.

"I gave the notice required by law. Give me my rightful heritage!" Richard Harlan shouted above the noise.

"You didn't give honest time for neutrals to get away from the fighting!" someone from House deVree shouted back.

"You broke the law. You set siege early." This came, violently, unexpectedly, from many voices in the Freemen's section.

"Freemen, stay out of Family business!" Richard Harlan roared.

Hareem Gashen stood before the Freemen's

speaking station, waving the Gild pix. "The laying of siege, the breaking of Council law is Freemen's business. It's the world's business."

"Order! Order!" Gormsby shouted futilely.

Karne vaulted onto the Halarek prep table. "The Nine have their laws." His voice carried above the others. "Our laws are harsh, but we've always obeyed them. Now one of the Nine wants exemption."

"Aye." The word came as a low growl of agreement from many parts of the chamber.

Karne felt victory at hand. The Council was leaning his way at last. Then Garren Odonnel stood and looked up at Karne.

"Lords and Freemen, Karne Halarek is not of age and has no right to speak in Council. Lord Chairman, I request he be barred from the room."

"Halarek stays to vote," the Earl of Justin said. "He is but eighteen days short of his majority, and he has spoken well."

Another roar went up in the chamber. Gormsby pounded again for order. "We'll vote on the right of Karne Halarek to—"

A roar of anger and disbelief cut off the end of Gormsby's sentence. Four men of minor Houses stood for recognition. The Freemen gathered in bristling clusters in their section of the chamber, waving fists and papers.

The Larga Alysha's high, clear voice cut through the noise. "We have an issue on the floor, Lord Chairman, the issue of the Harlan trusteeship." The novelty of a woman's higher voice speaking out in Council quieted the room.

Karne sprang from the table and strode to the

chairman's desk. He spoke loud enough for everyone to hear. "I had the floor, my lord, and I demand to be heard. House Harlan has broken the laws of feud by attacking me off-world, by attempting gang assassination, by laying illegal siege, by laying siege early. If Council grants Harlan exemption from our laws by lifting the trusteeship, no one will be safe."

"Exemption!" Harlan snarled. "I'll 'exempt' you, Halarek!"

He whipped out a knife. Karne watched, stunned, as the knife left Harlan's hand and flew toward him. He stood frozen, as if he and the knife and the room were in a nightmare. Death. In the Council chamber. From an illegal weapon. He wanted to move but seemed to have lost the power. Someone rammed into him from behind, the knife skimmed past his shoulder, he dodged at last and heard the knife thud into something soft. A little drawn-out sigh followed the thud. The hand that had pushed him slipped down his back and right arm, caught a moment in the sling, and fell away. Karne spun in time to see the Larga falling to the floor, the knife protruding from her side. He knelt quickly. She was not breathing. Council soldiers swarmed around him. A Council medical officer ran down the aisle, felt the Larga's pulse, carefully pulled out the knife, massaged her heart. He looked over at Karne. "She's dead, milord," he said softly, apologetically. "There's nothing I can do."

Karne saw the chamber through a red haze. He saw Richard wrestling silently against three men of his Family who were trying to get an illegal stunner out of his hand, the battle the fiercer for its silence.

Egil gone, and Jerem and Liam and Kerel, and now the Larga, all because of Harlan. Karne stood, ripped off the sling, rammed through the Council soldiers who surrounded him, and grabbed Richard Harlan by the throat. Hands tore at him, arms wrapped around his arms and body, trying to pry him loose. He felt his own hands squeezing tighter and tighter, trembling with the power in them. He shook Richard, watched with fascination the head, with its bulging eyes and gaping mouth, flop back and forth. Halarek men finally tore him away and bound his arms, but still he struggled. Even when they hauled him back across the room and pushed him down on the bench, it took four men to keep him there.

"He killed her! He killed her!" Karne's only thought was that Richard be punished for all the deaths, punished for them at once.

His rage and pain echoed in the cries of Council members. "Arrest the murderer!" "Aye, arrest Harlan!"

The Marquis of Gormsby beckoned a squad of Odonnel soldiers to the chairman's table. The uproar in the chamber increased at this clear violation of Council ground by Family soldiers. Gormsby spoke to the men and the uproar died in order to hear.

"Say it again, Lord Marquis! We of House Justin didn't hear you!" A young man at the prep table shouted.

Someone from House Konnor took up the cry. "Aye. We all want to hear what you tell a private army!"

"Say it again," the Duke deVree demanded.

Gormsby spoke with exaggerated care. "I said,

'Take Halarek out and hold him in protective custody until the session ends.'"

His reply was met by jeers and shouts of outrage.

"I'll bet you did!"

"Not Odonnel men, my lord. Council men or none."

"Odonnel hates Halarek. Council men."

"Council men! Council men!"

"Take him out!" Gormsby roared.

The Odonnel soldiers marched to the Halarek table, but the men of Justin and Halarek rushed between them and the young Lharr.

"Halarek stays," the Earl of Justin said firmly.

"Vote with Halarek or we're none of us safe," shouted someone from the back benches of Druma.

Some Council members roared approval of this, others reached for the knives and other weapons they did not have, had left with the guards outside the building. Gormsby pounded his gavel for quiet, called for more soldiers, ordered Karne's protectors to stop resisting. Three squads of soldiers in Council red marched down the side aisle with Hareem Gashen at their head. One squad split off and surrounded the Odonnel men near Karne. Gashen ripped the gavel out of Gormsby's hand and unceremoniously dumped the marquis out of the chairman's chair. The chamber quieted in shock. Gashen rapped the gavel once, sharply.

"The Nine Families will never again control this Council. While you have mocked law and justice for your own clan's ends, we of the Freemen and minor Houses have voted and have revoked the right of the Nine to the chairmanship."

"Treason!" shouted someone from Kingsland.

"Nay, lord!" Gashen shook his head emphatically. "Justice for the majority on this world is not treason. You of the Nine have seen murder done and tried to remove the intended victim instead of the murderer. Some of you have twisted procedure to push through action that would place a criminal, whose House has broken many laws, in control of vast political and financial power. The young Lharr Halarek spoke truth today, as he did at Frosttime. You, none of you, helped him protect our world from these wolves. Some of you jeered. Some of you tried to silence him." Gashen threw long sheets of ballots on the floor in front of the chairman's table. "These are the unanimous ballots recording our vote. We of the freecities and the minor Houses are two-thirds of Council, my fine lords, and we vote with the young lord. The trusteeship continues." Gashen looked around the chamber. "But there is more, my fine lords. We tell you now that from this moment, the Nine and their Houses-in-Council will have power only over the Nine Families and their affairs, short of treason and murder. We, the Freemen, have taken permanent chairmanship of this, the World Council. Look you, and see what you have caused."

There was a rustling and whispering among the Freemen. Reed stood. "Davin Reed, freecity of Loch. Richard Harlan committed murder. We all saw."

Gashen turned to Richard. "Richard, son of House Harlan, the sentence in the law for murder is eight years. Because you are head-of-House, you will not serve the sentence of the law in Zinn: You will spend nine years in solitary confinement at the Retreat

House at Breven. Control of the affairs of House
Harlan are, from this time until your release, in the
hands of loyal vassals. This sentence, too, will pass
by at least two-thirds." Gashen looked at the prep
tables with ill-concealed scorn. "Will you test it,
Noble Nine?"

Baron von Schuss spoke out of the shocked silence. "I, Emil von Schuss, say we will not test it.
Those who agree, speak."

There were six "ayes."

Gashen nodded. "It will be recorded so. Soldiers
of Council, arrest Harlan and take him to Breven."

The moment Council soldiers touched Richard,
his face contorted with rage and he flung out his
arms and legs, punching and kicking. Karne
turned away from a display so embarrassingly
outside Family codes. "Loose me now," he told the
men who still held his arms and shoulders. "I
won't do anything foolish."

When they loosed him, Karne stood and faced
the chairman. "Frem Gashen—" Karne paused to
swallow the lump that threatened to choke his
voice and expose his grief for all to see. "Frem Gashen, I ask to be named, now, head-of-House.
Without either regent or lord, much evil could
happen to Halarek between this Council and the
next. A House needs a lord, Freeman." Karne held
the new chairman's eyes.

Gashen nodded. "Well said, young sir." Gashen
looked around the chamber. "What is the Council's
pleasure?"

"He's not yet of age for naming," Kingsland argued.

"Near enough," the lord of Konnor retorted.

Many other voices murmured or shouted agreement.

Gashen pounded the gavel. "Order!" he commanded.

Garren Odonnel looked at the chairman and then turned deliberately away to face the Nine. He laughed slightingly. "Lords of the Nine, what can happen between now and midsummer?"

A Freeman stood, glancing at Odonnel with an expression nearing contempt before turning to the benches of the Freemen. "Tashak, freecity of York. The Nine no longer control Council and Freemen do not bend, as do the Nine, to such slights of a man's courage. Halarek should be named now. His regent is dead and he has proven himself today. His physical attack on Harlan, being entirely understandable, may be excused. I move Council approve Karne Halarek's request to be named head of his House now."

There were some angry mutterings from the more conservative of the Houses, but the motion was adopted overwhelmingly.

Karne bowed his head a moment to silently thank the Allfather, then knelt by the Larga's body. Somewhere in the back of his mind he heard Harlan cursing and thrashing as he was dragged from the chamber, but that was not as important now as his mother's cold, stiffening face and staring eyes. Gently he pressed her eyes closed and crossed her hands on her breast as tradition demanded.

"I will rule, Lady Mother," he told her. "I'll bring

our House to its proper place and power. We have help now, and, by your sacrifice, we have time."

He stood and stepped back, aware suddenly of bone-deep weariness and of warm blood trickling down his right arm. He motioned two cousins to him. "Take her to her flitter. Our House is done here now."

The End?

The end of a book is never really *the end* for a person who reads. He or she can always open another. And another.

Every page holds possibilities.

But millions of kids don't see them. Don't know they're there. Millions of kids can't read, or won't.

That's why there's RIF. Reading is Fundamental (RIF) is a national nonprofit program that works with thousands of community organizations to help young people discover the fun—and the importance—of reading.

RIF motivates kids so that they *want* to read. And RIF works directly with parents to help them encourage their children's reading. RIF gets books to children and children into books, so they grow up reading and become adults who can read. Adults like you.

For more information on how to start a RIF program in your neighborhood, or help your own child grow up reading, write to:

RIF
Dept. BK-1
Box 23444
Washington, D.C.
20026

Founded in 1966, RIF is a national non-profit organization with local projects run by volunteers in every state of the union.

About the Author

Minnesota-based author C. J. Mills has created a canvas of interstellar intrigue in this, her first science fiction novel. With its thrilling action and suspension of reality, *Winter World* will ensure C. J. Mills a place in the science fiction hall of fame.